NEIGHBOURS

Danielle Steel has been hailed as one of the world's most popular authors, with nearly a billion copies of her novels sold. Her recent international bestsellers include *Royal*, *Expect a Miracle* and *All That Glitters*. She is also the author of *His Bright Light*, the story of her son Nick Traina's life and death; *A Gift of Hope*, a memoir of her work with the homeless; and the children's books *Pretty Minnie in Paris* and *Pretty Minnie in Hollywood*. Danielle divides her time between Paris and her home in northern California.

By Danielle Steel

Neighbours • All That Glitters • Royal • Daddy's Girls • The Wedding Dress
The Numbers Game • Moral Compass • Spy • Child's Play • The Dark Side
Lost And Found • Blessing In Disguise • Silent Night • Turning Point
Beauchamp Hall • In His Father's Footsteps • The Good Fight • The Cast
Accidental Heroes • Fall From Grace • Past Perfect • Fairytale
The Right Time • The Duchess • Against All Odds • Dangerous Games
The Mistress • The Award • Rushing Waters • Magic • The Apartment
Property Of A Noblewoman • Blue • Precious Gifts • Undercover • Country
Prodigal Son • Pegasus • A Perfect Life • Power Play • Winners • First Sight
Until The End Of Time • The Sins Of The Mother • Friends Forever
Betrayal • Hotel Vendôme • Happy Birthday • 44 Charles Street • Legacy
Family Ties • Big Girl • Southern Lights • Matters Of The Heart
One Day At A Time • A Good Woman • Rogue • Honor Thyself
Amazing Grace • Bungalow 2 • Sisters • H.R.H. • Coming Out • The House
Toxic Bachelors • Miracle • Impossible • Echoes • Second Chance • Ransom
Safe Harbour • Johnny Angel • Dating Game • Answered Prayers
Sunset In St. Tropez • The Cottage • The Kiss • Leap Of Faith • Lone Eagle
Journey • The House On Hope Street • The Wedding • Irresistible Forces
Granny Dan • Bittersweet • Mirror Image • The Klone And I
The Long Road Home • The Ghost • Special Delivery • The Ranch
Silent Honor • Malice • Five Days In Paris • Lightning • Wings • The Gift
Accident • Vanished • Mixed Blessings • Jewels • No Greater Love
Heartbeat • Message From Nam • Daddy • Star • Zoya • Kaleidoscope
Fine Things • Wanderlust • Secrets • Family Album • Full Circle • Changes
Thurston House • Crossings • Once In A Lifetime • A Perfect Stranger
Remembrance • Palomino • Love: *Poems* • The Ring • Loving • To Love Again
Summer's End • Season Of Passion • The Promise • Now And Forever
Passion's Promise • Going Home

Nonfiction

Expect A Miracle
Pure Joy: *The Dogs We Love*
A Gift Of Hope: *Helping the Homeless*
His Bright Light: *The Story of Nick Traina*

For Children

Pretty Minnie In Paris
Pretty Minnie In Hollywood

Danielle Steel

NEIGHBOURS

MACMILLAN

First published 2021 by Delacorte Press
an imprint of Random House
a division of Penguin Random House LLC, New York

First published in the UK 2021 by Macmillan
an imprint of Pan Macmillan
The Smithson, 6 Briset Street, London EC1M 5NR
Associated companies throughout the world
www.panmacmillan.com

ISBN 978-1-5290-2140-0

1 3 5 7 9 8 6 4 2

A CIP catalogue record for this book is available from the British Library.

Printed and bound by CPI Group (UK) Ltd, Croydon, CR0 4YY

MIX
Paper from
responsible sources
FSC® C116313
FSC
www.fsc.org

To my wonderful so greatly loved children,
Beatrix, Trevor, Todd, Nick,
Sam, Victoria, Vanessa,
Maxx, and Zara,

With all the wishes I have for you,
good people who love you,
good people for you to love,
Wisdom to make good choices,
Courage to face life's challenges,
and happiness, and luck,
May you be forever blessed,
I love you so much,
Mom / d.s.

NEIGHBOURS

Chapter 1

The massive stone mansion was hot even in the basement, as Debbie Speck bustled around the large, efficient kitchen, putting away the groceries that her husband, Jack, had just brought in. He was perspiring profusely. He was forty-four years old, somewhat overweight, with balding dark hair, and always reeked of after-shave that covered the faintly boozy smell of the cheap scotch he kept in his room and drank at night. It came through his pores the next day, when he exerted himself. Debbie usually joined him with a drink or two at night. She preferred gin and tonic or vodka she kept in the freezer in the basement apartment where their employer, Meredith White, never ventured. She respected their privacy, which was ideal for them. Debbie was also heavy and dyed her hair blond herself.

They had been employed as property managers and live-in housekeeping couple by the famously reclusive, now retired movie star, for the past fifteen years. Meredith had still been working when she hired them. She was going from one movie to the next, frequently on location, and her husband, Scott Price, actor and producer, did the same. Sometimes they were apart for months, working on separate movies.

It was the perfect job for Jack and Debbie, working for often absentee employers in an immense, luxurious home, where at least one of their employers was away most of the time, and busy when they were home. They didn't have time to supervise Jack and Debbie too closely and trusted them. They'd been young then, just twenty-nine, but already knew the hidden benefits of that kind of job. The perks felt like plucking ripe fruit from the trees. The stores and workmen they patronized for whatever their employers needed kicked back handsome commissions to them or provided services, which were free to them, but unknowingly paid for by their employer, when bills were padded by dishonest suppliers. And there were plenty of those, as Jack and Debbie knew well. They had set up a whole network of profitable relationships within months of starting the job. It was common practice and Jack and Debbie had no qualms about ripping off their employers. They had done it before. They selected their employers by how profitable they would be, and how busy, distracted, or absent they were.

Meredith had been one of the most highly paid actresses in the business when Jack and Debbie took the job, and she was generous with them. In the beginning, they occasionally had to drive her thirteen-year-old son, Justin, somewhere, but there were tutors to keep an eye on him and a young graduate student who stayed at the house and drove Justin to school when both his parents were away. His parents took care of him themselves when either one of them was at home. Their daughter, Kendall, had gone to college in New York seven years before and never came back to live in San Francisco. She was twenty-five years old when Debbie and Jack took the job, and she only came home for Christmas. She was married and had Julia, a little girl of her own, by then. Meredith and Scott were away so much it was hard to find a good time to see them when they weren't busy.

It was a perfect situation for Jack and Debbie. The mother-in-law apartment they were given had a separate entrance and was attractively furnished. The house was in Pacific Heights, the best residential neighborhood in San Francisco, and it was the biggest house in town. Working for two big movie stars was prestigious, and profitable for them. Meredith and Scott had moved to San Francisco when their son was born, and their daughter was twelve years old. They didn't want to bring up another child in L.A., Meredith had told them. San Francisco was a smaller, conservative, wholesome city, with great schools for Justin and Kendall, good weather year-round, and the house and grounds gave them space and privacy, behind the tall hedge they had planted when they bought the house.

Over the years, Debbie and Jack had taken full advantage of all the benefits of their job. They had an impressive nest egg saved up from the many years of commissions. A few treasures had also found their way into their apartment, particularly two very valuable small French paintings, which had disappeared from the main part of the house, and had hung in their bedroom for a dozen years now. Meredith had never noticed their disappearance. Debbie liked them so she "relocated" them to their quarters. In addition, Meredith had a bank account dedicated to paying household expenses. Debbie had volunteered years before to pay those bills and relieved Meredith of the tediousness of it. Debbie deposited small amounts to her own. The amounts were so minor that even Meredith's accountant hadn't questioned them. Debbie and Jack were clever thieves.

Jack and Debbie were attentive to their employers' every need, and appeared to be deeply sympathetic and kind when Meredith's life fell apart fourteen years before. Her golden world unraveled rapidly after they arrived and lay in ashes at her feet within less than a year. It had made her less cautious about her accounts, and easily distracted.

Fourteen years before, Meredith's husband, Scott, had had a highly publicized affair with a young Italian actress who was starring in a movie with him. She was twenty-seven, and he was more than twice her age at fifty-five. His marriage to Meredith had seemed solid, when Jack and Debbie took the job. They seemed unusually stable for people in show business. They were devoted to each other and their children, from what Jack and Debbie had observed, and then Scott left for location in Bangkok for a picture. By the time he came back, their marriage was a shambles. Once he was home, he left Meredith for Silvana Rossi, and moved to New York with her.

Meredith had been deeply wounded by the betrayal, but kept a brave face on for her children. Jack and Debbie were surprised that they never heard her maligning Scott to their son, but Debbie saw her crying alone in her bedroom more than once, and put her arms around her and gave her a warm hug.

Humiliated by the stories about Scott and Silvana in the tabloids, Meredith stopped having any kind of social life, rarely went out, and turned her full attention to her son, driving him to school and sports practices, spending time with him, having dinner with him every night. Debbie overheard her turning down a movie she'd been offered. Meredith wanted to be at home with her son until the excitement over the scandal of the separation died down. Justin was very upset. He talked to Jack about it, and flew to New York to see his father several times. He came back every time saying how much he hated his soon-to-be stepmother. Scott was planning to marry her as soon as the divorce was final. At fourteen, Justin had called her a cheap whore when confiding in Jack about her, which Jack had reported to Debbie. Justin had said that his older sister, Kendall, didn't like her either. Jack and Debbie hardly knew Kendall, since she had moved to New York before they arrived.

Meredith refrained from talking about Silvana with Debbie. She was a dignified, discreet, respectful woman, although Debbie guessed that Meredith must have hated the young Italian starlet, and Scott was hell-bent on a divorce. Their previously, seemingly happy marriage had evaporated into thin air. Meredith put her massive career on pause, to spend all her time with her son. Although Debbie didn't know her well at the time, she admired her for it.

Jack and Debbie had no children of their own. They had worked in Palm Springs for an elderly couple, both of whom had died within months of each other. Jack and Debbie had met in rehab in San Diego two years before getting that job. They had both grown up in Southern California, but never met. He had had a number of arrests for petty crimes, mostly credit card fraud to support his drug habit. Debbie had been prosecuted for shoplifting, petty theft, stolen credit cards, and possession of marijuana with intent to sell. The courts had sent them to the same rehab program. They were both twenty-two at the time and spent six months there. While in rehab, they formulated a plan to work together, which ultimately turned into love, or harnessing their ambitions to the same wagon. They got married because they could get better jobs that way, as property manager and housekeeper, as a couple. Jack had suggested that working for rich people in their homes could be lucrative, and a rare opportunity for grander schemes in future. Debbie was adamant that she didn't want to be a maid, scrub toilets, or wear a uniform, and he explained that as property managers, they would have the run of people's fancy homes. They could do whatever they wanted, hire other people to clean toilets, the house, do the gardening, and skim a nice living off the top. They could even pocket a few valuables while their employers were away, blame someone else, and steal some cash, and at the same time earn a handsome salary for living well in someone else's home. He made it sound so appealing that they tried it when they got out of rehab. They went to a reputable employment agency in L.A. with fake references Jack had written for them, on stationery he had made, allegedly written by a couple who had died, leaving no heirs to check their story with. The agency was cavalier about checking references and did no criminal check, unless the client requested it.

They got fired from their first job, for general incompetence and not knowing what they were doing. They rapidly learned what was expected of them, and moved on to the job in Palm Springs, for the couple who really did die. They were so old that they paid little attention to what Jack and Debbie were doing. Their children were grateful to have friendly, caring, responsible people with their parents, and the couple even left them a small bequest when they died. This time, their references were genuine when they applied for the job with Scott and Meredith in San Francisco, who were looking through an L.A. agency they trusted and knew well. Jack and Debbie were in no hurry since they were living on the money they'd been left by the elderly couple. When they were offered the job with Scott and Meredith, neither of them could resist it. It was a major step up for them, and they knew what was expected of them by then. They understood how obsequious they had to be to ingratiate themselves into the lives of their employers. Scott hadn't liked them when they started. He told Meredith he thought they were slimy, but it didn't matter in the end, since less than a year later, Scott left for Bangkok, on location, and after that he was gone for good. Meredith bought their act more readily than he did.

They'd been in the job for fifteen years now, and Meredith had become completely dependent on them to shield her from the outside world, and attend to whatever needs she had, which were minimal. She was not a demanding person, and spent most of her time reading in a study just off her bedroom, or sitting in the garden. She never entertained anymore. The world had passed her by in the past fourteen years, or more accurately, she had removed herself from it, and preferred to live a more quiet life than the one she had lived as a star. But the world had not forgotten her. She became a legend once she was a recluse.

Six months after Scott moved to New York with Silvana, and filed for divorce so he could marry her, their son, Justin, went to stay with his father and Silvana at a house Scott had rented in Maine for the month of August. Kendall and her husband were going to come and stay with them, with their daughter, Julia, for the last two weeks of August. Kendall didn't like Silvana any more than Justin did, but she was close to her father and adored her little brother. She was unhappy about the separation, but she was closer to her father than her mother, and happy he was living in New York now. Kendall was married to a successful investment banker, and they had a very nice life in New York.

There was a speedboat Scott was looking forward to using at the house in Maine, and a small sailboat he knew Justin would love, since he had gone to sailing camp in Washington State two summers in a row. He was a fairly adept sailor for a boy of fourteen. Meredith had warned Scott that she didn't want Justin sailing alone in the unfamiliar and unpredictable waters off the coast of Maine. Scott assured her that he would sail with him, but said that Justin was a better sailor than most men twice his age, and, it was a sport he loved. Justin always said he was going to buy a sailboat of his own one day and sail around the world.

They had agreed to Justin spending the month of August with his father, he was looking forward to it, and spending two weeks with his sister, whom he idolized. He missed his father after he'd moved to New York, and the divorce was painful for him too. He loved the idea of a whole month with his father, in spite of Silvana's presence. He said she was dumb, and crawled all over his father like a snake, which Justin found embarrassing. He did his best to ignore her. Her English wasn't good, so he had an excuse not to talk to her.

Ten days after Justin arrived in Maine, Scott was hungover one brilliantly sunny morning, after a party he and Silvana had gone to the night before at the home of new friends they'd made. Loath to get out of bed with a pounding headache, he let Justin take the small sailboat out. It was barely more than a dinghy, and Justin promised to stay close to the shore and come back in time for lunch.

An hour later, a squall had come up, the ocean erupted in unexpected waves, and Justin was out farther than he'd meant to be, carried by the currents and battered by the waves in the small boat. Scott had called the Coast Guard when he got up at noon, saw the fierce waves and realized Justin hadn't come home. There was no sign of the dinghy when Scott stood on the dock, with the knot in his stomach growing. It was too rough to take the speedboat out to look for him.

The Coast Guard found the boat capsized that afternoon. There was no sign of Justin. His body washed up on the beach of one of the small neighboring islands two days later. Kendall had flown up to Maine by then to wait for news with her father, while Meredith sat by the phone and prayed in San Francisco. Her worst fears had come true. Scott was sobbing when he called Meredith the day it happened, and when they found Justin's body. Kendall was distraught when she talked to her mother. They all were. Scott was devastated when he and Kendall flew to San Francisco with Justin's body for the funeral Meredith had planned for their son. Kendall was deeply sympathetic to her father, knowing how guilty he felt, and she believed her mother was strong enough to weather it better. Scott wasn't.

Fourteen years later, it was a blur of memory, which still haunted all of them. Meredith had barely spoken to Scott since. Kendall felt sorry for him and had grown even closer to her father. She visited her mother once or twice a year, dutifully, for a few years after Justin's death, but she blamed her mother for how hard she'd been on Scott, and the toll it took on him. His own guilt had nearly destroyed him.

Scott sank into a downward spiral of drugs and drink for a year or two after Justin died. He had finally gotten back on his feet with Kendall's and Silvana's help. Meredith had blamed him entirely for their son's death, which Kendall thought was cruel. It had been an accident. He didn't murder him. But it had been foolish and negligent and he'd broken his promise to Meredith, and Justin died as a result. Meredith had filed for divorce soon after.

Scott had married Silvana when the divorce was final. He needed her more than ever then. Two years after Justin's death, sober again, Scott resumed his career. Now, at sixty-nine, he produced and directed more than he acted, and was even more successful than he'd been before.

Silvana's fledgling career had tanked and she'd been forgotten before he got back to work. She lived the life of the wife of a successful Hollywood personality now, and was content with that, at forty-one. Her looks had faded, and she had gained weight. She was no longer beautiful and was a tiresome woman with no talent of her own. She was one of those people who looked as though she had probably been striking in her youth, but now she tried too hard, had had too much plastic surgery, and more than anything, looked cheap. But they were still together after thirteen years of marriage, and she loved her role as the wife of a famous actor and producer. They still lived in New York, where he was able to spend time with Kendall and his granddaughter. Meredith doubted that Scott was faithful to Silvana, but didn't care anymore. She and Scott no longer had any reason to speak, with Kendall grown up and Justin gone. They hadn't seen each other since Justin's funeral, an agonizing memory for all of them. Scott had never forgiven himself for Justin's death, and had never had more children with Silvana. She didn't want any, and was content in the role of Scott's child herself, with twenty-eight years between them. She played the role of baby doll, but didn't look it.

Kendall had never forgiven her mother for how hard she'd been on her father for the accident, and she rarely came to San Francisco now. It depressed her to see the house where she and Justin had grown up. His room was kept as a shrine, and her mother was shut away from the world and living like a ghost. The two caretakers, Jack and Debbie, gave her the creeps, and acted like they owned the house, which her mother didn't seem to notice. And as a result of Kendall staying away, Meredith treated Debbie almost like a daughter. Debbie was only four years older than Kendall. Meredith could easily have been her mother, and they lived in the same house and saw each other every day. Her contact with Kendall was minimal, and they had drifted apart, much to Meredith's regret.

* * *

Meredith's immensely successful career had ended when Justin died. She remained behind closed doors for two years, mourning her son's death. It was another three before she felt even remotely like herself again. She never forgave Scott for not keeping his promise not to let Justin sail the boat alone. He had obviously ventured too far from the shore, and when the storm came up suddenly, the boat had capsized in huge waves, far from the coast, and he drowned. She'd had nightmares about it for years, and finally, slowly, achingly made her peace with it.

By then, making movies was no longer of any interest to her. She and Scott had invested her money wisely, she had few needs and didn't have to work. Pursuing her own stardom seemed like a travesty to her after her son's death, and without actually intending to, she became a recluse. She went for days without speaking to anyone except for a few words to Jack and Debbie, who efficiently kept the world at bay, as she had instructed them to. They shielded her from the public life she no longer wanted any part of.

For the first five years after Justin's death, Meredith noticed little of her surroundings and didn't care about them. She never noticed that a few paintings had disappeared from the walls of her living room since she rarely entered the room, and paid no attention to what was there. When Debbie told her that several of her fur coats had been stolen by a maid she'd hired, Meredith didn't care and let Debbie fire the maid. She couldn't imagine wearing anything that glamorous again. She lived in blue jeans now, and old parkas when it was cold, and she sat in the garden. She wore sneakers or her gardening boots. When she went for her long walks, no one recognized her. People in the area knew who lived in the house, what had happened, and that she almost never left the grounds anymore. It was one of those tragedies that happen in life, and from which some people don't recover. Apparently, Meredith was one of them.

Her career had come to a screeching halt when she was forty-nine, and the rest of her life with it. She shut out her friends, had no family except Kendall, who lived three thousand miles away with her husband and daughter, had her own busy life, and almost never came to San Francisco anymore. Kendall remained close to her father, and excluded her mother from her life. Her husband's betrayal with Silvana, her son's death, and her daughter siding with her father and abandoning her were cruel blows for anyone to weather, and drove Meredith deep into solitude.

Fourteen years after Justin's death, at sixty-three, Meredith lived quietly and was content to do so. Her agent died before she ever spoke to him again, and she had refused to see him before that. She had no interest in working again or being the star she had been.

She was no longer tormented by Justin's death. She had learned to live with it, and accept it. She believed she would see him again one day. She didn't travel, and was content to stay in San Francisco, in the house where Justin had lived his whole short life. His room was untouched, on the top floor of the house. She rarely went into it now, except to look for something, a photograph or something of his. She just liked knowing that the room was there, and still looked the same as it had when he lived. Nothing in the house had changed in fourteen years. It gave her the illusion that time had stood still after Justin's death. But the years drifted by nonetheless.

Jack and Debbie had become Meredith's protectors, her shield against the world and prying eyes, and took free advantage of it, for their own benefit, which Meredith didn't question or even notice. They had decided to let the hedge grow taller, and no one could see behind her walls. For the first five years, Meredith had been morbidly depressed. Now she was a quiet woman with a famous past, a tragic story, content to walk in her own garden, or drive herself to the beach on blustery days, for fresh air, with the wind on her face. She had no desire for companionship, or the friends she hadn't seen in years. Their lives were too different from hers now.

Meredith had watched some of the movies Scott had directed recently, and was surprised by how good they were, and relieved that he wasn't in them. She had no desire to see Scott's face again, all the photographs of him in the house had long since disappeared. There were photographs of Justin everywhere, at every age, for his brief fourteen years, and of Kendall, though more of him. Debbie spoke to Meredith of Justin with reverence, and made herself essential for Meredith's comfort. She knew how she liked everything, what she liked to eat, and when, and how she liked it served, how she liked her bed turned down, the kind of books she liked to read, and supplied them. Debbie introduced her to several new TV series, and watched them with her. Debbie had become a filter for her, screening out everything Meredith didn't want to deal with and making her life easy, while Jack assured her that he kept her safe, and she believed him. The world seemed dangerous and unfamiliar to her now. Meredith hadn't meant to become dependent on them, but without intending to, she had. They made everything so easy for her, and she was grateful to them. They hadn't abandoned her, which Scott and Kendall had. They had even woven heavy netting through the main gate, so the curious couldn't look in. She was something of a legend in the neighborhood, the big movie star whose son had died and had become a recluse.

"They probably think I'm some kind of witch by now," Meredith said sometimes, laughing about it. At sixty-three, she was still beautiful, with the huge blue eyes her fans had loved and remembered, sandy blond hair, and the elegant, delicate face. She was still very attractive, energetic, and in good shape, and didn't look her age. She spent hours gardening, which she enjoyed, and reading.

She had been in the garden all morning, trimming her roses, despite the heat. Heat waves were rare in San Francisco, and she had enjoyed it. She was wearing a big floppy straw hat when she came into the kitchen for something to drink, and smiled at Debbie, who was making Meredith's favorite chopped salad for lunch. She had kept her figure, although in the early years of her seclusion she had been too thin, and Debbie had to coax her to eat. Everything the devoted couple did proved to Meredith again and again how much they cared about her, and how kindhearted they were. More so than her daughter, who hardly even called her, sometimes not for months at a time. Meredith felt her loss acutely.

"Wow, it's hot out there," she said and smiled at Debbie. It had been a long foggy summer, and the September heat was a nice change. "It's real Indian summer," she said, grabbing a bottle of cold water from the fridge and taking a long drink.

"Earthquake weather," Debbie said, handing her a glass, as Meredith shook her head. She didn't need one.

"I hope not," Meredith said, setting the bottle down. "I've lived here for twenty-eight years, and there's never been a major earthquake, thank God," Meredith said. "We missed the one in '89 by four years. That sounded pretty nasty." It still shocked her to realize that Justin had been gone for half the time she'd lived in San Francisco now. He would have been twenty-eight if he'd lived, which was harder to imagine. In her mind's eye, he would always be a boy of fourteen. She remembered him smiling, and laughing, and playing pranks on her. He'd been playful, and happy, and funny. It gave her comfort to know that she and Scott had given him a happy childhood, with no sorrows until the divorce. The memories of him were gentle now, not of the imagined horror of the day he drowned.

"This house won't move an inch if there ever was a quake," Jack said, as he walked into the kitchen for a glass of water himself. He and Debbie were forty-four years old now. They hadn't weathered the years as well as she had. Meredith hardly looked older than they did, and had fewer lines in her face and around her eyes than Debbie, who always had a slightly hard expression, bleached her own hair a brassy blond, and always seemed to have an inch of dark roots before she dyed it again. Jack was growing bald and had a beer belly, which always surprised Meredith, since he wasn't a drinker, as far as she knew, and Debbie had put on more than a few pounds. Meredith was still naturally slim, with a good figure since aside from her daily walks, she went to a yoga class in the neighborhood, where no one ever recognized her. She had become comfortable with her solitude, embraced it, and at night she read voraciously. She and Debbie would talk about the books the next day. Debbie had never been a big reader, but she knew it was a way of bonding with Meredith, so she read what she knew Meredith liked. It seemed odd, but they had become her best friends.

The house was over a hundred years old, and made of stone. It was the largest house in San Francisco, sitting on a sizeable plot of land, which took up half a block. Between the gate and the hedge, and the imposing structure and grounds, people who were unfamiliar with the neighborhood wondered who lived there. Jack's comment about the house reminded her of something from the distant past.

"Speaking of earthquakes, do we still have the emergency supplies for one? We were worried about earthquakes when we moved here, and we stocked up a bunch of tents, and rope and crowbars, and some canned food, bottled water, and first aid supplies, and put them in the garden shed. Do we still keep them up to date?" She used to keep clothes for Justin out there too, when he was small, but after they'd lived there for several years, they stopped worrying about earthquakes, and had forgotten about updating the supplies. She hadn't thought of them in years. "We had battery-operated lanterns too." She also remembered that Scott had wanted to keep a gun with the supplies too, in case anyone tried to loot the house, but she wouldn't let him. They'd kept an envelope of cash in the safe for emergencies. She still did, for when she occasionally needed petty cash to give Jack or Debbie.

"I keep up with the first aid supplies, and the tools," Jack answered her. "I donated the tents to a homeless shelter years ago. We wouldn't want people camping out on the grounds anyway. And I threw the clothes away." She nodded, knowing they were Justin's from when he was a child. "And we have all the food and water we need in the house, if there ever is a quake. We keep the house well stocked." Debbie kept a large supply of meat they froze, and canned goods. "We don't need to feed the neighborhood," he said with a stern expression, implying he was protecting her from curious strangers. "We have everything we need for us, to keep going for a long time. The house is sitting on granite, you'd barely notice a quake here, and we have an emergency generator if we lose power," he said confidently. Scott had it installed when they bought the house.

The rest of the houses on the block were handsome Victorians, all wooden structures. They were lovely, though less solid, and might not fare as well. Meredith had never met her neighbors, and didn't want to. Scott had been more neighborly and concerned about the neighborhood in an earthquake when they moved in, but her life had changed radically since then. She had no idea who lived on her block in the string of pretty Victorian houses, and she suspected Jack and Debbie didn't either. They were even more reclusive than she was, and always seemed suspicious of their neighbors and passersby who tried to peek through the gate. They shielded and protected her.

She sat down to lunch with them at the kitchen table, as she did every day. Meredith ate her meals with them now, and had for many years. It didn't seem right to cause Debbie extra work, serving her in the dining room for just one person, and it seemed unfriendly, given how kind they'd been to her, at the hardest time in her life, through the divorce and her son's death. They made up for the fact that she never saw her daughter. At first, she had taken her meals on a tray in her study, but for years now, she had eaten lunch and dinner with Jack and Debbie, even though their backgrounds and histories were different from hers. They had grown up simply in poor families, never went past high school. Debbie had graduated, Jack dropped out in tenth grade, and were almost twenty years younger than she. But they had become her only friends. Sometimes Debbie watched one of their favorite TV series with her in the den. It was more fun than watching alone, and they could talk about it afterward. Jack didn't like the shows they watched. He pooh-poohed them, and would go to their apartment to watch sports, which Debbie hated. She and Meredith liked the same TV shows, and read the same books, because Debbie made the effort to do so. She was more intellectually ambitious than Jack. In some ways, she was like a daughter to Meredith, or a sister or a friend. Jack was more taciturn, a man of few words, and less chatty than Debbie, who engaged Meredith in conversation, and so was better company. He was bright, but not talkative.

Meredith went back out to the garden after lunch, to finish her gardening. She didn't mind the heat. She liked it. Debbie came out to check on her progress around four o'clock, and brought her a glass of ice-cold lemonade. Meredith accepted it gratefully and smiled at her. She took a long drink and drank half the contents of the glass before she stopped.

"My God, that's good. I was dying of thirst, but I didn't want to stop and come inside." She had tossed her hat on a garden chair, and was enjoying the sun on her face.

"Your roses are looking beautiful," Debbie complimented her, and Meredith was pleased.

"I never thought I'd be spending my days gardening. I actually enjoy it." She cut a particularly lush dark red rose and handed it to Debbie, and the two women exchanged a warm smile. They were entirely different. Meredith came from a distinguished family, though not from great wealth. But she had an aristocratic air and innate grace. Debbie had grown up in abject poverty, in a trailer park, and still looked it. There was a coarseness to her, with her bad dye job and black roots. And yet, Meredith believed that they understood each other, and were friends. "I've been thinking about taking a Chinese cooking class, since we all like Chinese food so much. There's no reason why you should have to cook every night," she said generously. Except that Meredith was her employer, and Debbie was paid to cook. Since they spent so much time together, it was easy to forget that. The boundaries got blurred when you lived in such close proximity and saw no one else.

Debbie went back in the house a few minutes later. It was too hot outside for her, and the air had gotten humid, heavy, and muggy. It really did feel like what people called earthquake weather, but Meredith knew it was just a myth. She'd never heard any evidence that the weather had been muggy during the 1906 quake, which was the biggest one of all. The '89 quake happened during the World Series, so it might have been hot and humid then too. Meredith wasn't worried about it. It was just trivial conversation, something to say about the weather.

As she picked up her basket of gardening tools at five o'clock, she thought of calling Kendall that night. Meredith still made the effort. They hadn't talked in a long time. Kendall rarely called her. The last time they'd spoken, Kendall had been battling with her nineteen-year-old daughter who wanted to drop out of college at NYU and not go back for junior year. She hated school, although she was majoring in drama at the Tisch School at NYU.

If she had dropped out, she was following in her mother's footsteps. Kendall had done her junior year in Florence, for her year abroad. She'd been twenty, had fallen madly in love with George Holbrook, the eldest son of an important and very wealthy banking family in New York. They were both students in Florence at the same time. Afterward, Kendall had refused to go back to Columbia. They had gotten engaged at Christmas and married a few months later. Kendall was stubborn. She never went back to school. Both sets of parents had been afraid the marriage wouldn't last and thought they were too young to get married. But twenty years later, they were still together and Kendall said they were happy. They'd had a baby, Julia, ten months after their wedding day, which didn't seem prudent to Meredith either, to rush into becoming parents, especially so young, but Kendall always did what she wanted, and she and George were a good match as it turned out. They were conservative, very social, and somewhat stuffy, in Meredith's opinion.

Kendall was on all the important charity committees in New

York. George's parents hadn't been thrilled that Kendall came from a family of actors, and Kendall had never gone back to school or worked. She was the classic society wife, which their daughter, Julia, detested. Julia wanted to follow in her grandparents' footsteps, go to L.A. and try to become an actress. She wanted to try her wings and fly, and her parents weren't happy about it. Meredith smiled, thinking about it. It was Kendall's turn now to have a daughter rebel, take off, and reject everything her parents stood for and had achieved.

Kendall had never liked her parents' acting careers, particularly since their work had taken them away from her so often when she was young. She also didn't like her parents being so recognizable and well-known. She hated their being stopped on the street by strangers for autographs. Meredith didn't deny that she had been on location a lot of the time. Kendall had been born just when Meredith was first becoming a major star. Justin was born twelve years later, when she was more mature and could handle it better. She was just as busy, but Justin never seemed to mind their absences the way Kendall had, or their being recognized. Sometimes he even liked it and often said he was proud of them. Kendall wasn't. She was embarrassed and jealous of her mother, although Meredith was discreet, and never made a fuss about her fame, which was impressive, given what a big star she was.

By the time Justin came along, she and Scott were trying to alternate the films they did on location so that at least one of them would be at home with him. When Kendall was a child, they were often both away at the same time, which she held against them later, especially her mother. She blamed her mother for all the ills in her early life.

Justin had a more easygoing nature than Kendall. Kendall had always been upset about something, and she resented her mother's career, although Meredith underplayed it at home. Kendall didn't resent her father's fame. But even now, when they spoke, Kendall made caustic comments about when her mother was a star. She was proud of her father's career now, but she never really acknowledged how famous and successful her mother had been. What she remembered most about her mother was how harsh she had been with Scott when Justin died. All Kendall's sympathy and compassion had been with him. She chose to overlook that any part of her brother's death had been her father's fault, and that Scott should never have let him go out in the sailboat alone. She couldn't bear to think that her father had been responsible for it at all, although she had loved Justin passionately. She considered his death an act of fate, or the hand of God. Her father was her hero, and she liked to believe that he was a saint. She never talked about how Scott had walked out on her mother, and had an affair with Silvana that was on the front page of every tabloid around the world. And, married by then herself, Kendall had been old enough to understand it, but chose not to.

Meredith thought of Julia and wondered what she was like now. As shocking as it seemed, she hadn't seen her granddaughter since she was ten years old. Meredith hadn't fully recovered from Justin's death until then, and Kendall always made it difficult for her mother to see her only grandchild, and kept her away. The timing was never convenient to visit them, and she never brought her to San Francisco to see her grandmother, except once nine years before for a few days, and hadn't been back since.

Meredith hadn't traveled anywhere in fourteen years, and for years now, Kendall had spent the holidays with her husband's family and not her own. She and George had bought a house in Aspen, so now they spent Christmas there and had never invited Meredith. She didn't force the issue, and didn't want to beg Kendall to come home. She knew it wasn't exciting to come and visit her, and for Kendall, the memories of her brother there were just too painful. She always told her mother she was "too busy" to come out. For Meredith, the outside world had lost some of its reality, like a TV show she hadn't watched in a long time, and had lost the thread of the plot. The characters had become unfamiliar to her, and she felt as though she had missed too many episodes in their lives to re-engage in the story now.

She had just turned the TV on to one of her favorite series, which she watched religiously every week during the entire season. It was the third year, and she hadn't missed a single episode, and re-watched it all again at the end of the season. She was tucked into a comfortable chair in her bedroom, when there was a strange groaning sound, as though it came from the depths of the earth. The television began to shake and the screen went black. The chandelier overhead was swinging wildly from side to side. When she looked up and saw it, she realized what was happening, just as everything slid off the coffee table in front of her and fell on the floor, and a painting came crashing down. She wasn't sure what to do at first. There was the sound of breaking glass around her, as the groaning in the earth continued and got louder, and she could hear things falling and breaking all around the house. Remembering what to do in an earthquake, she rushed to her bedroom doorway, and stood there shaking, as two more large paintings fell. Her feet were bare, and she had cut her foot on a piece of glass as she ran across the room. She didn't even feel it. All the lights had gone out by then, and she could see out the window that the whole neighborhood had gone dark. It felt like it went on forever, and after what seemed like an eternity, the groaning stopped, and there was a brief final shake. Meredith stood in the dark with a sea of broken glass around her, and she could hear Debbie calling out to her. A moment later, she heard Debbie coming up the stairs. She was breathless when she found Meredith in the doorway, and they stood there staring at each other for a moment. Debbie was carrying a powerful battery-operated lantern, and shined it around the room, at the fallen paintings and broken glass.

"Holy shit, that was a big one," Meredith said, sounding calmer than she felt. "I guess it was earthquake weather."

"Are you okay?" Debbie asked her. She looked badly shaken herself.

"I think so," Meredith answered. "Are you? Where's Jack?"

"He's behind the house at the meter, trying to turn off the gas." As always, he knew just the right thing to do, and Meredith was grateful to have them there. "It was like climbing a roller coaster, trying to get up the stairs to get to you," Debbie said, still breathless from the shock of what had happened.

"Thank you for coming up."

"Jack said we should go out to the courtyard, in case things keep falling in the house for a while." They heard a loud crash downstairs, and when she shined the light on the chandelier, it was still swinging. She handed a flashlight to Meredith, who turned it on to look for her shoes, found them, and as she put them on, she saw that her foot was bleeding. "Are you okay?" Debbie asked her, and Meredith answered that she was and followed her to the stairs. When they shined their lights on the big chandelier in the main hall, it was still swinging from side to side, and all the hanging crystals sounded like chimes as they bumped into one another. "Don't walk under it!" Debbie warned her, as they made their way gingerly down the stairs, and saw the paintings on the floor in the hall. The large frames on several of them were broken.

They walked around them, and opened the front door. Meredith could see, as she had from her bedroom window, that the entire neighborhood was dark.

"I wonder how big it was," Meredith said as they stood in the doorway, and Debbie shined the lantern outside.

"Big," she said, as they walked cautiously into the courtyard, and Jack found them a few minutes later.

"Are you two okay? The gas is off in the house now," he said in a reassuring tone.

"We're fine," Meredith said, starting to feel calmer. They could hear people talking in the street, and she wondered if they should open the gate.

"Don't go out in the street," he warned them both. "There are power lines down. One of them is shooting sparks. I saw it when I moved some of the netting on the gate to take a look." As he said it, all three of them could feel a mild aftershock, and Debbie looked panicked.

"What if there's another big one?" she asked, clutching Jack's arm. "What if that was just the first one? A warm-up?"

"There won't be another one," he said, sounding more hopeful than certain, trying to calm them, as Meredith wondered what the rest of the night would have in store for them, and how much damage had been done to the house, as paintings and fragile objects fell.

"We ought to check on our neighbors," Meredith said, concerned. "Somebody could be trapped, or hurt. Where's the first aid kit?" she asked Jack, and he glanced at Debbie before he answered.

"You can't go out there, Meredith. Everyone knows who you are and that you live here. You don't want people shoving their way inside. We don't know how bad it is outside. There could be looters." He made it sound ominous, as though there were people waiting to invade them. Meredith didn't care.

"Get the first aid kit, and we're going to open the gate, Jack," she said in a voice he'd never heard before. It was the voice of unquestionable authority. He hesitated and then disappeared into the house, as Debbie looked terrified.

"Don't open the gates. We don't know what's out there."

"No, we don't. But we're going to find out," Meredith said in a calm, firm tone that left no doubt in Debbie's mind.

Five minutes later, Jack was back with the first aid kit, and a stubborn look on his face, as Meredith took the key and manually opened the gate. It resisted at first, and then slowly it swung open. Meredith walked through the gates to the street, and Debbie and Jack followed. This wasn't what they wanted to happen at all. But Meredith was in charge now, for the first time in a very long time, and her eyes were bright and alive.

Chapter 2

Tyla Johnson was just taking a meatloaf out of the oven when Andrew came home from work. She knew he wouldn't like it, but she had promised the children. It was her grandmother's recipe and one of their favorites. She served it with mashed potatoes and corn on the cob. She had a steak in the fridge for him if Andrew preferred it.

"It's like coming home to a second-rate diner," he grumbled as he went to wash his hands with a sour expression. She hated it when he came home like that. She wondered if something had gone wrong at the office. She could usually tell. She had worked for him for three years as an O.R. nurse before they started dating and he married her. She'd gotten the job right out of nursing school. She was thirty-eight now, and he was forty-seven. He was an orthopedic surgeon at one of the best hospitals in the city, and had a booming practice.

Andrew was tall, blond, athletic, and handsome, with powerful shoulders. He had grown up in Southern California in a blue-collar suburb of L.A., and had lived in Venice for a while, which he thought was the perfect beach town, with lots of college girls to pick up, who were dazzled by him. Even now, as a busy physician, he ran three miles every day to stay in shape before he went to work.

Their daughter, Daphne, was seven, and their son, Will, was eleven. They both went to private schools, and Andrew never let them or Tyla forget how much it cost him. His parents had been poor when he was growing up, and had scrimped and saved and borrowed to put their only son through medical school, and now he was one of the most successful orthopedic surgeons in the city. From where he had come from, it was a huge achievement.

Tyla was from a poor Irish family in Boston, and had gotten a full scholarship to nursing school. She came to San Francisco as soon as she graduated, and when she married Andrew, her whole life had changed. Andrew was obsessed with money and success and worked hard.

They'd bought the house on Washington Street when Daphne was two. Tyla had stopped working when Will was born, and Andrew reminded her regularly how lucky she was to have a husband like him, who provided for her, and an easy life. He was proud of the money he'd made, and owning a house like this. He paid a hefty mortgage. He watched every penny she spent, and Tyla was never extravagant. She loved their house, and the advantages they could give their children that she had never had growing up. Her mother had stretched every dollar, made their clothes, and put food on the table for them by working as a maid in one of the finer houses in Boston. One of her brothers was a plumber, and the other one was an electrician. Both of her sisters were domestics as her mother had been. Tyla was their pride and joy, married to a doctor, living in a big house in San Francisco. She would have continued working to help him, but Andrew didn't want her to, and made enough money that she didn't have to work. He was proud of that too.

He came back to the kitchen after he washed his hands, took his jacket off, loosened his tie, and rolled up the sleeves of his white shirt, as the children came to dinner, wearing their school uniforms. Daphne looked up at her father with a wide toothless smile, her hair in pigtails, and Will looked serious, as they both sat down, and their mother put their dinner on plates and set them on the table in front of them.

"Meatloaf or steak?" she offered Andrew.

"Meatloaf is fine," he said, without smiling at his children. He hadn't kissed Tyla when he walked in, which was never a good sign. She didn't ask him how his day had been. She could see it. At other times, he spun her around and kissed her, but not tonight. She sat down after she had put his plate in front of him and served herself. The children had already started eating. The meatloaf was hot and delicious, and they were enjoying it as their father slammed his fist down on the table, and all three of them jumped. "What kind of rude kids are you? You started eating before we did. Where are your manners?"

"Sorry, Dad," Will said under his breath, pausing for a moment, as Daphne looked as though she was about to cry, and they continued eating in silence, while Tyla chatted to break the tension, and Daphne ate her mashed potatoes first, keeping her eyes on her plate. They were used to his outbursts, but it made dinner more stressful than pleasant when he was like that. It happened a lot, more and more these days.

"How was school today?" he asked them, looking pointedly at his son. In second grade, Daphne wasn't likely to have much to tell him about her academic accomplishments.

"It was okay," Will answered for both of them, and avoided his father's gaze.

"How was the math quiz?" He remembered.

Will hesitated. He knew he wouldn't escape his father's interrogation, and if he lied it would be worse. Tyla hated it when he put Will on the spot like that. Lately, he had developed a stammer, and his teacher had suggested speech therapy. "Not so good," he answered in barely more than a whisper. Will resembled his father, with the same handsome blond looks. Daphne had dark hair and green eyes like her mother.

"What does 'not so good' mean? What did you get on it?"

"A fifty-five, Dad," Will said, his eyes brimming with tears. "I got an F. I didn't understand it. I have to meet with Mr. Joppla tomorrow after school."

"Didn't you work on it with him before?" Andrew said to Tyla, turning his laser beam eyes on her. "What the hell do you do with them? He's in sixth grade. This is serious."

"I tried. I don't understand the way they do the math now either," she said quietly. "We really did work on it, Andrew. He might need a tutor," she said cautiously, suddenly feeling too sick to eat.

The kitchen was bright and cheery, and the dinner was delicious, but when Andrew was in one of his moods, no one could eat. He was spoiling for a fight tonight.

"We had math in school today too," Daphne said gently, trying to distract their father to give her brother some relief. "And reading," she added. Andrew didn't bother to answer her, and continued to harangue his wife about how irresponsible she was, and said that maybe she needed a tutor more than Will did, if she was too dumb to figure it out. He told Will that all he had to do was pay attention in class. He was smart enough to master the material, so obviously he was just lazy.

"He's not lazy, Andy. He's first in the class in English. He got an A+ on an essay last week. Math just isn't easy for him." Tyla tried to intervene on his behalf.

"And what's an A on an essay going to get him? A job as a schoolteacher? He needs to work on math and science. I'm not paying private school tuition to have him flunk a math quiz." There was dead silence at the table. They knew better than to answer him when he was on a rampage, and he was getting there.

The plates were still half full when Tyla cleared the table. She had made brownies and served them with ice cream for dessert. Andrew's cellphone had vibrated with messages all through dinner. He glanced at them, but never responded while they were eating, unless the hospital was calling him in for an emergency, which wasn't the case so far tonight. Will almost hoped they would call him back in. He knew his father would hound him all night about the math quiz.

The children asked permission to leave the table. Tyla gave it to them, and they scampered up the stairs, whispering to each other. Tyla saw Daphne give her brother a quick kiss to make him feel better.

"You have to stop being so hard on them," she said softly, as she sat down next to him, after she'd removed their plates.

"Why? Do you want an idiot for a son? Do you want him to wind up a plumber like your brother?" he said nastily.

"My brother is dyslexic, and he makes a damn good living," she said in defense of her younger brother. Andrew didn't like her family, and viewed them with contempt.

"It's your job to see that Will studies and gets decent grades," he said accusingly, checking his messages again.

"I do it with him. Math isn't his best subject. He's gifted in English, and he loves history." Andrew ignored her to answer a text, and then he looked at her more calmly for a minute, but there was a light in his eyes she didn't like. She knew where it led.

"It's my job to put them in good schools. It's yours to see that they learn something." She didn't argue with him, she knew better. She was about to tell him again that he needed to go easy on Will. He had come home twice in the last week with severe stomachaches, and Daphne had started biting her nails. They all knew that Andrew had a fierce temper. He controlled it at work and with his patients, but he took it out on them. All the pent-up rage that had been gathering momentum throughout the day was unleashed on them as soon as he got home.

Tyla had just opened her mouth to speak when the house started shaking. It felt as though someone had picked it up and was shaking it from side to side, and then up and down. The lights flickered and went out. There was a hideous groaning sound, like a beast about to eat them, and Tyla could hear Daphne scream as she started to run out of the kitchen toward the stairs. Andrew grabbed her arm to stop her and yanked her back. He hurt her arm when he did it.

"Get under the table!" he shouted at her as she pulled free of him, and ran upstairs to her children. The house was still shaking when she got upstairs. Will was holding Daphne tightly in the doorway, while she continued to scream, and Tyla reached them, and held them in her arms until the shaking finally stopped. Daphne was crying, and there were tears swimming in Will's eyes. It had felt as though the house was going to fall down, and they could hear dishes smashing in the kitchen, as they fell out of the cupboards and crashed on the floor.

"Get down here!" Andrew shouted at them, and the three of them walked cautiously down the stairs. The house had stopped shaking, and the groaning sound was receding, but they could still hear it.

"I smell gas," Tyla said as she walked into the kitchen. It was dark in the house, and Andrew found a flashlight and shined it on them. It was pitch black outside, and the old wooden house was creaking loudly as it settled after the earthquake.

"I need a wrench to turn the gas off. What did you do with the tools?" he asked her. He looked startled but not frightened. "Stop crying," he said to Daphne, as Tyla pulled her close. She was shaking.

"I don't know. I think they're in the garage where you put them." He pulled open the front door, and they could see wires shooting sparks in the street, and people gathering with flashlights. He told Will to come and help him in the garage, and Tyla held Daphne's hand as they walked outside. People were talking to one another and everyone looked shocked by the force of the quake, and panicked as an aftershock brought another wire to the ground across the street.

"Where the hell did you put the wrench?" Andrew asked through clenched teeth when he came back to them, with Will trailing behind him, looking scared. He wasn't sure what was worse, his father or the earthquake, or the pitch black outside, and the live wires across the street. "I can't turn the gas off without one," he said to Tyla.

"I don't use it," she said quietly, trying to calm Daphne, "maybe we don't have one."

"Well, we'd damn well better find one before the house explodes or catches fire," Andrew said, as people began coming out of their houses and walking into the street.

Daphne started to wail then. "Our house is going to burn down, and I left Martha inside." Martha was her favorite doll, and Tyla didn't dare go inside to get her, in case something fell, or the house exploded from the leaking gas.

"We'll go inside soon to get her," Tyla said, holding Daphne close to her, "and the house isn't going to burn down. Daddy's going to turn off the gas."

"Daddy needs a wrench and he can't find one," she continued to cry, as Tyla held her, and she saw Andrew walk to the house next door, and bang hard on the door. No one answered. They were either out or injured, or too frightened to open the door. Andrew continued pounding, and Will came to stand next to his mother. She could feel his whole body shaking as he huddled next to her, as Andrew went on banging his fist on the door. He wasn't going to leave until someone answered, so he could borrow a wrench.

Peter Stern was hunched over his old manual typewriter, typing as he did every night in his small bedroom in the attic. He worked in the advertising department of a local magazine by day, and had worked for Arthur Harriman at night for the past year. Peter considered it an honor to work for him, and the night job he had with him had saved his life. He made a very small salary at the magazine and lived on the commissions he made from selling advertising. Both amounts combined weren't enough to allow him to pay rent for even a studio apartment in a decent neighborhood, and he didn't want to live with half a dozen strangers as roommates anymore, particularly since he wanted to write at night. He'd been working on a novel for the past two years. At thirty-two, he didn't have a job he loved, but writing was his passion, and completing a novel and getting it published was his dream. He hoped to be a successful writer one day.

He'd been living in a seedy apartment in the Haight-Ashbury with five roommates he'd found on Craigslist, and with all the comings and goings of his roommates, it had been almost impossible to write.

He'd found the job working for Arthur Harriman in the *Chronicle.* He needed someone to sleep in his home at night, and provide occasional assistance. His housekeeper of many years, Frieda, stayed until eight P.M., and cooked him dinner. She arrived at seven in the morning. A man came to assist him on weekends. He needed someone to sleep in his home seven days a week, in exchange for a small salary and a bedroom. He was a world famous concert pianist, and had been blind since a car accident when he was eighteen. He was eighty-two years old and managed very well on his own. He just needed to know that there was someone in the house, but he was very independent and extremely self-sufficient. Peter had expected to meet a frail old man when he came to interview for the job, and was astounded to find him walking all over the house, managing the stairs with ease, with more energy than people half his age.

Peter was nothing more than a presence in case of an emergency of some kind, but there had never been one. They had long philosophical discussions, and often Arthur practiced at night. He was interested in the subject of Peter's novel, and he was vital and alive, well informed, and had someone to drive him when he needed to go out, who also traveled with him when he had a concert scheduled in another city. When he traveled, Peter had time off, but he rarely went out at night. He was intent on finishing his novel.

When the earthquake hit, Peter stopped typing for a minute while he wondered what was happening. The moment he realized it was an earthquake, he lurched toward the stairs across the floor that felt like it was rippling beneath his feet, and shouted as loud as he could.

"I'm coming, Mr. Harriman! I'm coming!" He slid down the stairs, reached the floor below within seconds, and found Arthur

Harriman sitting underneath his grand piano, looking surprisingly calm. "I'm here, Mr. Harriman, I'm here. Are you all right?"

"I'm fine. It's a big one, get under here with me!" He'd been playing when it happened. "Are you hurt?"

"No, I'm fine," Peter told him.

"Do you have shoes on? There will be broken glass everywhere." The sound of the earthquake tearing the earth beneath them was awful, and unconsciously, Peter held tightly to his arm. He'd never been in an earthquake before. He had come to San Francisco from the Midwest two years before. He was a good-looking young man with dark hair and brown eyes and had a boyish quality to him and a gentle manner. He had grown very fond of the older man he worked for every night. He reminded Peter of his own grandfather, who was a dignified old gentleman, a lawyer in the small town where they lived. Peter had gone to college at Northwestern, and had dreamed of moving to San Francisco for years. Growing up, his family life had been wholesome. His father ran the local newspaper and his mother was a teacher, but their small town was lackluster and dull. His brother and sister had moved to Chicago after college and Peter had dreamed of coming West.

"I have shoes on," Peter reassured him. "Where I come from, we have tornadoes. That's even worse. They just pick up houses and they fly away."

"It'll be over in a minute, son. Don't be afraid," Arthur said in a kind voice, listening and waiting for it to pass. "Is the power still on?"

"No, it's dark, in the house and outside."

"It's a big one," Arthur confirmed. They could hear something heavy fall in the house, and the Victorian wooden structure was groaning, but it had survived the quake of '06, so Arthur wasn't worried. "You have to be careful of falling objects afterward, and broken glass. The aftershocks will shake loose whatever this one didn't. Do you know how to turn off the gas?"

"I'm not sure. What do I do?" Peter asked him, as the earth and the house stopped shaking and the noise receded, like a wounded beast going back into its lair underground.

"The valve is on the side of the house. You need a crescent wrench. We have one in the tool closet. Let's go outside first, and see what's happening there. Someone will be able to show you how to do it." This was precisely why he hired a person like Peter. His last night man had worked for him for four years, and had gotten married shortly before he hired Peter. It was for times like this that he needed someone with him, and occasionally to help him get to bed, if he was exhausted after a concert. But most of the time, he preferred to manage on his own, as long as he knew Peter was upstairs. He used an intercom to call him. He wasn't a demanding employer and Peter loved working for him, and living in the handsome old house. Moving there had been a godsend for him, and in some ways reminded him of his boyhood home in Illinois. He still missed it at times. He rarely went home now. He didn't want to leave Arthur alone. After a year of working for him, he felt responsible for him. "Let's go outside," Arthur suggested to Peter. "Be very careful if there are live wires down. Don't step on them!" he warned him, and Peter helped him out from under the piano, led him carefully down the stairs and out the front door.

When he opened it, there was a man standing at their front door and a woman with two young children standing in front of the house next door. Peter suddenly realized that the man had been pounding on their front door, and in the excitement, and the noise at the tail end of the earthquake, they hadn't heard him.

"What took you so long?" Andrew almost shouted at Peter.

"We were busy," Peter answered him, leading Mr. Harriman to a cluster of people standing outside his house and talking. He was gregarious and an extrovert, and Peter knew he would want to talk to them.

"We need a wrench to turn our gas off," Andrew said, once he realized that the older man was blind, and bringing his tone down a notch.

"So do we," Peter said. "I think we have one in a tool closet. I'll go back inside and look in a minute. You can come with me. We need a crescent wrench and I'm not sure what that looks like. You can use ours if we find it." Andrew followed him into the house a few minutes later, as Arthur chatted with their neighbors, and Tyla and the children walked over to him. He was telling them all about the quake of '89.

Andrew used a flashlight to guide them through the Harriman house, and they found the closet easily. Andrew pointed to the crescent wrench they needed, and Peter handed it to him. Then he looked at Peter.

"Is that Arthur Harriman, the concert pianist? I didn't know he lived next door to us." He seemed surprised and impressed. "Or does he just look like him?"

"No, it's him. He's very discreet, and he travels a lot for concerts.

He's had the house soundproofed so the neighbors can't hear him practicing."

"Are you his son?" Andrew asked him, curious. He spoke to Peter in a pleasant tone, and smiled warmly at him. Andrew could be very charming when he wanted to be. He had been much less so when Peter opened the front door. His tone had been harsh, but not now.

"I work for him," Peter said with a smile. "I'm his 'sleeper.' I sleep at the house at night, in case he needs anything. But he manages fine on his own most of the time, except for something like this."

"I don't suppose our other famous neighbor will make an appearance tonight. The gates hardly ever open, and I hear she never goes out," Andrew said cryptically.

"Who's that? Mr. Harriman never talks about his neighbors."

Andrew looked surprised Peter didn't know. She was a legend in the neighborhood, and the city. It was a name everyone knew, all over the world.

"Meredith White, the famous movie star," Andrew told him. "She's been a recluse for the past ten or fifteen years. No one ever sees her. She's like a UFO. People wait for sightings, but she's elusive. My wife thought she saw her at a yoga class once, but it's not likely. I don't think she'll come out unless her house falls down, and that's not going to happen." He pointed toward the mansion on the corner, surrounded by the tall hedge, and Peter looked surprised. Arthur had never mentioned her. Maybe he didn't know, and Peter never wondered who the neighbors were.

"I didn't know she lived there. My mother saw all her movies. I'll have to tell her." Peter smiled at the thought.

The two men walked out of the Harriman house together, and Peter went with Andrew to help him shut off the gas at his place. Then Andrew followed him to turn off the gas for Arthur's house. They could hear helicopters overhead by then, flying low, checking the city.

"It sounds like a war zone," Andrew commented.

"Where are we all going to sleep tonight?" Peter asked him. "I'm not sure any of our houses are safe, even with the gas off."

"I have to show up at the hospital pretty soon," Andrew told him. "It's our protocol for citywide emergencies. I'll have to figure something out for my wife and kids." He looked pensive. "I think there may be shelters set up at the public schools. The auditorium at the hospital will probably be set up too." He could always take them there. They were discussing it when they joined Arthur, Tyla, and the children.

Joel Fine and Ava Bates had been making love when the earthquake hit. For an instant, Joel thought he had hit new heights with her, and then they both realized what it was, leapt out of bed, and rushed to the doorway where they stood and kissed, still naked.

"That was a good one, babe, wasn't it?" he teased her, while Ava looked panicked and clung to him, as the sound of the earthquake roared around them, and all the books fell out of his bookshelves and crashed to the floor. Joel had founded two brilliantly successful startups and made a fortune. His house had been decorated by a famous interior designer, and he had a Bentley and a Ferrari in the garage. Ava had been living with him for two years. He was forty-two years old and Ava was twenty-nine. She was a tradeshow model they had hired to do ads for his most recent startup, and she had caught his attention immediately when he attended a photo shoot. He had taken her to Vegas for a weekend, and she never left. She was going to college online now, and wanted to be a graphic designer. When he met her, Joel thought she was a gorgeous girl, and had applied all the same rules to her he always did. Give them a great time, concentrate on having fun, keep them around as long as they're amusing and easy to be with, and future plans not included. He never dragged out a relationship once it stopped being fun, and Ava had lasted longer than most of his women. He was divorced and had no interest in getting married again, and said so. His first marriage had cured him. So had his own parents' bitter divorce. He had spent his youth as an only child in Philadelphia as a pawn between parents who hated each other, and he fled gratefully to college at UC Berkeley. He had married after business school in their entrepreneurial program. And when he caught his wife cheating on him, he had divorced her, before they could turn into his parents. He had learned his lesson early. Marriage wasn't for him, and he had no intention of trying again.

He was always honest about what he had to offer. He promised nothing except great sex and good times. He had no kids and didn't want any. His mother came from an old Main Line family, and his father was in investments. He had grown up with privilege and money, and had stayed in California to make a fortune of his own. He had exceeded all his expectations. His parents were stunned.

As soon as the shaking ended, he walked into his bathroom with Ava right behind him, handed her a robe, and put one on himself.

They both put on running shoes. There was broken glass everywhere.

"We'd better get our asses out of here, before the place blows up. I have no idea how to turn the gas off," he told her. They could already smell it. She tied the robe around her with nothing under it, she couldn't find her underwear in the dark and he didn't have a flashlight. The house was pitch black.

They groped their way out of his bedroom and down the stairs. It was the consummate bachelor pad, full of expensive art and sleek furniture, selected by his decorator. They made their way out the front door and onto the street a minute later, and walked straight to the small knot of people standing outside, an older man with a mane of white hair, who looked like Einstein, two younger men, and a woman and two children. The younger men stared as Ava walked up to the group. Peter could guess that she had nothing under the bathrobe. Joel was a handsome man, who exuded confidence and looked as though he owned the world. Peter wondered if they'd been in the shower when the earthquake hit. The woman looked nervous and shaken by the experience, and the man looked as though he was enjoying it. There was a fearless quality to Joel, which Peter almost envied. He'd been shy and had asthma as a child. He couldn't do sports because of his asthma, and he lived through reading books, and came alive once he started writing. He exchanged a shy smile with Ava, while Joel talked to the others and seemed to forget about her. He acted as though he owned her.

"We should have someone out here serving drinks," Joel suggested, and Andrew smiled. They all introduced themselves, and stood chatting for a few minutes about what had happened in their homes, and what they'd been doing at the time. They were talking animatedly when a blond woman walked up to them in a white shirt and jeans and running shoes. It was a warm evening after the hot humid day, and she smiled when she saw them. They hadn't seen the gates open, or the woman slip through. There was a couple following behind her at a discreet distance, and she was carrying a first aid kit, and a large powerful flashlight.

"Hi, is everyone okay here? Anybody hurt or need assistance?" They all stopped for a minute to look at her, and Tyla said that they were fine, just shaken up. No one was hurt. "Does anyone need food or water?" Andrew looked at her carefully for a minute and realized who she was. He had never seen her in the flesh before, and couldn't keep himself from staring at her. She spoke to Arthur, who was laughing and good-humored, as Andrew whispered to Peter standing next to him, "Meredith White." Peter's eyes flew open wide and he tried not to stare at her and couldn't help himself.

"Oh," Peter whispered to Andrew, feeling starstruck, and as Tyla looked at her more closely, she recognized her too. It was the same woman she'd seen in the yoga class, although Andrew didn't believe her.

"I'm Meredith," she said easily. "Do you all have the tools you need to turn your gas off?"

"I don't," Joel said, standing in his bathrobe. "Does anyone have a joint? I'd much rather have that than a wrench. Or a drink?" They all laughed, and Ava looked embarrassed to be standing in a terrycloth robe with nothing under it. You couldn't see anything, but she knew, and Joel loved it. Meredith spoke to Will and Daphne then, and Daphne told her about her doll named Martha who was still inside on her bed. She looked worried about it, with her little brow furrowed, and her long dark pigtails with bows on them.

"I'm sure she's okay, if she's on your bed," Meredith said with a gentle smile. "She's probably sleeping." Debbie and Jack were watching the entire group from a little distance with a look of displeasure. They seemed awkward and out of place, and didn't mingle with the others. They kept their eyes on Meredith, as though she had escaped from jail, and they were eager to get her into custody again, but weren't sure how to do it without creating a scene. Only Arthur, who couldn't see her, and Joel and Ava seemed to have no idea who she was. Andrew and Tyla and Peter were stunned to be talking to Meredith White on the sidewalk, like any ordinary mortal. She didn't act like a recluse. She seemed like a very normal woman, and Daphne was smiling at her. Andrew said regretfully that he had to get to the hospital soon. He was enjoying talking to Peter and Joel, and he knew now who Joel was too, the current king of the high-tech startup world, and Ava was very nice to look at. She had long dark hair cascading down her back, and even the terrycloth bathrobe couldn't hide her figure. She kept having to tie the belt tighter to keep the robe from opening and revealing too much. Peter couldn't keep his eyes off her. He was even more fascinated by her than the famous movie star. It was turning into a very exciting night.

"I can't supply a joint," Meredith said, smiling at Joel, in response to what he'd said, "but I can offer you all a drink and something to eat at my place. We've got plenty of bedrooms if you'd like to spend the night. I mean the offer. Things may continue to shift and fall through the night, and my house is built like a fortress." It was the only stone house on the block. "You're more than welcome to come in. We've got an emergency generator, so we'll have some light."

"We'd love it," Joel said for both of them. It sounded like a party to him. And he was intrigued to see the inside of Meredith's home. Andrew liked the idea too. Daphne was holding Meredith's hand, and Tyla smiled shyly. They all looked grateful and relieved by her offer. Debbie and Jack looked horrified and exchanged a glance. The last thing they wanted was a horde of strangers coming in, and having to watch them to make sure that they didn't steal anything while they were there, or take photographs, which wasn't allowed. Suppliers had to sign a confidentiality agreement just to make deliveries. And now she was inviting strangers in. Debbie rolled her eyes at Jack. Meredith wasn't in the least worried about her neighbors, and was enjoying chatting with them.

Joel and Ava rushed into his house to get some clothes to bring with them. Tyla disappeared into theirs, and returned triumphantly carrying Martha, Daphne's doll, and iPads for both children. Andrew looked annoyed but didn't comment. They all locked their front doors, hoping that there wouldn't be looters or vandals later in the night. Then they followed Meredith to her front gate. She opened it with her key, Debbie and Jack had gone ahead, and the others followed her inside with a look of awe. Peter explained to Arthur where they were going, and when he said Meredith's name, Arthur looked stunned.

He turned and spoke to Meredith immediately and introduced himself and she was equally impressed.

"I've wanted to meet you ever since you moved in. But I never wanted to intrude," Arthur said warmly. "What a great pleasure it is to meet you, and how kind you are to invite us in. I'm beginning to think the earthquake was a stroke of good fortune," he said enthusiastically, and Meredith laughed, and ushered them all into her home. They stood admiring what they could see by flashlight, and she led them all down to the kitchen, where some of the lights were on. Their emergency generator had kicked in, which would power a few lights and appliances around the house.

She asked Jack and Debbie to come up with something simple to eat for all of them. "Sandwiches and cookies would be great," she suggested in an undertone. She could see they didn't look pleased. She knew how protective they were of her and the house, and they had a profound distrust of strangers. But all of her neighbors were highly respectable people, one of them was famous, and the others looked nice. Peter was obviously a sweet boy, and both women were very pleasant, and the two children were adorable. She and Daphne were already fast friends.

"And I have a special job for you two," she said to Will and Daphne. "Since most of the power is off, we'll need to eat everything in our big freezer over the next week or so. So how about if you two get a head start and eat as much ice cream as you can? I think we have five or six flavors," she said, as Will grinned and Daphne let out a squeal of delight. Meredith lifted her onto a stool, and scooped out the ice cream herself into two bowls in the flavors they wanted. And she added a plate of cookies while Debbie got to work on sandwiches with a sour look. Meredith had Jack get Joel a scotch on the rocks, Arthur asked for a brandy, both women had white wine, and Andrew said he couldn't drink since he was going on duty, and should already be there, but he didn't want to miss the gathering at Meredith's house. Peter had white wine, like the two women. Meredith poured herself a small glass of wine too, took a sip, and toasted them all to welcome them to her home. It was the first time she'd had guests in years.

Debbie set out a big platter of sandwiches a little while later. She had just done a big grocery run the day before, so they were heavily stocked with food. Debbie liked to buy in quantity as much as possible, so she didn't have to go often, except for produce and dairy products, but for now they had plenty of those too.

And Jack was pouring drinks like the bartender on the *Titanic*. He took a quick shot himself when no one was looking. The guests were all having a good time, and sat around the kitchen table talking. Andrew finally left them then to go to the hospital a few blocks away. After they'd all talked for a while, and eaten the sandwiches Debbie made, Meredith led them to the bedrooms she had offered to let them use. They were afraid to go back to their own houses, so they had accepted gladly.

She put Peter in a spacious room right next to Arthur. She had Debbie bring in a rollaway bed for Will, so he could sleep in the same room with his mother. And Daphne was going to share the canopied bed with her mother, and Martha, since Andrew had to stay at the hospital. Daphne told Meredith that Martha thanked her for the nice room and the pretty bed. Their rooms were on the same floor as Meredith's, whose suite was at the opposite end of the house. There was a little sitting room off her bedroom where Meredith sat and chatted for a few minutes with Ava and Tyla. She'd given Joel and Ava a handsome guest room, after he and Peter went to shut off the gas at his house, and returned. Meredith loved having them in the house. Suddenly the whole place seemed infused with laughter and chatter, and delightful people. It felt like an old-fashioned house party and the earthquake made them feel like friends immediately.

She finally went to her own room at midnight, after making sure that everyone had what they needed. The two children were fast asleep by then, with Daphne clutching her doll, and Ava looking even more stunning in a short white T-shirt that left her midriff bare, and tight jeans. She and Joel had changed into clothes as soon as they got there.

A few minutes after Meredith got to her bedroom, Debbie came to see her in the guise of checking if she needed anything. She looked like she had something else to say as she lingered with a disgruntled expression.

"I'm fine. And thank you for the delicious sandwiches." Meredith smiled at her, to cheer her up. She assumed that Jack had retired for the night, since their night security men were patrolling the house, making sure that no one tried to force their way in, come over the outer wall, or slip in a window. A night where most of the city had no power was an open invitation to intruders. And with the generator, Meredith's house wasn't dark. It was the only house with lights in the neighborhood, which made it stand out more than ever.

"You can't let these people stay another night," Debbie said boldly, taking Meredith by surprise. She had thought Debbie was upset by the earthquake, not the guests.

"Why not? Of course I can. Their homes may not be safe, and will have to be inspected before they go back in and can stay there. Heavy objects may be ready to fall on their heads, and there could be dangerous structural damage. There's no electricity in any of their houses. We at least have some light, and all our mechanical devices are up and running. Jack said so."

"But you don't know who these people are, Meredith. They could rob you blind during the night, or even hurt you."

"I can't imagine a famous blind concert pianist holding me at gunpoint, or any of the others for that matter. His young novelist employee, a doctor and his wife and two children, and an internationally known founder of high-tech startups and his girlfriend." Joel had made sure that everyone knew who he was. "They don't seem dangerous to me, and I want them to stay as long as they need to," she said clearly to Debbie. Meredith was in full control of the situation. She was enjoying their company, and even the sound of their voices in the hall. The house was no longer silent and it felt full of life. For an instant, she wondered if Jack and Debbie were jealous. They had been used to her full attention for so many years now, almost like children. Maybe they didn't want to share her with strangers. But Meredith was enjoying every minute of it. The earthquake had suddenly put new vibrancy into her home, and was making her feel needed. But she could see that she wasn't going to be able to convince Jack or Debbie to welcome their guests. They felt threatened by them, which seemed foolish and unfriendly to her. She was loving it. Their being there gave her a purpose, even if only for a few days, or however long they needed her. She was happy to welcome them and help them, whatever Jack and Debbie said.

When she went to bed that night, Meredith thought of Daphne and her doll, the fabulous concert pianist she was thrilled to meet, and all the others. There had been something endearing and vulnerable about Tyla. That drew Meredith to her and made her want to mother her. The two hotties in their bathrobes were intriguing too. Ava seemed like a bright girl, but Meredith could see easily that Joel didn't appreciate her fully as a person. He just wanted her as a toy to play with. Peter seemed mesmerized by Ava and couldn't keep his eyes off her. They were an intriguing group.

As she drifted off to sleep, after Debbie left the room, Meredith could hardly wait to see them all at breakfast the next day. She was sure they would want to check on their houses, and she'd ask Jack to help them.

Alone with Jack in the kitchen, Debbie was saying that she would have liked to poison them all and get rid of them. She reported that Meredith was being stubborn about them. They had a last drink from Meredith's bar, which was better than their own booze, and went to their apartment, convinced that their impromptu houseguests were going to be trouble, and they were determined to get rid of them as fast as they could.

What they didn't understand was that for the first time in fifteen years, Meredith was having the time of her life, and she wasn't going to let anyone interfere. Her home was full of life again, with people who needed her. There was a sense of community and caring, which made each of them feel stronger and braver in the face of adversity. Welcoming them into her home had made them feel safe and brought them comfort and had turned a trauma into an opportunity to make new friends. And Meredith intended to hold on to that for as long as she could. And no one was going to spoil that for her.

Chapter 3

Meredith's houseguests emerged shyly from their rooms the next morning, some of them having slept later than they had intended to. The events of the night before, the shock of the earthquake, and the steady stream of small- to medium-sized aftershocks had worn everyone out, and their rooms at Meredith's home were so comfortable that when they finally fell asleep, they slept for hours.

The weather the next day was cooler, and the sky was gray. The ongoing sound of helicopters overhead and the sirens of fire trucks in the distance were a constant reminder of the state of emergency and chaos that the city was in. The governor had come to observe some of the damage the night before, and the president had promised to come in the next few days. He was on a state visit to Southeast Asia at the time. The whole city was shut down and all businesses, schools, and offices were closed.

When Meredith came out of her room early that morning, in jeans and a T-shirt, and an old pair of gardening boots from the back of her closet, she found Daphne sitting on a chair politely in the hallway, all alone, holding her doll. She looked as though she was waiting for someone, and was afraid to move. The house was large and daunting, and she seemed happy when she saw Meredith, who smiled at her.

"My mommy and Will are still asleep," she whispered. "Martha and I woke up." She had dressed herself and was wearing pink jeans with hearts on them, and a gray sweatshirt inside out, which were the first things Tyla had grabbed out of a drawer when she went back into their house for some clothes for them. And Daphne was wearing the pink light-up sneakers she'd had on the night before. Meredith had admired them when they met.

"Did you and Martha sleep well?" she asked, stopping to talk to her with a warm smile. Daphne's long dark hair had been haphazardly brushed, and she nodded in answer.

"You have a very big house. Do you have children?" She was curious about her.

"I have a daughter. She's grown up, and she lives in New York." Daphne nodded, absorbing the information.

"You live here by yourself?"

"Jack and Debbie live here to help me. You met them in the kitchen last night."

"My daddy said you're a witch, before we met you. Like in Hansel and Gretel." Meredith was a little shocked and then she laughed. God only knew what others said about her, since no one ever saw her, or didn't recognize her when they did. "I think you're a good witch," Daphne added. "Martha thinks so too. She said so last night."

"Thank you." Meredith grinned, and held out a hand to her. "Would you and Martha like some breakfast?" Daphne nodded immediately. She'd been sitting in the hallway for an hour, waiting for someone to get up.

"She's very hungry."

"Me too," Meredith said. They held hands as they walked down the grand staircase, and then a smaller one to get to the kitchen in the basement. The generator provided enough electricity to run the basic equipment to prepare a simple meal, and Jack had one of the refrigerators running on it as well. Debbie was in the kitchen when they got there, looking on her phone at the news of the destruction around the city.

"Both bridges are closed," she announced, as Meredith and Daphne walked in. "It was an 8.2 quake. There's a lot of damage downtown. People are still stuck in elevators. It looks like a total mess. Half the streets are impassable, and there's been a lot of looting South of Market. The hospitals are jammed." Meredith had heard that the death toll was over three hundred the night before, thousands of people had been injured, and many were still trapped and buried under their homes. Emergency services were working overtime. Additional trained personnel had been flown in from other states, and volunteers and civilians were helping to dig out survivors. "The National Guard was called in to control the looters. Jack says we need to keep the gates locked," Debbie said with a severe expression. With Meredith's sudden spirit of generosity toward her neighbors, she and Jack were both afraid she'd try to bring more in, or throw open the gates.

"My daddy didn't come home from the hospital last night," Daphne said in a soft voice, her eyes big in her face. "My mommy was afraid our house would fall down. And Will said it would blow up if Daddy didn't turn off the gas." The news had reported fires raging all over town, and with water mains broken, the firefighters couldn't put them out. The fires burning out of control were what had caused most of the damage in the 1906 quake, and could again.

"Your daddy must be very busy at the hospital," Meredith said.

"He fixes broken arms and legs," Daphne said proudly, as her mother and brother wandered into the kitchen. They both looked sleepy and tousled, in oddly assembled outfits, but clean clothes. Tyla had been annoyed to realize that the only shirts she'd brought for herself had short sleeves. She usually wore long-sleeved ones, and she had absentmindedly grabbed Will's soccer uniform, which he was wearing to breakfast.

"Debbie, do you think we can manage pancakes?" Meredith asked.

"Sure," she said, setting out places for four at the kitchen table as Tyla and Meredith chatted. She noticed an ugly bruise on Tyla's upper arm in the short-sleeved, plaid shirt she was wearing.

"Ouch, that looks nasty." It was about the size of a salad plate. "Did that happen last night?" Meredith asked her. It seemed dark purple to be that fresh.

"I . . . I don't know . . . I fell in the garage a few days ago, I slipped on some oil, it might have happened then," she said vaguely, as Ava walked in, in bright pink exercise clothes, fresh and wide awake. The top looked more like a sports bra and her midriff was bare. She was in perfect shape and her muscles taut.

"Can I grab a cup of coffee?" she asked cautiously, her dark hair piled on her head. She was incredibly sexy. "I usually go to a spinning class today. I guess everything's going to be closed for a while," she said, as Debbie handed her a mug of coffee, and Meredith poured two, for Tyla and herself. Tyla was a pretty woman, but her style was plain.

Debbie had set out orange juice for the kids. Will drained his, and Daphne offered Martha a sip before she drank hers. Meredith smiled as she watched her, and they all sat down at the kitchen table. Ava poured herself a bowl of granola, when Meredith showed her where it was, and all Tyla wanted was a piece of toast and her mug of coffee. Debbie was using an electric stovetop to make the pancakes, since the gas stove and ovens were off.

They talked about the damage in the city, as the two kids ate their pancakes. And halfway through the meal, Andrew walked in, wearing scrubs, looking exhausted.

"I've been up all night," he said, as Debbie handed him a mug of coffee, and he sat down at the table with the women and children.

"Breakfast?" Debbie asked him, and he shook his head.

"I ate at the hospital cafeteria before I came home. I just stopped at the house. One of the beams in the dining room is on the floor. I don't think there's a dish left in the kitchen, and there's a tear in Will's bedroom ceiling. I called our insurance adjuster, and all I got was voicemail," he said, stretching his long legs out ahead of him.

He glanced at his wife's arm, and gave her a glance when he saw the bruise. "Why are you wearing your soccer uniform?" he asked his son, "there won't be a game today."

"It's what Mom brought me to wear," he said in a small voice. His father didn't look like he was in a good mood. He was tired after the long night. He'd been at the hospital working nonstop for twelve hours.

"I have to go back at three o'clock. We're all working double shifts. Half the people in the city must have broken something last night," and many were still buried. An apartment building in the Sunset had collapsed, emergency teams were still digging people out, and people who had left their offices late were still trapped in elevators all over the financial district. "They're estimating it will take five or six days to get to everyone downtown. And one of the bridges in the South Bay collapsed, they're still pulling people out of the water, but they're taking them to Stanford Hospital in Palo Alto, and Alta Bates in Oakland. We've got more than we can handle now." They'd had emergency drills for an event like this for years, but once it happened, it never went quite as smoothly as they hoped, or the way it had been planned. He spoke to his wife in a low voice. "I don't see how you and the kids can move back in until we get the mess cleaned up and some of the damage fixed, I don't have time to pursue it, and all of the contractors must be closed. But all the hotels are jammed, and a lot of them don't have power yet."

At the hospital, they had emergency generators, but even there, there were areas that were dark and they couldn't use. They'd had to send the last wave of injured to SF General and UCSF. They were over their maximum limit of patients they could deal with now, and people were still showing up in droves. It was going to be a very tough few weeks for health professionals all over the Bay Area. They were bringing in nurses from neighboring states, as fast as they could get them, and a flock of doctors from L.A.

He was still describing the situation to them when Joel Fine walked in, and the two men exchanged an appreciative glance. They had hit it off from the moment they met. Joel didn't greet either of the women, nor the two children, and started talking to Andrew as soon as he sat down, while Meredith watched them, and Jack showed up to help his wife in the kitchen. The two employees looked somewhat sullen, and anything but pleased to have a house full of guests, due to their employer's largesse, inviting neighbors she didn't even know to come and stay. And none of their houses were sound enough to move back into yet, and wouldn't be for some time.

Peter and Arthur Harriman walked into the kitchen as the others were finishing breakfast, and Debbie collected their plates and put them in the sink, grateful that the dishwasher was running, thanks to the generator. She felt like she was a one-man restaurant serving all of them. And if they stayed, they'd expect lunch and dinner too. Every restaurant in town was closed. And so were most of the grocery stores. Luckily Debbie had just done a massive grocery run right before the earthquake. And from her youth, she was good at making food stretch. She guessed that with canned and frozen food, as well as fresh, and a huge amount of pasta, she would be able to feed the whole group for several weeks, not that she wanted them to stay. But she could provide meals for them if they did. And all around the city, restaurants were giving away free food, before it could go bad. And a few generous grocery stores were open and doing the same, with frozen and perishable food.

Arthur thanked Meredith as soon as he heard her voice, and walked toward her, using his white cane. "I haven't slept that well in years. Thank you for putting us up so kindly. What can I do to help you today?"

"Not a thing, Mr. Harriman." She smiled at him. "It's an honor to have you here." They sat down at the table, and Debbie took their breakfast order with a somber expression, as Jack went to answer a pounding at the back door. The bell at the front gate wasn't working, and the gate had to be opened manually, using a key. When he returned, a tall erect man with salt and pepper hair, in a military uniform, walked in, looking businesslike and serious, and he smiled when he saw the two children. The adults were all surprised to see him in their midst. Meredith approached him quickly, and he introduced himself. She noticed a number of stripes and stars on his uniform and wasn't sure what they meant. She wondered if the city was now under martial law, and how it would affect them if so.

"I'm sorry to interrupt you," he said pleasantly. "I'm Colonel Charles Chapman, retired Air Force. I'm attached to the National Guard, as liaison to the Office of Emergency Services. I'm one of several retired officers walking the neighborhood today, going house to house to see if you need help. The National Guard troops have been deployed downtown to stop the looting, and it will be a while before the OES can get to all of you, but we're trying to assess how bad the damage is in the residential neighborhoods. Do you all live here in this house?" He looked around the group at the table, and wondered if they were a big family living in the enormous house. Everyone appeared to be hale and hearty, and he noticed Andrew in medical scrubs, and other than two large broken urns with plants in them at the back door, he hadn't seen any significant damage when he walked in. There was broken glass all around the house, and some broken windows, but Jack and Debbie had cleaned it up in the early morning hours before anyone got up. There were bags of it where they left their trash for the garbage collectors who hadn't come, and probably wouldn't for several days.

"Thank you, Colonel," Meredith said graciously as she walked up to him and they shook hands. "I actually live here, and these are my neighbors from the three houses adjacent to this one. They had quite a lot of damage, so they're staying here with me."

"How bad is the damage?" he asked, looking at the others, and Peter, Joel, and Andrew reported what they had seen so far, but admitted that they hadn't been able to assess it thoroughly the night before. "Your gas is turned off, I hope?" he asked them and they all nodded.

"We have our own emergency generator," Meredith explained to him, "but it's limited as to the power it gives us." Debbie was cooking on an electric stove, fortunately. Meredith guessed that the gas might not be turned on for several weeks. "The rest of the neighborhood was dark last night," she reported to the colonel, which he already knew.

"And it will be, possibly for weeks, or even months." There was a collective groan when he said it, and he smiled, and looked at

Meredith. "You're kind to take your neighbors in. Most of the houses I've been to so far have several additional people staying there, who couldn't get home across the bridges, or whose houses are too damaged to be safe. Was anyone injured here last night?"

"A few cuts and bruises, nothing major, Colonel," Meredith answered. "We were all very lucky. A lot of broken glass. I think we'll need an engineer to assess how sound our houses are before people move back in." But hers was solid and had withstood it well. On closer inspection, Jack had discovered a crack in the façade of the house, but it was more cosmetic than structural. Meredith's house was not at risk. "Would you like a cup of coffee?" she offered. He hesitated. He had many more houses to visit on his morning rounds, but it was tempting. They looked like a congenial group, and their hostess was an attractive woman with a gracious manner that was hard to resist.

"A quick one." He smiled at her. He'd been making home visits for four hours, and was grateful for a break. "You're a doctor?" he asked Andrew as he joined them and sat down, and Andrew nodded and smiled at him. His family knew what no one else did, that his mood could go from tropical sunny to arctic glacial or volcanic in an instant. At his best, Andrew was personable and appeared to be a great guy. His demons lurked just beneath the surface, carefully kept out of sight.

"I am. I'm an orthopedic surgeon. We're on emergency status with double and triple shifts. I'm going back in a few hours. We had a busy night."

"The casualties have been higher than we projected," the colonel said as he took a sip of the steaming coffee, "but the death toll isn't quite as bad as we feared with an earthquake of this magnitude." It had been an 8.2 on the Richter scale, which was serious business, and more powerful than the 1906 quake. But the city codes for earthquake-proof construction had protected many people, and reduced the potential damage. In poorer neighborhoods with old houses, and on landfill, many homes had collapsed. "They put us old dogs to work, checking out the neighborhoods. I live nearby, so I was assigned to this one. I've been knocking on doors all night." He didn't look tired and he had a calming manner that reassured them all. "I retired two years ago, but I stayed in the National Guard, for situations like this. I've seen some bad earthquakes in my time, in war zones and underdeveloped countries where there were no codes for their construction, and the devastation after an earthquake like this is heartbreaking." He had a relaxed, easy manner, spoke to all of them, asked Will about his soccer team, and asked Daphne if the Tooth Fairy had been to visit her for all the teeth she was missing, and she said she had, she had gotten a dollar for every tooth. When Colonel Chapman got up to leave, Meredith walked him through the main floor, out the front door, and let him out the main gate with her key. He handed her a card with his name, and OES cellphone number. "I've got the phone on me at all times. If you have a problem we can help you with, don't hesitate to call me. It's nice of you to take your neighbors in," he said kindly.

"It would be pretty awful if I didn't, with a house this size," she said modestly.

"Still, I'm assuming you don't know them, and you seem to like your privacy." He motioned to the gate, the wall around her property, and the tall hedge that almost hid the house from the street.

"I met them yesterday, and there's no privacy at a time like this. They're all very nice people."

He hesitated for a minute at the gate. "I know this sounds ridiculous, but I have the feeling we've met somewhere." There was something about her face that was haunting him, and he couldn't figure out what it was. "I was based in Washington, at the Pentagon, for the last ten years before I retired from the Air Force, and I moved out here two years ago when my wife died. I needed a change of scene, and figured it was time. I don't know if we met here or in Washington, but I have the feeling our paths crossed somewhere."

"I haven't been out much in a long time," she said cautiously, not wanting to explain it to a total stranger. She wondered if he had seen her movies in the past, and it hadn't clicked for him yet, and she wasn't going to tell him.

"Well, give a shout if there's anything we can do for you."

"I think we have everything under control," she said as she smiled at him, "but thank you." He walked through the gate then, waved and headed down the street at a good clip, crossed the street at the corner, and she saw him knock on the door of a large handsome house. An older woman answered and he went inside, and she went back to the others. They were milling around the kitchen, trying to figure out what to do next. They all wanted to go back to their homes and check out the damage in daylight. She heard Andrew Johnson growl at his wife in a barely audible voice, as they walked up the stairs so Tyla could get her bag.

"So which of the men here were you flirting with when I was working?" At first Meredith thought he was joking, but his tone said he wasn't. There was a vicious edge to it, she saw him grab Tyla's arm, and she winced. He had clamped his hand over the ugly purple bruise. There was nothing flirtatious about Tyla and no cause for what he'd said.

"Don't be silly, none of them. I was with the kids," Tyla said, as they disappeared into the room they were using, and Meredith went to her own room. Debbie showed up a few minutes later.

"So what am I supposed to feed them for lunch, now that I'm running a restaurant?" She knew she had to stretch the food supplies they had and make them last, since there was no way of knowing how long grocery stores would stay open and if their stock would run out. She looked sour and annoyed as she said it, and Meredith refused to give in to Debbie's displeasure at having strangers in the house, during a crisis.

"Sandwiches, salad, pasta, whatever is easy for you. And you can take some chickens out of the freezer for tonight. It doesn't have to be fancy. Just simple food to keep everyone fed." Debbie was usually much more pleasant than that, and Meredith was surprised by her attitude. Jack had been no better. Whenever one of the guests spoke to him, he answered them tersely and was barely civil. It was unlike them, they were always so kind to her. Debbie and Jack's unspoken hostility was a side of them Meredith had never seen.

"I wasn't expecting to run a hotel after the earthquake. There are shelters they could go to. They don't need to stay here. They're taking advantage of you." She was trying to instill fear and anger into Meredith, and it wasn't working. Meredith didn't respond. She had an idea and went to knock on Tyla and Andrew's door. Tyla looked startled and nervous when she opened it, and Andrew was standing right behind her.

"I was wondering if you'd like me to keep the kids with me, while you check out your house," Meredith offered, and Tyla turned to Andrew for the answer.

"No, they can come with us. Will can help me clean up, and Daphne likes to stay close to her mom," Andrew said. It seemed as though he didn't want Meredith to have time alone with them, but that was understandable too. They really didn't know her.

"Well, let me know if I can do anything to help, or if you'd like Jack to come with you," she said pleasantly.

"We'll be fine," he said, and closed the door before Tyla could, and Meredith heard his words before she walked away. "What did you tell her?" he said in a vicious tone to his wife.

"I didn't tell her anything. She's just trying to be nice," Tyla said in a pleading tone.

"Just keep her out of our business, and away from our kids," he said in a raised voice, as Meredith walked away as soundlessly as she could. A few minutes later, she saw Peter and Arthur Harriman heading down the stairs, and went to speak to them, still startled by what Andrew had said to his wife. What were they hiding?

"We're going to check my piano," Arthur explained to her. "I want to be sure it didn't get damaged in the aftershocks," he said with concern, as he made his way down the steps at a good clip, with Peter right behind him. For an eighty-two-year-old man, he was agile and alert, and had more energy than anyone in the group. "Peter doesn't think I should practice in the house in case something falls in an aftershock," Arthur said, faintly annoyed. Normally, nothing could keep him from playing.

"I have a piano here, in the drawing room, if you'd like to check it out. It's probably not up to your standards. It's a baby grand, a Steinway," Meredith offered.

"I'm sure it's a fine instrument. I'm used to mine. We have a long relationship. I've had it for thirty years. My wife and I used to play duets on it. She was an excellent pianist as well. We met at Juilliard when we both studied there. We were seventeen when we met. We were married for fifty-seven years."

"Do you have children, Mr. Harriman?" she asked when they reached the front door. She was touched by what he had shared with her.

"No, I don't. We had each other, and our work. For us, that was enough. We never felt ready to include children in our lives. We were devoted to each other."

"It sounds like a beautiful love story," Meredith said gently.

"Do you have children?" he asked her, curious about her too. "Peter says this is a very big house, I doubt that you always lived here alone," he said.

"I have a daughter, in New York. She's grown and married now, with a daughter of her own." She didn't tell him about Justin, the story was too sad and too personal to share with people she had just met, virtually strangers. "I love this house, and it is big, but I rarely go out. I have my own private world here." He frowned as he looked at her, almost as though he could see her.

"That's never a good idea, having one's own private world behind walls. The world needs you, Mrs. White. Look at us. We all need you now. Don't deprive others of your company, or yourself of the world. It's a troubled place these days, which is all the more reason for you to participate in it. You have a great deal to offer." He couldn't know that, and he knew who she was. He certainly didn't lead a secluded life. He still had a heavy concert schedule, and traveled constantly. There was nothing elderly or reclusive about him. She was mildly embarrassed that she had admitted to him that she was. She let him and the Johnsons out of the gate a few minutes later, and the house was very quiet after that. She went upstairs to her room, and dealt with some bank papers she had meant to take care of the day before and hadn't.

When she left her room again, she crossed Joel and Ava, and he was saying to her, "Come on, baby, let's go back to our place and finish what we started when the earthquake hit," and then he laughed.

"What if the house falls down on top of us in an aftershock?" Ava said, and Meredith was embarrassed to have overheard them.

"Wouldn't that be a great way to die?" Joel said, and didn't care who heard him say it. "Having sex." He acted as though it was all he wanted to do with her, and Meredith felt sorry for her. She was clearly a sex object in his life, and not much more. He could hardly keep his hands off her, and was always rubbing some part of her, her back, her waist, her neck, her bottom, in a sensual almost lewd way. Meredith felt like a Peeping Tom around them. It didn't surprise her now that they'd been naked, wearing bathrobes, when they'd walked into the street after the earthquake. It was as though he wanted everyone to know that he had sex with her all the time.

It was more than Meredith wanted to know about them. And she had a strong sense that there was much more to Ava than Joel Fine saw. She was a bright girl who was clearly trying to better herself. She was proud of going to college online, and had mentioned it at dinner the night before. She couldn't afford to go to a top design school, but she was applying herself diligently online. She had mentioned in passing that her parents had both died when she was a child, and she was brought up by a strict aunt and uncle in Salt Lake City, and had fled to San Francisco as soon as she was able after high school. She got work as a tradeshow model in San Francisco. She'd worked hard at it and got by for nine years. Her life had been altered unimaginably when she met Joel, and he introduced her to a whole new world of luxury, and his ability to have and do whatever he wanted due to his success. Joel paid for whatever he desired, and treated her as though he owned her, with no interest in how bright she was or her dreams.

Joel wanted Ava's company and her body at his beck and call. She realized now that she had become too comfortable in his lifestyle, and even addicted to it. She felt safe in his world even though she knew that one day he would tire of her, and it would be over, like all the women who had come before her. Joel was a golden dead end, she reminded herself of it constantly, but she never had the courage to walk away. It was too easy to stay, even though he offered her no future. But he was kind and fun and generous.

The people she'd grown up with would have envied her, but she had always wanted more for herself and still did. A career she could be proud of, a man who valued her as more than just decorative, or for sex. She wanted a husband and children one day, and

Joel was never going to be that person and had said so since the beginning. She knew she'd have to jump off the train one day, but Joel's life in the fast lane moved too quickly and it was too easy to stay, so she had.

She wanted to be more than she was now, with him. She refused to let go of her dreams, but there was no way to pursue them while she was with him. She knew she was settling for a man who wasn't capable of truly loving her, or anyone. She was part of the fantasy life he had created for himself, but she was not real to him. There were qualities of Joel's that Ava loved and she was grateful to him for the life he shared with her, even though she knew that the only person Joel would ever truly love was himself. She knew it, but always hoped a little that something would change, and he would see her as a person, and maybe even fall in love with her.

Joel and Ava left the house after Meredith saw them, and Jack let them out. He had been picking up more broken pots in the garden. Meredith went to check on her rosebushes. Some of them looked sadly battered, and one had literally been torn out of the ground. She was still checking on them and trying to repair them, when the others began coming back at one o'clock. Daphne was skipping and carrying two more dolls along with Martha, and Will was carrying his backpack full of his schoolbooks. His father wanted him to do some homework every day, even though his school was closed. Tyla looked tired, and had a bandage on her hand. She had cut herself throwing away mountains of broken glasses and dishes. She had a suitcase with changes of clothes for all four of them. Andrew was carrying his medical bag, in case any of them got hurt. He had bandaged Tyla's hand when she cut it.

There was a kind of vacant look in her eyes, and she seemed nervous when Meredith glanced at her, as though she was hiding a secret.

Arthur said he had been able to practice on his own piano, but he reported that Peter said that there were numerous cracks and fissures in the walls and ceilings, and a lot of plaster had fallen. They needed an engineer to check it out before they could stay there. And Peter was carrying his manuscript, in case Arthur's house caught fire.

Joel said his newly decorated house was a mess. Many paintings had fallen, a piece of neon art had been destroyed and half his furniture was broken. Ava was upset that her laptop with all her schoolwork on it had fallen off her desk and was broken. It sounded like there was a lot of work to do at their house too, and they hadn't been able to pick up all the broken glass everywhere, there was so much of it, along with their dishes. Joel was going to hire a service to do it. Meredith noticed that they had changed clothes, and wondered if they'd had sex again when they were at his house. Ava was wearing a different exercise outfit, in turquoise this time.

They all went to the kitchen, and Debbie had set out a buffet for them, of salads, a platter of sandwiches, potato chips, fruit, and cookies. It was a more than adequate lunch and Debbie commented to Meredith that eventually they'd run out of food, if the houseguests stayed for very long. But Meredith knew they had enough to provide many more meals for the group staying at the house. Their storage cupboards and fridges were full.

"If we do, the stores will be open again by then, and we can buy more food. It sounds like none of their houses are sound enough to move back into and won't be for a while," Meredith said curtly. She didn't like Debbie's inhospitable attitude at all, and knowing how kind she and Jack had been to her, it really shocked her, and seemed out of character for them.

They had almost finished lunch at two o'clock when Colonel Chapman appeared again to check on them. He said he was on his way home and had come to speak to Meredith. The others reported in greater detail the damage in their homes. It sounded structural at Arthur's house, and might be at the other two. They agreed that it would have to be checked out by professionals, and their insurance companies would have to be involved too.

"No one escaped this one," Charles Chapman said, looking more tired than he had earlier in the day. He'd been checking on people in their homes for fourteen hours. He seemed awkward with Meredith when he spoke to her, and after he shared coffee and a brownie with them, he quietly asked Meredith if he could speak to her alone.

"Is something wrong?" she asked him, worried. She wondered for an instant if he had found out something about her neighbors that he thought she should know. Maybe Jack and Debbie were right.

"No, not at all. Except that I'm an idiot. I mentioned your so generously housing your neighbors when I went back to the OES office to report in at the end of my shift. A lot of people are putting friends up, but you've got eight people staying here whom you'd never even met before. That's admirable, and not many people would do it, whatever the size of their home. They're still strangers, and you're letting them all stay here, and even feeding them."

"It seems the least I can do in the circumstances, and we had very little damage, other than a number of painting frames, which broke when they fell, and a few fragile antique objects. I'm a little worried about the chandeliers too, and want to get them checked out when we can get an engineer here, which probably won't be for a while, if what you've said is true."

"All the construction companies are going to be backed up for a long time," he confirmed. "But that isn't what I wanted to tell you. I mentioned your name at the office and my colleague's jaw dropped. He's a movie buff, and I've seen all your old movies too. I just didn't make the connection when I met you, and forgot that you live here." His co-worker had filled him in on the history too, that a bad divorce when her husband left her and a child who had died tragically had ended her career. Charles had heard long ago that she had become a recluse, but he wasn't interested in movie star gossip, and never made the connection with the warm, attractive, kind woman he'd met that morning. He'd been stunned when his colleague told him. "*That* Meredith White?" was all he could say. But when he thought about it, he realized that it was why her face looked so familiar. He had seen her in dozens of movies before she disappeared from the screen. His friend had asked him what she was doing now, and he had no idea, other than living in a big house and housing her neighbors after the earthquake. She had been so modest and unassuming that it never dawned on him that she was the movie star. But seeing her for the second time, it was obvious even to him.

"You must have thought I was an idiot when I said I thought I had met you before. My wife used to love your movies and so did

I. But we surely never met, unless you were one of my fighter pilots, or ran a squadron." He blushed and she smiled.

"Don't worry about it. That's fine. It's been a long time. I've been out of the movie business for fourteen years." He knew why now. He wasn't even sure if he'd known before. Eventually, she just stopped appearing in movies. He didn't question why. "I've probably changed a lot since then. I don't go out much, but when I do, people rarely recognize me."

"Do you wear a blanket over your head, or a hat and dark glasses? Now that I know who you are, I'd recognize you immediately."

"Audrey Hepburn used to say that if you don't make eye contact with people on the street, they don't recognize you. I think that's true. But I go out very, very rarely. I sneak into a yoga class once in a while, and go for long walks on the beach, but that's about it."

"What about your daughter in New York? Do you go to see her, or does she come here to see you?" She had mentioned Kendall to him before. She hesitated before she answered. He was so dignified, respectful, and distinguished looking that she was saying more to him than she would have normally. He had a warm style, and a kind manner with people.

"Actually, we don't see each other very often. She has a busy life, and I haven't traveled since . . . since I retired from films."

"It's probably not easy for you to go out with fans hounding you."

"It's a little more complicated than that. My daughter and I talk on the phone, I'll get to New York one of these days." But she didn't sound convincing, and he could see that she was sad as she said it.

He could feel her retreating and he was afraid he had upset her, particularly since he knew about her son's death now, from his friend at the OES office. He couldn't imagine her daughter not coming to see her. He saw his own children as often as he could. But he wasn't a movie star who had become a recluse, and hadn't been struck by tragedy. His wife had died, earlier than they'd ever expected, at fifty-three, but she had handled it with dignity, and he had done his best to live a good life since, and remain connected to the world after she died.

Meredith had retreated from the world and had been in hiding ever since. He wondered who her friends were, and if she had any. She had been so generous with her neighbors, he wondered if that was typical of her. The only thing he didn't like that he had seen so far was the couple who worked for her. The two of them looked like a nasty piece of work to him, and wanted to make everyone who crossed her threshold, including him, as uncomfortable as they could, to chase them away. He wondered what the story was there, and why she had them working for her. Most people didn't have that reaction to him, either due to his military rank, or his open, easy, friendly nature. Meredith was warm and welcoming to him too, despite her celebrity. But her two employees seemed hostile and downright unpleasant.

"Anyway, I wanted to apologize to you for not recognizing you. I was mortified when I made the connection. I wanted to stop by on my way home to tell you."

"It's nicer that you didn't recognize me." She smiled at him. "I don't want to be treated like some kind of historical relic," she said with a laugh, "although I suppose that's what I am by now." But she was sixty-three, not a hundred, and she looked even younger, without makeup, and with her blond hair.

"You're not a relic, you're a legend," he said, slightly in awe of her.

"Oh dear, that sounds scary too. I'm just a person who used to make movies. Now I spend my time gardening and reading, going for long walks. It's a peaceful life." But it sounded empty and sad to him, and yet she didn't look like a sad person. But her eyes told him that she had been through hell and come to a place of peace. He wondered if it had taken her all fourteen years of her retirement to do it.

"Well, your neighbors are very lucky that you're letting them stay here. And I feel fortunate to have met you. If it's all right with you, I'd like to drop by again. You've got a good group here. I'm a big fan of Arthur Harriman. It's a treat to have met him. He's remarkable for his age, and such an extraordinary talent. You've actually got quite an interesting group here. Joel Fine is certainly the king of high-tech startups." Meredith knew that. "I've read about him. He's a fascinating guy. He comes from a wealthy background, went to Harvard, and got an MBA at UC Berkeley, and made a fortune on his own with his startups. He hasn't had one fail yet."

Joel was very upset when he got back from his house inspection, as Charles Chapman was leaving. Something had fallen in his garage and dented his Ferrari. Will had asked him at lunch if he could see it, since he talked about it, and Joel said he could.

"Call me if you need anything," Charles Chapman said again when he left, and Meredith thought about their conversation and wondered if she had said too much, but he was easy to talk to. She didn't usually admit that she and Kendall didn't see each other and hadn't in years. They weren't estranged, since they still spoke on the phone from time to time, but they weren't close either. Kendall was close to her father, and the damage with her mother had never been repaired. Kendall had never tried to, and San Francisco was no longer on her map. Meredith had made her peace with that too. Her heart had taken a beating three times, when Scott left her for Silvana, when Justin died, and when Kendall stayed close to her father, blamed her mother for everything, and systematically cut her out of her life. Jack and Debbie had gotten her through it, and she felt indebted to them forever, even if they were being difficult now, about having the neighbors stay under her roof. They wanted Meredith to send them to one of the earthquake shelters and there was no way she would now. They were people to her now, and rapidly becoming friends, as they opened up to her.

After Charles left, Andrew went back to the hospital a little while later. Joel took Will to see his Ferrari and let him sit behind the wheel. He was basically a nice guy, he just didn't have a strong respect for women and saw them as sex toys. His father had been that way too, which had broken up his parents' marriage. Meredith could already tell that there was so much more substance to Ava than he gave her credit for. He was nice to her, and generous, but all he really cared about was her body. Meredith couldn't imagine being with a man like him, but Ava seemed devoted to him, and didn't seem to mind. She had sold her soul for the lifestyle he offered her, and Meredith wondered if most women would. And Joel was used to being seen as a prize of some kind, and a means to an end. Although she had no money, Ava wasn't with him for what he could give her or do for her. She genuinely cared about him and sometimes even believed she loved him. She wasn't cynical and thought the best of everyone. It came through in everything she said.

The one who worried her in the group was Tyla, who seemed so meek and vulnerable to Meredith, after knowing her for only twenty-four hours. She obviously adored her children, and was devoted to her husband and anxious to please him, but he seemed so harsh with her when he thought no one was listening. He was handsome, intelligent, successful, and charming to everyone else, but Meredith sensed a chip on his shoulder she couldn't identify, and a silent, deeply buried, underlying rage. She didn't know why, but she thought there was something dangerous about him, and she had noticed that his children seemed ill at ease around him too. She had heard Will stammer a few times when his father addressed him. She suspected that still waters ran deep in Andrew's case, and things weren't always as they appeared.

Later that afternoon, Joel went downtown to see if they would let him cross police lines to check out what condition his office was in. He didn't ask Ava to come, in case it was dangerous, and she ran into Peter in the kitchen when they both went to make a cup of tea. She was wearing very short shorts and a T-shirt stretched over her enormous breasts. He blushed as soon as he saw her, as though she could read his mind, and he had his manuscript with him. Arthur had gone to take a nap, and Peter was going to work on his manuscript by hand. He had left his vintage typewriter at Arthur's house.

It was too cumbersome to carry, and he had nowhere to set it up here. He had mentioned earlier that he never wrote on a computer, and loved his typewriter.

"How long have you been working on it?" Ava asked, when he mentioned his book to her. He seemed so intent and passionate about it that it touched her. He had loved writing since he was a boy and was determined to make his family proud of him one day.

"Two years. I have a job in the daytime, and I write at night when Arthur is practicing, or after he goes to bed. He doesn't need much help from me. I'm hoping to finish it in a few months. Working for Arthur has given me the opportunity to spend time on it and make some headway at night."

"I used to dream about being in film production, but it never happened," Ava admitted shyly. "I was freelancing as a tradeshow model, and Joel gave me a job as a receptionist at one of his start-ups. Eventually, after we started dating, he made me quit so I'd be available to him. I haven't worked in two years, so I'm taking classes now in graphic design, which I love, so I can get a better job one day, after . . ." Her voice trailed off and Peter understood. There was no future to her relationship with Joel, and she knew it. He wondered if she was with him only for his lifestyle and the perks, or if she loved him. But he didn't know her well enough to ask. She seemed like a sincere person, but Joel's lifestyle would be hard for most people to resist.

"It's nice that you have dreams," she said softly, as their eyes met, and Peter felt an electric charge run through him. Everything about her fascinated him, not just her body, but her mind, her drive to do something better with herself. She seemed like a sympathetic person. He liked talking to her. He wondered if Joel ever did. He made it so obvious that he was with her for her stunning body and her looks. It embarrassed Peter for her. He knew he had no right to, but he felt protective of her, although he barely knew her.

"You have dreams too," Peter reminded her, "or you wouldn't be taking classes." She smiled. He understood. She knew that her time with Joel was finite. He never stayed with a woman for more than two years. He had told her that in the beginning, and it had been slightly more than that now. She was on borrowed time. She knew that Joel didn't love her. He enjoyed her company, but women were interchangeable to him, like cars. And one of these days he would find a newer model, give her a generous gift, or an apartment, and be gone. She'd been thinking about it a lot recently. It made her work even harder on her classes, and she was hoping to graduate soon. She had to get a new computer now, so she could continue her classes and complete her design assignments. Several of her professors had said in their reviews of her work that she had real talent.

"I'd better get to work," Peter said as he stood up. "Before Arthur wakes up from his nap. I'm not usually with him in the daytime, just at night. He never stops." He smiled at Ava. It had been nice talking to her.

They walked upstairs together, and they each disappeared into their rooms. Peter had the pages of his book in front of him on the table, and a pen in his hand, and all he could do was stare at it and think of Ava. He'd never been as obsessed with any woman in his life, and there was nothing he could do about it. She belonged to someone else. He was asking himself how could someone like him compete with Joel Fine? He had no money, two uninteresting minor jobs, he was writing a novel, which would probably never get published, and he lived in someone else's house. He had nothing to offer her, or to dazzle her with. Ava, with all her beauty, brains and youth, was like Joel's Ferrari, totally beyond his reach, and all he could do was dream. He loved being in the same house with her, but he hoped they moved back to Arthur's house soon, before he lost his mind, obsessed with her. Just thinking about her made him long for a future that would never be even remotely possible.

Chapter 4

Charles Chapman's visits to check on them every day were beginning to seem familiar to all of them. He chatted with them, and kept them abreast of the progress around the city, to repair the damage from the earthquake. Three days after it had devastated the city, they were still digging people out. The next time Charles stopped by for coffee in the morning, Peter asked to volunteer for the Office of Emergency Services. He wanted to do something more useful than just keeping Arthur company. And Arthur was managing well with his white cane in Meredith's safe, comfortable home. And there were plenty of people for him to talk to. He had asked Arthur's permission, and he thought Peter volunteering was an excellent idea. There were enough people around to assist him if he needed help with some small task until Peter got back.

The others were startled when Peter mentioned it, and Charles was pleased. He told Peter where to report. He said they needed all the help they could get. Two hours later, Peter took off, in work boots and jeans, with a pair of gardening gloves Meredith gave him, and they wished him luck. He knew it would be rigorous work and deeply upsetting at times. Not everyone they pulled out of the rubble would be alive, but there had been amazing stories about infants pulled out of the debris, old people, small children. Many or even most of them had survived.

"We ought to do something like that," Ava said at lunch after he left, speaking to Meredith and Tyla.

"Digging people out of the rubble? I don't think I'm strong enough," Tyla said, worried.

"Not that, but we could serve food at one of the shelters that have been set up, or help at a first aid station. There must be something we can do." They all felt slightly guilty, living in comfort and safety in Meredith's palatial home, while others in the city were enduring unimaginable hardships and had lost everything.

"It's not a bad idea," Meredith commented. "Why don't we? Why don't we just turn up and offer our services?" She turned to Tyla then. "You're a nurse, at least you know what you're doing. But I could serve food, or hand out clothes." Ava nodded agreement.

"I haven't been a nurse in a long time," Tyla said shyly, but all three of them liked the idea, and decided to go down to the nearest shelter at a public school in the Marina, to see what there was for them to do. "Who could I leave Will and Daphne with?" Tyla asked Meredith.

"Debbie can keep an eye on them," Meredith volunteered, and went to explain it to Debbie after lunch. She looked anything but pleased at the idea.

"I don't know anything about kids. I'm not a nanny," she said, looking miffed.

"You don't need to be. They're not infants. Plant them in front of the TV. They have iPads. They can entertain themselves." Debbie told Jack about it after everyone left the kitchen.

"We have to get rid of them. These people are all over the house, and taking over her life. I'm watching fifteen years of hard labor and planning go up in smoke." He nodded agreement. He had been observing the same thing and trying to come up with a plan to scare them off and encourage them to leave.

"I'm working on some ideas."

"Meanwhile, I'm a babysitter now."

"Just go along with it. We'll get them out of here soon," he said, with a look that would have frightened Meredith if she'd seen it. They were desperate to reclaim their turf and their power over her.

"Not soon enough for me," she said under her breath with a murderous expression.

Joel was downtown meeting some of his employees at his office, since the police had let them in. They were trying to salvage what they could from the rubble in the office. Andrew was at the hospital, and Peter was volunteering with the OES. Meredith told Arthur that the three women were leaving for a few hours, Jack and Debbie were available to help him, and he said he'd try to entertain the children. Maybe a piano lesson, he suggested, and Tyla smiled.

"Good luck with that! I can barely get my kids to do their homework."

"Playing the piano is fun," he said to her.

Half an hour later, the three women left. They took Meredith's car, since their own garage doors were stuck and they couldn't get their cars out, and Meredith's wasn't. They took her SUV, and Jack was shocked. Normally, she had him drive her, but she didn't want him to. She had suddenly found independence, and now she had friends. He was as worried about it as Debbie, who looked sour as she turned the TV on for Tyla's kids when the women drove away. Arthur had suggested a piano lesson to them and they liked the idea. Debbie was going to take them all to the piano in the drawing room after they watched a TV show or two. Since Meredith was out, she helped herself to a beer, out of sight of the children. Jack had had a swig of bourbon after lunch and was in a better mood, and he had told Debbie he had a plan.

"What do you think it will be like?" Ava asked them as they headed down the hill toward the Marina. It was slow going with many streets blocked off, and part of the Marina closed, since it was on landfill, and rows of houses had collapsed. They had suffered the worst damage in '89 too. "Do you think it will be scary?" She was nervous now, but all three of them were excited, and liked the idea of lending a hand to help people in need.

They parked between two piles of rocks. Nothing was orderly when they got there, and they threaded their way through the crowds in front of the school. There were hundreds of people, men, women, and children, and close to a thousand more once they got inside. There were large rooms with food stations, a massive cafeteria, and everything else was set up as dormitories. There was a haphazard information area on rickety tables, with half a dozen people telling new arrivals where to go. There was a nursing station in the rear, where minor injuries were being treated. Those with anything more severe were being sent to local hospitals.

Meredith explained that they wanted to volunteer, and the woman they spoke to looked relieved.

"Great," she said, glancing at them. They were clean, sane, sober, and willing. "Any special skills?"

"I'm a nurse," Tyla said, and the woman told her to go to the first aid station. She left with a smile on her face and looked excited now that they were there.

"I'll do whatever you need," Ava said, "childcare, cafeteria." The woman pointed to the main cafeteria and Ava took off with a wave at Meredith, and the same woman sent her to a room full of children, where they needed someone to read them stories, so they could give their frazzled parents a break.

They assigned Meredith to about twenty five- and six-year-olds, with another woman to help her, and she read book after book, wiped noses, took them to the bathroom, and let them sit on her lap in turns. She felt like she'd been running a race all day by the time her shift ended at seven. The children thanked her, and she went to find Ava in the cafeteria. She'd been handing out sandwiches, yogurt, and bottles of juice and water all day. She told them she had to go, and they went to find Tyla, who was bandaging scrapes and cuts. She had just assessed a child with a concussion, and sent her and her parents to the hospital where Andrew was working. She finished a few minutes later, and the three of them left the shelter a little after seven P.M. They'd been there longer than expected, and could have stayed all night. The school was filled with people who were now homeless, or with damaged homes, and were in desperate need of food, clothes, and housing.

"Wow, what an incredible day," Ava said, as Meredith drove them home. All three of them were deeply moved by what they'd heard and seen.

"I hope my kids didn't drive Debbie nuts," Tyla said, on a high from working as a nurse again.

"I read stories to five-year-olds all afternoon. We spent more time in the bathroom than reading, but we went through a stack of books. I felt like Mary Poppins." Meredith grinned. They had all promised to go back the next day. It took them less time to drive home, because Meredith knew what streets to avoid now. She pulled the car into the garage, and they entered the house through the kitchen. The men were all talking at the kitchen table. Debbie was cooking dinner, and shot Meredith a dark look. They were home much later than they'd said.

"How was it?" Ava asked Peter, and he was beaming.

"We found a family of a mom and dad and a three-month-old. The baby was fine, the mom was pretty shaken up, and the dad had a nasty head injury, but they're going to be okay. Where were you?"

"At the shelter in the Marina." All three looked as excited as Peter did, and Daphne ran into her mother's arms.

"I can play the piano!" she said. "I played 'Twinkle, Twinkle, Little Star.' Mr. Arthur showed me how." Tyla smiled and kissed her, as Andrew looked at her coldly.

"You just walked off and left our kids? What if there'd been another earthquake?"

"I'd have come back if there were, and so would you," she said, less cowed by him than usual. She didn't want to let him spoil a great day where she'd done something useful and got to use her skills again.

Joel looked hurt as he came to kiss Ava. "Hey, babe, if you want to help, you can help me put my office back together. You don't have to go to some school with a lot of filthy homeless people. There are others who can do that."

"You have your staff to help with your office. They need everyone they can get at the shelters," she said, and kissed him. He looked like a boy whose feelings were hurt.

"You have talented children," Arthur added. "We had a very good first lesson," he told Tyla and Andrew.

"I really liked it, Mom," Will said.

"Me too." Daphne grinned.

Debbie had hamburgers ready for them ten minutes later and they all sat down to dinner. Andrew said he'd had an exhausting day, and didn't speak to his wife all through the meal. He left the table as soon as they finished eating, and signaled to Tyla to come with him. She followed a few minutes later with the children, who didn't want to go upstairs, but thanked Debbie for dinner, and did as they were told. Peter, Ava, and Meredith were full of tales about what they'd done that day. And they all went to bed early. They were exhausted, and Joel made it obvious that he wanted alone time with Ava, which left Arthur and Meredith alone in the kitchen for a little while, until he went upstairs too. Meredith walked him upstairs, and Peter was waiting for him with the bed turned down, and his pajamas.

"It sounds like you had a good day," Arthur said to Meredith as they walked upstairs together.

"I feel alive for the first time in years," she admitted. "It's terrible to say, but the earthquake is the best thing that's ever happened to me. I feel useful again."

"That's something to think about, isn't it?" he said wisely, kissed her cheek, and walked into his room with Peter.

He was right, Meredith realized. She sat in her room, physically tired but wide awake, thinking about her afternoon at the shelter, but at the same time, she was worried about Tyla. She didn't like the look on Andrew's face when he went upstairs and gestured to Tyla to follow him, like a child who had done something bad and needed to be punished in private. She hoped he wasn't being too hard on her. Something about him frightened her for Tyla, but she hadn't complained about him. It was the look of terror in her eyes that Meredith didn't like.

As she thought about it, she went to her closet and pulled out piles of old sweaters and jeans, some warm jackets and shoes to take to the shelter the next day. They needed them more than she did.

Downstairs, in their separate apartment, Jack was telling Debbie his plan. She smiled when she heard it. "It's perfect. I like it. That should do the trick."

"It will," he said confidently. "I'm tired of helping all of them, and she hardly speaks to us now, now that she has them. She'll want them out after this." Jack toasted Debbie with his flask of bourbon, and then lifted it to his lips, and drained it before he set it down again. It was a silver flask that had belonged to Meredith's father. Jack had found it in a box in a storeroom shortly after they arrived. She had never missed it or asked him about it. It had become his in the last fifteen years, like a lot of other things that Meredith had never missed.

Andrew had locked both children in the bathroom as soon as they got to the room. He had given them both their iPads and told them to put their earphones on. And as soon as he locked the door, Andrew had hit Tyla so hard she had literally flown across the room. She hadn't expected it, not here, where someone might hear them, and she hadn't braced herself for it. She fell over the rollaway bed that Will had been sleeping in, hit her head, and was dazed for a minute. Daphne was going to be sleeping on an inflatable mattress they had brought from home, since the children didn't want to sleep alone. The room was big enough for all of them.

Tyla didn't have time to recover before he hit her just as hard again. She cowered on the floor this time, with her arms over her head. She had learned how to protect herself and not to cry out, since their children were usually in the next room when he hit her. When she looked up at Andrew, her nose was bleeding from both nostrils, and her eyes were glazed. There was hatred in her eyes, but there was unbridled rage in his.

"How dare you go down to that filthy place without my permission. You probably got lice and God knows what else."

"I administered first aid all day," she said weakly. "I'm a nurse."

"You're nothing. You probably don't even know how to put a bandage on by now. You haven't worked in eleven years. You left our kids with that bitch of a housekeeper all day, and a blind man. Are you insane?" Tyla didn't answer. He wanted to control every second of her day, and anything that might give her pleasure or make her feel good about herself was forbidden to her. "You don't take a shit unless I tell you to! Do you hear me?" She nodded, and felt a pounding in her head where she had hit it on the rollaway. He was a master in the art of wife beating and knew how not to leave marks on her unless he wanted to. He bruised her breasts when he felt like it, and left marks up and down her arms and legs. He had left a footprint of his shoe on her back once, and almost broken it and could have crippled her. But he usually didn't leave any telltale signs on her face. The rest she could cover with pants and long sleeves.

He had been beating her for almost ten years now. For a long time, she thought it would get better, but now she knew it never would. It had gotten significantly worse after Daphne was born. She wanted to leave him, but she saw no way out. She hadn't worked in eleven years since Will was born. Andrew didn't want her to. So she had no money to go anywhere or escape. She couldn't ask her family for help. They needed what they had for themselves and their children. And the only money she had was the allowance Andrew gave her for the house. She had looked into safe houses for women once or twice, but without a job she would have had to go on welfare, and she couldn't do that to the kids. With Andrew, they lived in a nice house and went to private schools. They had extracurricular activities, and a future. He would pay for college one day in the not-so-distant future. She told herself she would leave him when Daphne left for college in eleven years, if she was still alive by then.

Her family was poor and couldn't take her in. Her two brothers made a decent living as a plumber and electrician, but one had four kids, and the other six. And her sisters were both single moms and worked as maids to support their kids. She was their success story, married to a rich doctor. He wasn't rich, but to them he was. He made a healthy living, and having grown up poor himself, he saved every penny he could. He accused Tyla of coming from scum, of being shanty Irish, of being stupid, a bad mother and sleeping with other men, which she never had. She had never cheated on him, even once, and wasn't sure the same was true of him. But whether he did or not, he was brutal with her. He had never laid a hand on the children, or she would have left him, poor or not, but she was sure that they suspected what he did to her. They knew. But she stayed with him to ensure their future. It never dawned on her that a college education and private school weren't worth it. He was damaging all of them. She couldn't believe that he had the guts to beat her while they were staying at someone else's house. He pulled her off the floor by her hair, and threw her on the bed, and didn't care that her nose and mouth were bleeding on the sheets. He gave her one more hard slap across the face, and then went to let the kids out of the bathroom. He was laughing when he did, as though something funny had happened.

"Your mom fell over the rollaway," he said, "and bumped her nose. Isn't that silly?" Both children saw that she was bleeding and she hurried past them into the bathroom to wash her face.

Will looked panicked. He had seen her that way and worse, many times before. "Are you okay, Mom?" he whispered when he came to stand next to her at the sink with a heartbroken look.

"Your mom is fine," Andrew said, and dragged him out of the bathroom by the neck, as Daphne stared at them with wide eyes. Tyla had washed the blood off by then, and tried to act like nothing had happened, but she needed ice to put on her face and nose and didn't have any. She didn't want to go downstairs and get it, in case someone was in the kitchen and saw her. She had splashed cold water on her face instead. She could see a bruise starting on the side of her cheek when she looked in the mirror. She'd have to cover it with makeup. She had become an expert at that.

She put the children to bed and there was silence in the room. Andrew went to take a shower, and while he was gone, Will whispered to her from the rollaway. "Are you really okay, Mom?"

"I'm fine," she said in a steady voice. "I just tripped." One day, she would tell him. She had to, so they knew never to let it happen to them, especially Daphne. She was clinging to her dolls, and lay in bed with a sad expression.

"Does your nose hurt, Mommy?" she asked her.

"No, sweetheart, it's fine," she lied to them, as she had all their lives. And now she had to lie to the people at Meredith's house too.

When Andrew came out of the bathroom, she locked herself in and took a hot shower. She wanted to get clean of him. He made her feel dirty every time he beat her, and even worse if he made love to her afterward, or raped her, which he did sometimes too, but not in front of the children. He called her a whore when they weren't listening. His mother had cheated on his father when he was a boy, and then ran away when Andrew was seven, and he had a profound hatred of women. Tyla always wondered if his father had beaten Andrew's mother too, if that was why she had run away with another man. Andrew had never forgiven her for leaving him. They had never heard from her again, and if Andrew was anything like his father, she didn't blame her. She hoped to do the same one day, and run away, but not with another man. She would never leave her kids, and especially not with him. Her children were growing up in a house filled with hate and terror, but she kept telling herself it was the sacrifice she had to make so they could go to private school and get a good education.

Her own father had been a drunk and died when she was three years old. She didn't remember him. He had died driving home from work drunk in a snowstorm, and left her mother a widow with five children. She didn't know if he had ever beaten her, but her mother never said much about him. She had supported them all by being a domestic, as Tyla's sisters did. It was odd how history repeated itself. But she didn't want her history to repeat itself for Will and Daphne. Tyla had learned to live with terror, for their sakes.

She lay awake for a long time that night, staying as far away from Andrew as she could in the bed. He had to be back at the hospital again at six the next morning. She was glad she wouldn't have to see him when she woke up. And hopefully, one day, she'd never have to see him again at all.

Chapter 5

Meredith got up early the next morning, and was surprised when she saw Daphne sitting in the hall again. This time, she was wearing a pink nightgown, and was holding all three of her dolls in her arms.

"You're up early again," Meredith said with a smile. Daphne nodded and didn't say anything. She didn't look as happy as she had the day before. "Are you hungry?"

"A little. Can I have cereal?"

"No pancakes?" She shook her head. "Do you want to get slippers?"

"I don't want to wake Mommy. Daddy went to work. Mom and Will are still asleep." Meredith took her hand and they walked downstairs to the kitchen. No one was up yet, and it was peaceful, as Meredith got out a bowl and filled it with cereal, and then poured milk into it. She folded a napkin, put a spoon next to it, and Daphne ate the cereal, as Meredith made herself a cup of coffee.

"My mom fell down and got a bloody nose last night," Daphne said out of the blue, and Meredith looked at her, wondering what part of it was true.

"How did she fall down?" Meredith asked, trying to sound casual. She didn't know why, but she didn't believe the story, not all of it.

"She fell over Will's bed and bumped her nose." Daphne said it as though she didn't believe it either, and expected Meredith to question her about it. She wasn't sure if she should, or what the right protocol was if a child was seeing her mother abused.

"That must have hurt." Daphne nodded, her little face serious. She seemed so small in her nightgown.

"She falls down a lot," Daphne added, her eyes never leaving Meredith's, and then when Meredith least expected it, Daphne's voice dropped down to the merest whisper. "Sometimes he hits her." She looked down into the bowl then, and neither of them said another word for a minute. It confirmed what Meredith had been thinking and was afraid of.

"I'm very sorry to hear it," Meredith whispered back. "Does he ever hit you?"

She shook her head. "He shouts at us, he doesn't hit us. He only hits Mommy." Meredith couldn't imagine what that must feel like to a child, knowing that their father hurt their mother, and not being able to stop it. How terrifying it must be for them. Meredith wasn't sure what to do about it, but she knew she had to do something. She couldn't call Child Protective Services because he wasn't hitting his children, "only" his wife. Meredith went to sit next to her, and pulled Daphne onto her lap and just held her, her arms around her, holding her tight. She could feel Daphne relax in her arms, and hadn't realized how tense she was.

"If you're a good witch, can you fix it?" Daphne asked her, and it brought tears to Meredith's eyes.

"I'm not sure I'm that kind of witch. But I can try."

"Will you put a spell on him?" Daphne liked the idea.

"I have to think about it." Daphne nodded and got back in her own chair, and then looked seriously at Meredith again.

"Why do you only have a girl, and you don't have a boy too?" Daphne asked her, and Meredith felt as though she had been hit in the solar plexus. "Like me and Will," she explained. Meredith decided to tell her the truth.

"I had a boy too, but he's with the angels." Daphne's eyes widened and she looked at Meredith.

"Did he get sick? My friend Stephanie's grandma is with the angels now. She got cancer."

"No, he had an accident."

"That's very sad," Daphne said solemnly.

"Yes, it was very sad. His name was Justin. And my daughter's name is Kendall. And I have a granddaughter named Julia." As she said it, she realized that Kendall was almost the same age as Daphne's mother. Kendall was forty, and Tyla was thirty-eight. It was odd how women the same age as her daughter kept coming into her life. Like Debbie too.

They sat quietly together for a while, thinking about their confidences to each other, and then Will and Tyla walked in. Will looked very pale, and Tyla was exhausted. She had on makeup, and if you looked closely, you could see that her nose was swollen, but only slightly. Her son looked worse than she did. Tyla went to make him some tea, and said that he had a stomachache.

"He gets really bad stomachaches sometimes." Meredith could guess why, but didn't say anything, and Daphne shot her a glance, which Meredith pretended not to notice.

"Should he stay in bed?" Meredith asked solicitously.

"No, I think he'll be okay in a while."

Tyla made him a piece of toast, and Peter and Arthur came in after that. Arthur promised them another piano lesson. When Ava and Joel came to breakfast, the three women agreed to go to the shelter again. All three of them had loved it, but Meredith looked questioningly at Tyla.

"Are you sure you want to go? I got the feeling Andrew wasn't too pleased about it." Tyla looked her straight in the eye, and there was something determined in her face.

"I'm going. They need us there," Tyla said firmly.

"Yes, they do," Meredith agreed.

"I think it's wonderful," Arthur commented. Peter was going back to volunteer at the OES, and Joel said he was going back downtown. They were still shoveling broken glass, computers, and parts of the ceiling out of his office. He didn't comment about Ava going to the shelter.

"You can come with me if you want," Joel offered Ava, but she shook her head and said she was going back to the shelter in the Marina, they needed her more, and he didn't argue with her, but didn't look happy about it.

The others all went upstairs after they'd eaten, and Arthur lingered for a few minutes. "I hardly know you, but I'm proud of you," he said to Meredith. "I know you've been hiding behind your walls for a long time, but maybe this is what you needed. The world needs you."

"I needed some time to myself for a while, but I think I stayed that way for too long. My husband left me for someone else, and I didn't expect it. And my son died a few months later. It was all too much to deal with at once, so I folded the show, gave up my career, and I've been hiding for a long time. Too long." She realized that now her life was suddenly full of people she barely knew, but who needed her. Kendall had shut her out for so long that she had forgotten what it felt like to be wanted.

"It's a lonely life, being alone like that," Arthur said gently. He felt able to say it to her because of his age, if nothing else, and he had grown fond of her in a few days. He could tell that she was a kind, generous, honorable woman, just from the fact that they were all staying with her, and she was taking good care of them.

"I wasn't alone. I had Jack and Debbie here with me," she explained to him and he shook his head.

"I have my housekeeper, Frieda, and Peter. That's not the same thing. They work for me, and that gets complicated. You need meaning and purpose in your life, and friends. You gave up a career that must have been rewarding and gave millions of people enormous pleasure. I'm much older than you are, and I had a wonderful marriage. I have those memories to keep me warm, and I don't mind being alone now, as long as I still have my work. But you're too young to do that."

"I'm not that young," she said, thinking about it.

"If you'll allow me to say so, you're too young to lock yourself away forever. You need to come back into the world in some way that means something to you, whatever that is. It's never too late to start over."

As he said it, Peter and Ava arrived back in the kitchen at the same time. He had a thick stack of papers in his hand, and handed it to Ava. It was his manuscript. She had promised to read it, and ran back upstairs with it to put in her room. He left for the OES office a few minutes later, and Arthur smiled at Meredith. They were friends now, and she took seriously what he'd said to her.

"I may be blind," he said softly, "but I smell romance in the air," he said, referring to Peter and Ava, and she laughed.

"You could be right. I don't disagree with you. But she and Joel seem quite involved. I'm not sure how that would work out."

"You never know with people. He never lets anyone read his manuscript."

Meredith escorted Arthur to his room after Peter left, and as soon as she got back to her study, Debbie appeared with a somber expression and said she had to speak to her.

"Is something wrong?" Debbie nodded, with a devastated expression, as though the world had come to an end. She had been unusually dramatic lately, ever since their unexpected houseguests had arrived. Both she and Jack had been acting strangely and bordering on rude with them. It was the first time she had had any guests in fourteen years, and Meredith had been startled by their behavior.

"I was cleaning in the main living room this morning," she began, and Meredith was certain she was about to report on some treasure that had been broken in the earthquake. "I don't even know how to say this to you, but the heart-shaped pink enamel Fabergé box is missing."

"Missing or broken?" It was something Meredith had paid a fortune for years before and had always loved. It had diamonds and pearls on it, and an inscription inside from the czar to his mother. It was an extremely valuable collector's item, and it was too large for someone to slip into a pocket.

"I hate to say it, but I think one of your guests must have taken it. I saw the sex bomb looking at it a few days ago. I don't know if it was her or one of the others. I know it's very valuable and how much you loved it." None of their day workers had been able to come to work since the earthquake, so it couldn't be one of them, and they had worked for Meredith for years, and were trustworthy.

"When was the last time you saw it?" Meredith asked her, trying to sound calm about it, although she would be sad if it had been lost.

"I was in the room the afternoon of the earthquake and saw it, and now it's not there. I looked everywhere for it, in case someone picked it up and set it down in the wrong place. It can only be one of the people staying here," she said solemnly, and Meredith looked shocked, but something felt wrong about the story. She wasn't sure what. "Do you want me and Jack to search their rooms if they go out today?" she asked hopefully.

"Certainly not! They're all respectable people with fine homes of their own. They don't need to steal valuable objects from me. I just don't understand it. It will probably turn up."

"Not if someone plans to sell it. Should we call the police?"

"I'm not ready to do that yet," Meredith said.

"I think you need to ask them to leave, if you don't want to search their belongings." Debbie looked disappointed. She and Jack had been sure she'd be willing to do that for the Fabergé box, with a bunch of strangers in the house.

"And where would they go? None of the hotels are up and running, half the city doesn't have power yet. I won't send them to the shelters. From what Colonel Chapman tells me, most people have earthquake victims staying in their homes."

"But not people they don't know."

"It can't be one of them," Meredith reasoned with her. "Andrew Johnson is a respected physician, his wife is a lovely woman. Arthur Harriman is one of the most famous musicians in the world. Peter may not be rich, but he seems like an honorable young man. Joel Fine has made a half a billion dollars on his two startups. He certainly doesn't need to steal a Fabergé box from me. He could buy his own."

"And his girlfriend?"

"I just can't believe that," Meredith said firmly.

"Who do you suspect then? Jack and me?"

"Of course not. You've worked here for fifteen years, and been the best friends I've ever had. I don't know where the box is, but it's here somewhere. Maybe someone put it in a drawer so it wouldn't get broken in an aftershock and forgot to tell me. I'll ask everyone tonight. These people are friends now, Debbie, and I just don't believe they're stealing from me."

"You're being naïve," Debbie said angrily, "you've been isolated for too long. You've forgotten what people are capable of. One of your new friends has stolen something valuable, while staying in your home. If you had any sense, you would throw them all out, before they take something else." Meredith was angry at the way she said it, and the presumptuousness of telling her what to do. The boundaries between them had dissolved a long time ago, and Debbie had forgotten that she was an employee and did not call the shots. Meredith didn't like her tone. She stood up to indicate that she wanted her to leave the room. The conversation was over. Meredith was not about to throw her new friends out of her home. If anything, she wanted Tyla to stay longer, until she could figure out how to help her with Andrew. After what Daphne had told her, she was seriously worried.

Debbie walked out of the room and slammed the door behind her. She was fuming in a black rage when she got downstairs, found Jack in the living room of their apartment, and told him what had happened.

"Do you realize I told her that one of them had stolen it, and not only does she not believe me, she doesn't care. I think she's losing her mind."

"Or reclaiming her independence. Personally, I'd prefer it if she was senile. And the old man has been telling her to open her doors wider. I heard him. We're never going to have the influence we did before, if she does that. We've been the only voices in her head for fourteen years since her boy died, and her only friends. Talk about ungrateful. What do we do about the box now?"

"Hang on to it, sell it, whatever we want. It won't do us any good to put it in one of their rooms. She forbid me to search their rooms with you. She trusts them. Shit, a week ago she didn't even know them. Now they're her best friends." Jack took a long swig of bourbon from his flask then, and Debbie held a hand out. He handed it to her, and she finished the rest.

"I want to get those bastards out of here," Jack said with a venomous look. "She won't listen to us again until we do." She was slipping through their fingers, and they both knew it. For fourteen years, they had had control of her, and now suddenly she was slowly moving back into the world, and once she did, it was over for them, and everything they loved about the job would be ruined.

Meredith was still angry after Debbie left the room. She sat thinking about it for a minute, asking herself if she thought one of her current guests had stolen the Fabergé box, and she couldn't imagine it. She didn't want to believe it of them, but she couldn't think who else it would be. And no one else had been in the house except Jack and Debbie since the earthquake. None of their day cleaners had come in, and they were all longtime employees too. The box had to be misplaced somewhere, put away for security. It was the only possible explanation, and she trusted Jack and Debbie implicitly.

She was still thinking about it when the phone on her desk rang. Debbie usually answered, but she didn't, so Meredith answered it herself, sounding distracted, and she was stunned to hear her daughter's voice on the line. They hadn't spoken in at least two months. Kendall never answered her calls, and even when Meredith left her a voicemail, she didn't return the call, or waited a month to do so. She'd been planning to call her the night of the earthquake, but her last two calls to her had gone unanswered. Kendall called her when she felt like it, at her own convenience.

"Kendall?" she said, sounding surprised. The phones hadn't been working right after the earthquake, except for cellphones, and now full service had been restored.

"Mom? Why didn't you let me know you were okay?" She sounded annoyed not to have heard from her mother.

"Our Internet was down at first, and the house lines didn't work. I could have called you on my cellphone, but you never pick up anyway."

"You could have sent me a text," she said practically.

"True. And you could have called me. I pick up when I see your number." Unlike Kendall, when she saw her mother's.

"If Jack and Debbie don't get it first. I always think they don't give you my messages."

"Why would they do that?" She knew Kendall didn't like them. Meredith had always suspected she was jealous of how close her mother was to them. But they had always been there for her, and Kendall never was.

"Are you okay? Is the house okay?"

"A lot of broken glass, but this house is solid, nothing major broke, some of the paintings fell down and the frames broke. We don't have full power yet, but hopefully we will in a few days, or maybe in a week or two. It was a huge shake-up and quite frightening. I have six of my neighbors staying with me, and two little kids. Their houses took a harder hit than mine did, and are pretty severely damaged, so I invited them to stay here."

"Your neighbors? Do you even know your neighbors?" Kendall

sounded shocked. Her mother, the famous recluse, had neighbors staying with her?

"I didn't until the earthquake, but I have room for them, and they're very nice. Arthur Harriman, the concert pianist, lives next door, and he's one of them."

"Isn't he blind?" Kendall sounded amazed by everything her mother was saying to her.

"Yes, he is. He has a young man living with him to help him, but he's busier and livelier than the rest of us, at eighty-two."

"I was worried about you. The coverage on TV looked awful, fires burning out of control, the bridges damaged and closed, people buried under houses."

"I'm fine. How are you? We haven't spoken in a while."

"We're fine. I've been worried about Julia. She dropped out of school, and is trying to be an actress in L.A. Dad has seen her a few times. She's been very difficult about it. I think she wants to follow in your footsteps." Kendall didn't sound pleased about it. She still blamed everything on her mother, and never on Scott.

"Or your father's." Kendall never blamed him for his career, only her mother.

"I want to come out and see her one of these days."

"Why don't you come to San Francisco when you do? You haven't been here in ages." Kendall hadn't, and she still didn't want to. It had depressed her profoundly every time she did. Her brother's room was still intact, her mother hiding from the world. Jack and Debbie, who acted as though they owned Meredith. It was too much for her.

"Maybe you could meet us in L.A.?"

There was a long silence at Meredith's end, and then she answered. "Maybe I will. I'd like to see Julia."

"She looks a lot like you." So did Kendall, but she never acknowledged it. "Well, I'm glad you're all right. I was afraid you might be hurt when we didn't hear from you." But it had still taken her several days to call her mother. Her instinct never was to just reach out and call her.

"It was very unpleasant, but I'm fine. Actually, I'm volunteering at a shelter for the people who lost their homes, or can't get into them because they're damaged. The city is going to be a mess for a long time."

"I'll let you know if I go to L.A.," Kendall said to her in a gentler voice. "Julia says she's not ready to see me yet. I think she's afraid I'll try to talk her out of an acting career."

"And will you?"

"I tried, but she says it's the only thing she wants to do. I'd rather she was here in New York, going to school, or in a sensible job, but that's not what she wants. Dad thinks she has talent, and he's arranged a few auditions for her."

"That's nice of him," Meredith said coolly. She still didn't like hearing about Scott, or even the mention of his name. "I see that his last two films did extremely well," Meredith said generously.

"He won an Oscar for both of them, which is pretty amazing," Kendall added. Meredith had won an Oscar at the height of her career, but Kendall had never been proud of her. She hadn't gotten the mother she wanted, a normal, ordinary bourgeois mother who wasn't a movie star. They had both been unlucky. Meredith had a daughter who never wanted to talk to her, but at least she had called to make sure she was alive. "Take care of yourself, Mom. It's probably still dangerous, with things falling. It sounds like a lot of people got hurt."

"I was never in danger," Meredith said gently. And Jack and Debbie took good care of her, which she didn't say to her.

"I'm glad," Kendall said. "I'll call soon." It had shocked her that it had never occurred to her mother to get in touch with her after the earthquake, and say she was okay. Kendall hadn't tried to call her for the first few days either. It was sad for both of them that their relationship had deteriorated so severely over the years. They both hung up feeling nostalgic, remembering the old days when Kendall was young, and Justin was still alive, before everything changed and Meredith's world fell apart. Meredith was still sitting at her desk, staring into space, thinking about it, when Ava stuck her head in the door and asked if she was ready. It woke Meredith out of her reverie.

"Sorry. My daughter called from New York. I forgot to call her to tell her I was okay. It never occurred to me," she admitted, feeling guilty. All it did was tell them how far they had drifted apart in the last fourteen years. And she barely knew her granddaughter, Julia. Meredith recognized that some of it was her fault. She had disconnected from the world, and everyone in it, even her daughter. Maybe Arthur was right, and it was time to reconnect again. She almost felt ready to.

She grabbed a denim jacket and put sneakers on, and took the pile of clothes to donate, and two minutes later she was out in the hall, where Ava and Tyla were waiting for her.

"Where are the children?" she asked Tyla.

"They're with Debbie, she said she'd make cookies with them, and Arthur is going to give them another piano lesson." Tyla smiled and Meredith wondered if it was worth risking her husband's fury to work at the shelter, but Tyla seemed to think so and was taking a stand.

They drove to the Marina and spent the day there, each one at their assigned tasks. Meredith was sent to the children's room again, to entertain them and give their parents a break. She read them stories, put them down for a nap, and fed them lunch with the other volunteers. Tyla was at the first aid station, and Ava was in the kitchen this time, helping to make soup in enormous vats, and washing pots afterward. They all looked tired and rumpled by the time they drove back to Meredith's home again.

"I'm exhausted," Meredith admitted. Several times during the day, she had thought of the Fabergé box, and tried to imagine any of her new friends stealing it. She just couldn't. It didn't compute. Even for Peter, who had no money to speak of. They all seemed like honest people, and stealing something of value from her home seemed so out of character. She couldn't imagine it, and was sure it would show up at some point and prove her right, especially to Debbie, who thought them all profiteers and thieves, out to take advantage of Meredith. She appreciated how protective Debbie was of her, but in this group, she was sure it wasn't necessary.

All the men came home shortly after they did, and looked just as tired. Peter had run into Charles Chapman at the OES office, and had invited him to dinner, and hoped Meredith wouldn't mind. She didn't, and was happy to see him when he came. Even Andrew seemed more subdued that night. He had dealt with a steady stream of emergencies at the hospital, and didn't comment when Tyla told him she had gone back to work at the shelter.

Debbie had prepared a simple meal of pasta with basil from the garden, and she'd defrosted steaks for those who wanted them. Meredith noticed that Charles and Arthur were engaged in a long conversation, and he and Peter seemed to have made friends. Then over coffee, Charles came to sit with Meredith. She had talked to Tyla and Ava all through dinner about what they'd seen and done that day at the shelter. It was exhausting, but invigorating to be helping people.

"How are you faring with your hotel here?" Charles asked her with a warm smile. "Arthur has been trying to talk me into going to his concert in Shanghai in November. He almost has me convinced. Are you going?"

She laughed. "Shanghai is a little extreme for a woman who's officially been a recluse for fourteen years."

"It might do you good. And it would be interesting. He's playing at a new concert hall there. He certainly hasn't slowed down. He's also playing in Paris, Hong Kong, and Sydney this winter. My life is embarrassingly dull compared to his. I hear you've been working at the shelter in the Marina."

"It feels good to be doing something to help."

"I think you're already doing quite a lot here." He smiled at her. "We're hoping that this part of the city will have power by next week."

"We're lucky we have the generator," she said. "And I've gotten used to battery-operated lanterns all over the house."

"Certain parts of the city won't have power back for at least another six months," he said.

"There seems to be so much reconstruction to do," she said thoughtfully. "Some of the people at the shelter have lost their homes, and have no earthquake insurance. It costs a fortune, so most people don't have it."

"The city will be hurt for a long time," he said. "We're swamped at OES." They were still digging people out of the rubble, and the financial district was a shambles with many people still trapped in office buildings. Rescue teams were working frantically to get them out before they died. The stories on the news were still fraught with drama every day. "I'd love to take you to dinner sometime, when the restaurants get going again. How does that fit in the life of an 'official recluse'?" he teased her a little and she laughed.

"A week ago, it wouldn't have," she said, "but that seems to be changing. My neighbors have gotten me out from behind my walls."

"That's lucky for me." She noticed that he was watching Debbie as she worked in the kitchen cleaning up. She hardly spoke to Meredith that night, after their conversation about the Fabergé box, and Charles said something to Meredith, when she walked him through the courtyard to let him out the front gate. "I feel a little odd saying this to you, but I get a funny vibe from your housekeeper. I saw her looking at you strangely tonight. She doesn't seem too happy about your guests."

"She's not, and neither is her husband. They're not used to houseguests. Admittedly it's been a big group, although they're all very easy, and Will and Daphne are adorable and well behaved. Actually, I had a run-in with my housekeeper this morning. She's convinced one of them stole a valuable object from the house. I just don't think that's possible with this group. I think the object she thinks is stolen is tucked in a drawer somewhere. They're very protective. They've been through a lot with me. They've been with me for fifteen years and have been the mainstay of my existence for most of it, my only friends. They worry about people taking advantage of me, or chasing me because of who I am. That's not the issue here. These people all needed help and a place to stay, and they've all been respectful and discreet, but of course it's more work for Jack and Debbie than when I'm alone in the house."

"This may sound strange, but some people who live in other people's houses as a way of life often try to take control of them at some point, and isolate them. The tables turn, and suddenly the employees are running the show. It sounds odd, but it has happened to some very capable, intelligent people. Be careful, Meredith. That woman looked daggers at me several times, and she was almost seething when she watched some of your guests. How much do you trust them?"

"Totally," Meredith said without hesitating.

"Maybe they took the missing object and are trying to point the finger at someone else," he suggested, and Meredith looked shocked.

"They would never do that. They had flawless references when I hired them, and they've never done anything that concerned me in fifteen years."

"Just keep your eyes open," he said as gently as he could. He thought that something about Debbie was almost frightening, Meredith was more vulnerable than she realized, and at the mercy of whoever worked for her. They could influence her, or isolate her without her realizing it, steal from her cleverly, or even hurt her. She wouldn't be the first famous person it had happened to. There was something about Debbie and her husband that had struck him viscerally from the first time he'd seen them and Jack had let him into the house. They almost seemed to feel that it was their house as much as hers.

"I'm sure they'll relax again when my guests leave."

"When do you think that will be?" he asked her.

"When their homes are up and running, and safe again. They all had considerable damage, but their houses aren't ready to fall down. They've been calling construction companies all week. I think Joel is meeting with his contractor on Monday, and Arthur has someone coming to assess the damage later in the week." She hesitated for a moment, and then told him something else. "I'd like to keep Tyla and the kids with me as long as possible. Since we're talking about following our instincts, I think Andrew can be a very different man from the charming doctor we see at dinner. He's very hard on Tyla. I've overheard him say some things to her I didn't like, and their little girl says he hits her. If she needs help, I'd like to keep an eye on things for as long as I can." Charles nodded as he listened to her, sad to hear what she said, and touched by how concerned Meredith was about her, after only knowing her a short time. And he agreed with her.

"It's funny, I have the same feeling about him. Underneath the smooth exterior, I think he's a very angry guy." Meredith nodded and unlocked the gate, and Charles hugged her. "For a recluse, you seem to have a good eye for the people around you."

"I used to," she said quietly. "I might be out of practice, but don't worry about Jack and Debbie. Trust me, they're good people. I would trust them with my life."

"I hope you're right." He felt concerned for her now, he liked her, and he also realized how alone she was. She had one daughter, whom she wasn't close to and never saw, three thousand miles away, and no one else, except the couple he didn't trust.

He walked home from Meredith's house, and thought about her all the way. He wondered if she'd really go out to dinner with him. He wanted to spend time with her without half a dozen other people around. He wanted to know more about her, and what had driven her behind her walls. He hoped she would stay engaged in life now, for her sake, as well as his.

When they went to their room that night, Tyla saw the familiar look in Andrew's eye. She knew it well. He started to say something to her about going to the shelter again, and she turned on him with a look he'd never seen before. Will and Daphne were brushing their teeth and for a minute they were alone. She hissed at him almost like a snake.

"If you touch me, or hit me again, I'm calling the police, and I'll tell everyone in this house what you do to me." He pulled his arm back to hit her, and just as quickly realized that she meant it.

"Who have you been talking to?" he said to her, taking a step toward her menacingly, but he put his arm down.

"I don't need to talk to anyone. I'm never going to let you hit me again." She said it coldly and clearly as their children walked back into the room. Andrew didn't say another word. He got into bed, and turned his back to her, and he didn't lay a hand on her that night.

Chapter 6

Arthur was the first of them to get his contractor to come to the house, ten days after the earthquake. He had cleverly used his age, the fact that he was blind, and preparing for a concert in two weeks to get the owner of the company to come and assess the damage. There were deep tears in several ceilings, two of which had to be torn out and reinforced. His bathtub was cracked right down the middle, his kitchen cabinets had come loose from the wall, and all his plates were broken. The floors had been torn up, and several light fixtures were hanging by a thread. In the midst of all of it, miraculously, his beautiful piano was untouched. His housekeeper, Frieda, had hired a crew to remove all the broken glass. She had made a list of furniture that had to be repaired or replaced. Frieda was elderly but efficient, and Peter helped with whatever he could in the evenings.

The contractor estimated two to three weeks of work in the house, but once the windows and bathtub were replaced, Arthur could live there while the work continued, which he wanted to do, so he could rehearse for his concert on his own piano. He had invited the entire group to attend his concert, since it was in San Francisco.

The contractor got a glazier there in record time, and installed the bathtub, and two weeks after the earthquake, Arthur told Meredith, regretfully, that he was moving back to his house the next day. The power on their entire street had come on two days before, while three blocks away, the residents still had no electricity. The gas lines had been checked at all their homes and found to be intact, so the gas and electricity were on, and they had lights. Arthur was genuinely sad to leave the group. They had become a family after living through the aftermath of the earthquake together.

Meredith organized a dinner for him the night before he left and planned the menu carefully, since the grocery stores and most businesses were open again. Debbie was still being chilly with Meredith, ever since she had refused to believe that one of them had stolen the Fabergé box that was still missing. Meredith decided not to worry about it. She had more important things to do.

The dinner for Arthur and Peter was a festive affair, and she served her best wines and champagne, which irked Jack immeasurably. He acted as though his personal reserves were being depleted. He and Debbie occasionally drank some of Meredith's best vintages when they could get away with it, and had become connoisseurs of French Bordeaux. He preferred Lynch-Bages, while Debbie favored Chateau Margaux.

Arthur was very touched by the trouble Meredith went to, and since the power was back on, they ate in the dining room. The dinner was elegant and stately, even though they all dined in jeans and sweatshirts and the rough clothes they'd been wearing for two weeks. And in spite of herself, Debbie prepared a delicious dinner. Meredith knew what everyone liked to eat by then, and went out of her way to pick a dinner Arthur would love. The next day, Meredith, Jack, and Peter helped Arthur move back to his home. There were workmen everywhere, and the repairs were underway. He looked ecstatic the moment he sat down at his beloved concert grand piano.

Ava was heartbroken when Peter moved out, and she went to the house every night, with the excuse of helping Arthur. Five days later, Joel and Ava moved out, and went back to his place. They were tearing the house apart, and putting it back together. All of which left only Tyla and Andrew still with Meredith three weeks after the earthquake. They'd had trouble getting a construction company to come and start working on their house. They finally found a small outfit that agreed to do it, and a month to the day after the earthquake, they were ready to move out and go home.

Meredith helped Tyla get the children settled in, and she felt bereft when she went home to her empty house. She had dinner on a tray in her study that night, and only picked at it. Debbie was offended when she declined to eat with them, but she had lost the habit of sharing her evenings with them. All she could think of were Will and Daphne, and she was worried about Tyla. Andrew was back to his normal office schedule by then, and in a better mood, but alone with Tyla at night, Meredith had no idea what he would do. Daphne's admission that her father sometimes hit her mother had terrified her, and Tyla still hadn't admitted it to her.

The only thing that cheered her was Arthur's concert at the symphony at Davies Hall the day after the Johnsons moved out. They had all agreed to have dinner together afterward. Meredith invited Charles Chapman to join them, and he was delighted. The OES was still swamped, but he said that things were slowing down a little. They were still trying to help people find short- and long-term housing, but the shelters were closing down one by one, schools were open again, some in temporary government locations, and Meredith was back to her quiet life behind her walls. She dropped in on Arthur occasionally, and noticed that Ava was there whenever Joel was busy or out of town. The night of Arthur's performance, she looked incredible in a short sexy black dress that showed off her breathtaking cleavage and her long legs. Peter looked stunned when he saw her.

Arthur's performance was superb, and dinner afterward at a Greek restaurant they all loved was a jovial affair. They were the last ones in the place and Charles, Peter, Arthur, Joel, and Ava came for drinks at Meredith's house afterward. Andrew and Tyla had to go home to let their babysitter leave, and at two A.M. Arthur finally conceded that he was tired. Peter took him home to go to bed, and then went back to Meredith's to join the others. In the past month, they had become their own little family block party, and Tyla planned to invite Meredith to dinner whenever Andrew allowed it.

The morning after Arthur's concert, Tyla told him that Meredith was coming to dinner that night, to test the waters.

"Again? Why?"

"We lived with her for almost a month. She's alone now. The least we can do is have her to dinner occasionally."

"Haven't you seen enough of her? Why don't you just have her move in with us?" Andrew said, and then slammed the door to their bedroom when he went to dress for work. The day was off to a bad start but he didn't forbid it. Meredith could feel the tension when she arrived, and Tyla looked nervous when she put dinner on the table. Andrew was furious when she burned the rice, and snapped at Will and told him to get his elbows off the table. Daphne was clutching Martha to her, which Meredith knew now she did whenever she felt anxious. She never let go of the doll for an instant the day after her father had hit her mother. It was always the same day Will had one of his bad stomachaches that kept him home from school, so he could be with his mother.

Meredith had been slightly late for dinner because Debbie had made a fuss when she left the house.

"You're going out *again*? Why didn't you tell me? I made your favorite dinner." She looked like she was going to cry, and Meredith felt terrible to hurt her feelings.

"I left you a note in the kitchen this morning," Meredith said gently.

"I didn't see it." She made a great show then of throwing out the dinner, which made Meredith arrive twenty minutes late at the Johnsons, after apologizing profusely to Debbie. She ran down the street to the Johnsons, and left Debbie looking mortally wounded in the kitchen. As soon as she left, Jack broke out a bottle of Debbie's favorite Chateau Margaux, and she had dinner for him in the oven.

"She'll get tired of them," he reassured her, "or they'll get tired of her. They're not going to want an old woman hanging around all the time, and she's not going to want to hang around an eighty-two-year-old man. Peter and Ava are going to be sneaking around seeing each other. They won't want an audience for that. All Joel wants is to get laid. He won't want Meredith underfoot either," Jack said smugly.

"What about the colonel?" Debbie asked him, concerned, as they drank the wine and ate the dinner she'd hidden in the oven. "He seems pretty interested in her." Debbie didn't like the look of him. He was always watching her and Jack as though he was suspicious of them.

"She's almost ten years older than he is. How long do you think that will last?" Jack said cynically. "He's got his eye on Ava. I think he wants a piece of that himself."

"And she wants Peter." Debbie laughed. "They're all so screwed up. You're right, they'll get bored with each other in no time, and she'll come crawling back to us," Debbie said, getting drunk on the wine, while Meredith had dinner with the Johnsons.

The atmosphere stayed tense between Andrew and Tyla all through dinner, and not wanting to make it worse, Meredith came home as soon as the children went to bed. The house was quiet by then, and Meredith could see the lights on in Jack and Debbie's apartment as she walked home. She hoped that Debbie had forgiven her for not eating the dinner she'd prepared. She hated upsetting her. She knew it had been a hard month for them with everyone staying there after the earthquake. She'd given them extra days off as soon as the guests left. It had been a good month for her, but challenging for them, and they acted as though their own home had been invaded. She still remembered Charles's words about them, and knew he was overreacting and had misjudged them. They had been moody while the guests were there, but they weren't evil people.

She was thinking of him when the phone rang. It was only nine o'clock. It was Charles, calling to check on her, and thank her for inviting him to Arthur's concert.

"How are you doing without your houseguests?" he asked.

"I miss them. I just had dinner with Tyla, Andrew, and the children."

"How was that?"

She sighed when she answered. "Tense. I worry about her, and the kids. It's like living on the side of a volcano. She still claims that everything is fine with them, but I know it isn't. She burned the rice and he had a fit. Poor Daphne looks terrified whenever she's around him. I just want to scoop them up and take them home with me."

"Before you do that, how about dinner with me tomorrow night? You can scoop me up and take me home," he said, and she laughed. They had never had dinner alone and she was nervous about it. He made it sound like a date, and she didn't know if she was ready for that. She hadn't been out on a date since before she married Scott. She felt ridiculous going on a date at her age, especially with a man eight years younger. She wanted to be friends with him, and thought it was probably better if they left it at that, but she was embarrassed to say it to him. "Are you comfortable going to a restaurant, or will everybody recognize you?"

"I'm not sure. I don't go out much. Almost never," she said. He had seen a few heads turn the night before, at the symphony, and the Greek restaurant, but no one had bothered her. They just stared at her for a few minutes and whispered to one another when they realized who she was. Her looks hadn't changed much since she had stopped making movies, and she was easily recognizable, particularly when she was dressed up like the night before. She had worn a simple black dress, with her hair pulled back and diamond earrings. Everything about her was sleek, elegant, and understated. For an instant, he had felt overwhelmed, realizing he was out with Meredith White, but she was so open and easy to be with, that she made it possible to forget what a big star she was, and what an icon. In some ways, she had become even more famous, by being so mysterious and disappearing from public view when she went into seclusion.

"I know a little Italian restaurant out in the Avenues. No one will bother you there. Or would you rather go someplace fancier?"

"I'm a pizza and hamburger girl myself," she said simply.

"You make things awfully easy. I can cook for you at my place too. I've become a decent cook in the past two years."

"We can eat here, if you like," she suggested, but he didn't want to do that. He wanted to get her away from the watchful eyes of Jack and Debbie, and to make it a real date.

"I'll figure it out. Pick you up at eight?"

"That would be perfect," she said, and regretted it as soon as she hung up. She felt ridiculous going on a date with him at her age. She was past all that, or she had been for the past fourteen years, but he was slowly pulling her out of seclusion, against her better judgment.

She made a point of telling Debbie the next morning that she was going out to dinner again, for the third night in a row. She felt dizzy thinking about it. She was sorry she had told Charles she would go out with him. She was planning to make it clear to him at dinner. They could be friends and nothing more. She wasn't interested in romance at her age. She was thinking about it when she went to the drugstore to buy toothpaste and nail polish remover. She had found what she needed when she almost collided with Tyla, who had just picked up a bottle of foundation and an ice pack. Meredith looked shocked when she saw the bruise on the side of her face. It hadn't been there the night before, and Tyla looked instantly embarrassed and turned her face away.

"I walked into the bathroom door last night. I forgot where I was, and Andrew had left it half closed," she said immediately.

"Are you okay?" Meredith asked her as they walked to the checkout counter together.

"I'm fine. I'm sorry dinner was so lousy last night. I've forgotten how to cook, after staying with you and being spoiled for a month." She smiled and Meredith saw that her lip was slightly swollen too.

"Dinner was good, I was going to call you in a little while. But, Tyla, I'm worried about you."

"You don't need to be. We're fine. I know I look terrible. I just bruise easily. I'm always walking into things, or falling over my own feet." Meredith felt sick as she listened to her, and she was sure the children were upset too.

"Tyla, you don't have to put up with anyone hurting you." Meredith tried to make it sound as nonjudgmental as possible.

"Andrew doesn't hurt me," she said, coming to his defense immediately. She knew that if she told anyone, he would kill her, just as he said he would. If she left him, where would she go and what would she do? She couldn't deprive her children of their father. They needed him too.

They chatted for a few more minutes, and then Tyla scurried off and said she had to pick the kids up from school.

Meredith was still worried about her when she dressed for dinner, and Charles could see that something was bothering her when he picked her up that evening, and drove her to the Italian restaurant he had mentioned to her. She told him about it over dinner, and it disturbed him too. He commented that no one defends an abuser like their victim.

"I don't know what to do to help her. She's never admitted to me that he hurts her."

"You can't do anything until she tells you," Charles said. And then they spoke of other things. Charles knew a lot about movies, and had seen all of hers. He admitted that he'd had a crush on her when he was first in the Air Force. "I was just a kid then, and so were you. I never thought I'd be having dinner with you one day." He told her about the missions he had flown, being in military intelligence, and winding up at the Pentagon. He had had a distinguished military career. His son had gone to West Point, and was in the army now, and his daughter was a private pilot for a major corporation and lived in Texas. She was married to a commercial airline pilot and had two children. "I guess I gave her the flying bug when she was a little kid." He sounded proud of her.

"Maybe it's hereditary. I hardly know my granddaughter, but she's trying to be an actress," Meredith said softly.

"Do you miss it?" Charles asked her.

"Sometimes. Not much anymore. It was another lifetime. I loved it when I was doing it. It was thrilling. And then I stopped. Everything stopped . . . when my son died." She looked at him with eyes that told the whole story of loss and bottomless grief, and he didn't press her about it.

"Would you ever go back to acting?" he asked her and she shook her head.

"Not now. It's too late." And then she remembered Arthur telling her it was never too late. "I'm not even sure I could do it anymore, or that I'd be any good. It's been too long, and there aren't a lot of great parts for women my age."

"You could make a comeback if you wanted to. Even kids who never saw your movies know your name."

"It's the only job I ever knew, or that I wanted. I loved it," she said, and her eyes lit up. It was the first time in years that she had admitted it, even to herself. "I just couldn't make myself go back after Justin died. It seemed so insignificant compared to losing him."

"Most jobs are insignificant," Charles said quietly, "unless you're saving lives or curing cancer. I had a lot of fun flying, and my daughter does too. But we weren't changing the world. We just had fun doing what we got paid for." He had a relaxed, practical point of view about things, and she liked that about him. She admired the fact that he volunteered for the OES now, and that he'd had the courage to come to San Francisco, knowing no one, to start a new life and his own business. While she had retreated behind her walls, his reaction to grief and losing his wife was to try something different. He was braver than she was. He owned a private security agency, providing protection for high-profile people, like her. He had kept the agency small and had select clients, and he enjoyed it.

The evening sped by, and the dinner was as good as he had promised. What she noticed most of all was how comfortable she was with him. He felt like an old friend instead of someone new. She didn't have to tell him her whole history. He already knew most of it, and could sense the rest. He was intuitive about people, at ease with himself, and comfortable in his own skin. She realized as he drove her home that she had forgotten to tell him she didn't want to date him. She laughed when she thought of it.

"What's funny?" he asked as they stopped at a light.

"I was going to tell you that I didn't want to go out with you, that I'm too old to start over, and too old for you." She was smiling at him.

"And? You think that's funny?" He didn't look amused.

"I was having such a good time with you, I forgot to tell you."

He laughed too then. "And now?"

"I'm still too old, but I had a really nice time. I like being with you." He looked pleased when she said it.

"So do I. Shall we leave it at that and not make any major policy decisions just yet? And you're not too old by the way. I don't actually give a damn how old you are, if that's okay with you. My wife was five years older than I am and it was never a problem for us. I don't see what difference eight years makes. And you look great. So can we scratch that one off the list?"

She nodded with a grin. "Apparently."

"Anything else you seriously object to? I think your recluse status is somewhat at risk. You went to the symphony two days ago, and out to dinner at a restaurant tonight. So that's kind of a flimsy excuse. Let's just take it easy and see where it goes. How does that sound?"

"Interesting," she said with a mischievous look, and when they stopped at her gate, she took the remote out of her purse, opened the gate, and they drove in. When he stopped the car, he leaned over and kissed her. She was startled by how it made her feel, suddenly young again and as if there was hope for the future. She hadn't felt that way in years. She had been so sure that the best of her life was behind her, and now she didn't think so.

"I love being with you, Meredith," he said softly.

"Me too," she whispered. He kissed her again, and then a night security guard appeared and waited discreetly for them to get out of the car, and stayed in the courtyard. He had been less aware of her security right after the earthquake than he was now.

"I'm not sure how fast I'll get used to how famous you are," he said as he followed her into the house, and they said good night in the front hall. "I'll call you tomorrow," he promised, and she knew he would. She wanted him to. That was the best part. He left then, and she went upstairs with a smile on her face, and as she did the years melted away, and the heavy burdens she had carried for so long. Suddenly she felt young again. She wondered if maybe Arthur was right after all. It was never too late. She realized that now.

Chapter 7

The night Meredith had dinner with Charles, Ava dropped in at Arthur's house to return Peter's manuscript to him, and tell him that she loved it. She thought the story gripping, and the characters insightful. She said she couldn't put it down, and whenever she had to stop reading, she couldn't wait to get back to it. He was thrilled to hear it.

"You're the only person I've given it to," he said, looking nervous. Arthur called down to him then as they stood inside the front door, and asked who it was.

"It's Ava," Peter called up to him, hoping he wouldn't mind. She hadn't called first to ask if she could come by.

"Tell her to come up," he said in answer. She followed Peter up the stairs, and she went into the room Arthur used as an office, with his piano prominently in the room. It was the first room he had Peter and the cleaning team put back in order, and where he most liked to be. Ava greeted him warmly and apologized for dropping by unannounced. "You're welcome anytime you want to," he said warmly. She kissed his cheek and he noticed the exotic scent of her perfume. Even without seeing her, he was aware of the sensual quality about her, and Peter even more so. It was the way she spoke, the slightly husky timbre of her voice, the long silky hair that brushed his cheek, which Peter looked at longingly. He had the benefit of being able to see her enticing figure, which Arthur didn't.

"Why don't you two go into the living room and play, or wherever you want to." Peter looked embarrassed when Arthur said it. He would have liked to take her to his bedroom, but didn't dare.

They heard him practicing after that, and were surprised how fast the time went, as they sat there talking. It was two hours later when she glanced at her watch, and looked regretful.

"I'd better get back. Joel had a late meeting tonight. He'll be home by now. He likes me to be home when he gets there." He wasn't unreasonable or overly possessive, but she was there for a reason and he never let her forget it. He lived with her because he enjoyed her company, and her body. He usually made love to her as soon as he walked in the door at night. She felt differently about it now than she had in the beginning. At first it had flattered her, and now she realized it was more about his needs than any deep feelings he had for her. She knew he stayed with women for about two years, and she was nearing her expiration date.

He had opened new horizons to her, and had been very generous. He made up for the salary she had lost when he asked her to give up her job. He wanted her to be fully available to him, and he didn't want to be sleeping with one of his employees, or not for long anyway, so he didn't want her to work for him.

Joel had always told her that marriage wasn't an option, and he wasn't a "long-term guy," as he put it. He had learned that lesson once, and been burned. Ever since his divorce, he liked to "keep things fresh," and move on before the relationship got too demanding or maudlin or boring. She wasn't with him for the money, it had been exciting and fun to be with him, he was handsome and sexy, and she liked the difference in their ages. He was a grown-up, and not some young kid who would jerk her around. He never did, and lived up to his promises. But in the past year she had begun to feel like a body he thought he had bought and paid for. He didn't want anything too exotic, but he acted like he owned her. And there was always the unspoken message that she was disposable.

She had thought of leaving him, but it was never the right time. They were always about to go on a fantastic trip, or he was in the middle of a complicated deal and she didn't think it was fair to leave him then, or it was a holiday like his birthday or Christmas. And what would she do when she left him? She lived in a gorgeous house with him, hadn't worked for two years, which would be hard to explain. He had promised her a reference saying that she had been his personal assistant when they separated, but people knew about their arrangement. She met all his business contacts when there were social aspects involved, and she held up her end of the deal too. She looked fantastic, and every man was envious of him. She supported Joel in everything he did, she appreciated everything he did for her, and she had an easy, sunny disposition. He had even said to her more than once that if he was still a marrying man, he would marry her, but he wasn't.

He preferred his bachelor life with a revolving door of women like her. He knew that if he married her, he would always feel that he had missed something, and eventually his own curiosity would get the best of him, and he would cheat on her, and then it would all come tumbling down around his ears again, and he'd be giving her a house and paying spousal support and they'd end up hating each other, just like his parents and his ex-wife. He never wanted to go through that again. In his mind, it ruined everything. Ava didn't think he cheated on her, but she didn't know for sure. If he did, he did it carefully. She thought she loved him at first, but now she wasn't sure. It was an arrangement that worked for both of them, or had. But at twenty-nine, she was coming to a fork in the road. She wanted marriage and babies one day, and a home of her own.

Joel wasn't the man she wanted to be with forever, and now she knew it more than ever. From the moment she'd met Peter, her heart had been engaged. He was ten years younger than Joel, but he seemed like a boy in comparison. His dream was to be a successful novelist one day, and in the meantime, he eked a living out of mediocre jobs. Peter fully realized that his writing wasn't going to be lucrative for several years, or maybe ever. He could barely support himself now, and couldn't have supported her, and she didn't care. She wanted to be with him every moment of the day. She dreamed of him at night, and she could hardly breathe when he walked into the room. She thought Peter was the most beautiful, sexiest man she'd ever seen. The only thing she didn't know was what they could do about it. He needed the job with Arthur so he could continue to write, but he'd made almost no money on his writing so far, except some freelance articles in obscure literary magazines. His real career hadn't even begun yet, and hers as a model had been on hold for almost two years, and she wasn't a graphic designer yet. They had some lean years ahead of them if they tried to make a life of it.

Neither of them had an apartment. He lived in a tiny room in Arthur's attic. They had talked about it, and Peter was sure that Arthur wouldn't let her live there with him. She didn't know whether to wait until Joel ended their relationship sometime in the next year, which seemed inevitable, or to throw caution to the winds, leave him, have Peter leave his safe haven with Arthur, find an apartment together and try to get better jobs than they'd both had previously. Peter felt an allegiance to Arthur now. He really liked him and didn't want to let him down. When she'd gotten involved with Joel, she was twenty-seven, but two years later, she didn't want to make a mistake.

Peter kissed her, and held her tight afterward. He had tears in his eyes when he whispered to her, "What are we going to do? I hate your going back to him." They hadn't made love at Meredith's, because she didn't want to sleep with two men at the same time. She was in love with Peter, but she lived with Joel. It had been bearable and even fun most of the time until the earthquake, but since then, everything had changed. It worked when she saw Peter every day, but every night in bed with Joel, she ached for Peter and fantasized about him. Now she couldn't bear to be away from him, two houses down on the same street. And he was going crazy, thinking about her. "Maybe I should give Arthur notice," he said miserably. He had come to love him almost as a father, and he knew Arthur needed him, or someone who really cared about him, to make his life easier. But he wanted to be with Ava. He could see himself marrying her one day, if another guy with a Ferrari didn't see her first.

"We'll figure it out," she said, trying to calm him. They had known each other for a month, and it already felt like a lifetime to both of them. He hated her being with Joel, but he was well aware that materially he had nothing to offer her. He was literally a starving writer, living in a garret. It was picturesque in a novel, but not in real life.

He walked her down the stairs, and she left a few minutes later, after they lingered for a few more minutes. He walked up the stairs to Arthur's study to check on him. Arthur was reading some papers in Braille at his desk, and looked up when he heard Peter walk into the room. He had intensely acute hearing, despite his age, which helped him compensate for his blindness. He joked about it at times, and said thank God he wasn't Beethoven, who was deaf. In some ways it was easier since he had been sighted as a young person, so he knew what things looked like.

"Everything all right?" Peter asked when he checked on him. Arthur could hear the sadness in his voice, despite the cheerful tone he used to cover it. He knew that he was troubled, and he could guess why, as he had said to Meredith.

"Come in, son," he invited him to come in and sit down. "I'm fine, but what about you? What's happening with you two?" They both knew he meant Ava. It was the only subject on Peter's mind at the moment, and superseded even his unfinished novel. He had figured out the ending since he'd met her, and had told her about it, but hadn't written it yet.

"Nothing," Peter responded to his question, as his voice sank to a lower register, which Arthur heard too. "It's an impossible situation. It's complicated for her too. I have nothing to offer her, and she has an ideal situation with Joel."

"Is she in love with him?" Arthur got right to the heart of the matter.

Peter hesitated. "She says she isn't. We're in love with each other, but it's not going to get us anywhere. I can't, in good conscience, encourage her to leave him. He can do everything for her that I can't and never will. I'll probably never make what he does."

"He doesn't love her," Arthur said with certainty.

"How do you know that?" Peter was intrigued. Arthur had an uncanny instinct for people that transcended vision.

"I can hear it. He has fun with her. She's probably interchangeable to him, and one day she'll be disposable, maybe sooner than she thinks. He's the kind of man who believes that women are toys to play with. She's not in love with him, I can hear that too. She was probably foolish to get tangled up with him, and impressed and dazzled. That doesn't last long. What the two of you have are possibilities, hopes, dreams. It deserves to be explored if you can figure out a decent way to do it. I'm not looking to get myself shot by an angry, jealous lover, but if you need to spend time with her, and want her to stay here from time to time, do it. I trust you to handle it, and still keep your ears open for me. You can have her here whenever you want to." Peter's face lit up like a child's on Christmas, and Arthur didn't need to see it to know it. "I hope she's a smart girl and handles it sensibly. We don't need a lot of drama around here." But what he wanted to do was give them an opportunity. And he didn't want to lose Peter. It was the wisest thing for him to do, so Peter didn't bolt and run in his enamored state, just so he could spend the night with her. She had to deal with her situation with Joel soon. "I hope she cleans it up in a reasonable time. It's not smart to let situations like this linger. They have the potential to get nasty and then it's like lighting a match to dynamite."

"I don't think she'll do that. I have faith in her."

"Good. I trust your judgment, unless she proves otherwise. And remember, the Ferrari is not what matters here. You're a good man, Peter, and an honorable one. She'd be lucky to have you."

"Thank you," Peter said, both touched and jubilant. He couldn't wait to tell Ava that Arthur was willing to let her spend the night with him, if they could figure out her end of it.

Ava only had a short distance to go from Arthur's house to Joel's, and her mind was full of Peter as she walked. She had no idea what to do about Joel, and had been tormenting herself about it for weeks. At least at Meredith's, they saw each other constantly, but now that they had moved back into their respective houses, her heart was down the block with Peter at Arthur's, and her body belonged to Joel. She could tell he had just come in, and was putting some papers on his desk. The house was a shambles, with the repairs just starting and dust everywhere.

"Where were you?" he asked as he looked up at her, when she walked into the room. He was in a good mood. He'd had a few drinks at the meeting. On the whole, he was an even-tempered, good-natured person, who liked to have a good time, which was why he was opposed to marriage now. He hated drama and dissension and heartache in his life. He'd had enough of that to last a lifetime with his ex-wife. He had given her a fortune when they divorced. He was glad they'd never had children. He had decided children weren't for him. He had no desire to leave another generation behind for posterity. He lived in the moment, and wanted no part of the headaches his friends had with teenagers, or crying babies at night.

"I dropped something off to Meredith," Ava lied to him, and hated herself the moment the words were out of her mouth. She had never done that before. She had always been truthful in their relationship, and her confusion over Peter was slowly turning her into someone different, a person she'd never been before, to protect what she felt for Peter and hide it from Joel. "How did your meeting go?" She was always interested in his business, and impressed by how creative he was in his field. He was a genius in the Internet world.

"It went great." He smiled at her. "We're buying three new Internet companies and absorbing them to wipe out the competition. Everyone's happy with the deal. We're going to London and Berlin next week by the way, and New York on the way back." He always told her, he didn't ask her. She had no voice in the matter, and followed him everywhere, and he let her shop to her heart's content. She didn't take undue advantage of it. It was one of the perks of being with him. She knew that one of these days she'd have to give that up. Hearing about their trip made her heart race, and all she wanted was to find an excuse not to go. It would give her time to be with Peter, and maybe figure things out.

"I don't think that's smart, with the construction going on here. I think one of us needs to be here, to keep an eye on them, or they'll never finish," she said.

"That's nice of you, but you don't have to sacrifice yourself to sit here with the workmen. The contractor can do it."

"I think I'd rather be here," she said, and he smiled and walked over to kiss her, and then they walked upstairs to their bedroom, and that was getting harder too. She felt like a liar and a fraud all the time now. Peter was in her heart and mind, and Joel didn't deserve her lies to him. She knew she couldn't go on this way for long.

"Are you okay?" he questioned her. She seemed quiet lately, or distracted. He wondered if they were approaching the witching hour when things turned serious, and girls forgot his warnings in the beginning, when he told them he would never marry them. It usually happened when they were around Ava's age, twenty-nine or thirty. He hoped it wasn't happening to them yet. He enjoyed her more than most of her predecessors, but not enough to want a future with her. And if she pressed him, he knew he'd run.

"I'm just tired," she said vaguely, "and the dust gives me a headache. Everything is such a mess."

"They'll be finished soon. Maybe we should go to Paris for a weekend, before New York." He was considerate of her, and thoughtful, to a point. In the end, it was all about him, which was why she was there, to entertain him sexually and otherwise. But he held up his end of the deal and gave her a golden life.

"Let's see how the repairs are going by then," she said, clinging desperately to the only excuse she could think of for not going with him. He didn't answer, went to take a shower, and came to bed. She was in tears while he was in the bathroom, and forced a smile when he got back, as he walked naked across the bedroom. He had a fabulous body, tall and powerful, and in good shape. He worked hard at it with his trainer. He spent enough time at the gym to keep it that way. Peter was more human and what she loved about him had nothing to do with how fit he was, or his muscles, although he was good-looking too. But he was real. Her relationship with Joel had been satisfying for two years, but seemed superficial to her now, and artificial, and with her recent lies, fraudulent. She was the fraud. Joel had always been honest and straightforward with her about what he would never offer her. He believed in truth in advertising, and never promised what he didn't intend to deliver. What it boiled down to was that Peter had heart. Joel didn't.

He was quiet for a minute when he got into bed, and then asked her a question she didn't understand at first.

"Do I hear a clock ticking?" She glanced at her bed table, and the same clock she'd always had was there. It was electronic and didn't tick. "I don't mean that one. I mean yours." He knew women well enough, and what they expected.

"Oh." She didn't answer for a moment. He was handing her an opportunity, and she was afraid to seize it. It was too soon. She hadn't even slept with Peter yet. "I don't know . . . maybe . . ."

"I didn't think you were there yet." He sounded sad as he said it. They both knew what that meant to him.

"I wasn't. I don't know why, but I think the earthquake changed things. It shook me up." He hadn't suspected her interest in Peter, and didn't consider him a threat. No money, a night guard for a blind old man, a novel he'd never get published. He didn't see much there, neither the heart, nor the brain, by his standards. Andrew would have concerned him more. He was better looking than Peter, but he was no match for Joel either, in what Joel considered the real world. He assumed that Ava's strange mood was about her, not other men.

"You know, even if you're getting poetic about marriage, even if you find a guy and are married for fifty years, in the end one of you dies, and you wind up alone. What's the point?"

"The fifty years before that, of companionship," she said softly.

"We have that, you don't need to be married for that, except if you want kids. And people don't marry for that anymore either. Not that I want a baby." They both knew he didn't. He wanted a woman, and that was it. It was almost generic for him. He turned to look at her more closely then. "Is that what's happening? You want to get married and have kids?"

"I think so. Eventually. I always thought I would." He nodded. He had heard it all before from others, and he was glad Ava wasn't given to scenes. She was a sensible girl he could talk to.

"So have we hit that wall?"

"Maybe," she said in the smallest voice, feeling like she was on a roller coaster, panicked over what she was doing. She hardly knew Peter. Maybe she was insane to risk Joel for him. "I don't know."

"Maybe we should quit while we're ahead," he said quietly. "I didn't see this coming," he said with regret.

"Neither did I," she answered, meaning Peter. She hadn't seen it at all, until she walked out to the sidewalk, naked under her bathrobe, five minutes after the earthquake, and saw Peter looking at her with a stunned expression. If she was ever going to believe in love at first sight, he was it. The past month at Meredith's had only strengthened their feelings for each other. And now she was putting her comfortable, easy relationship with Joel on the line. She thought she had truly lost her mind, and now she was about to lose her security with it. She had a little money put aside in the bank, but not much. She hadn't started to save for her exit yet.

"I hate dragging things out till they get nasty. Been there, done that. And I saw my parents do it that way. By the time you get to where you are now, we're screwed. Is that why you don't want to come to Europe with me?"

"Maybe. I don't know. It would give me time to think."

"Don't overthink things, Ava. It's been terrific. We never thought it would last forever. I'll be gone for two weeks. That'll give you time to figure out where you want to go. Find a nice apartment. I'll pay for the first six months, and the security deposit." He'd done this before. And he would have paid a year's rent if she asked him to, but she didn't. He'd done enough in the last two years. She didn't want to take advantage of him.

"Do you want me to move out when you're gone?" she asked him, terrified of what she was doing, and wondering if she'd regret it. But it was going to end at some point anyway. He had never told her he loved her. She had said it to him, and thought she did when she said it. Now she knew she didn't. She loved Peter, as she had never loved any man before.

"That's probably a smart game plan," he said about her moving out while he was away. He put an arm around her. "I'm going to miss you," he said, as though she were an old friend leaving on a trip. "I never thought that the roof that would fall in during the earthquake would be us, but it was bound to happen sooner or later. That old expiration date. Suddenly one day it's staring you in the face." In his world that was how it worked for him. No woman was ever going to own him again. He didn't care how much the relationship cost him, at least she wasn't his wife, and he didn't have to pay her a big settlement, or spousal support. No fuss, no muss, no kids, no bother. Thanks for a good time, and don't let the door hit you in the ass on the way out. That was his take on relationships, and she'd always known it. She just hadn't expected it to end so fast and simply. He was a businessman, and to Joel, everything was a deal that either worked or didn't.

He tried to make love to her when they turned the lights out, and she didn't want to. She had too much to think about now. He didn't insist. He knew when it was over. It was like taking a jar of mayonnaise out of the refrigerator and finding that the date had expired. Oh too bad, and you threw it in the trash. And when you had time to think about it, you bought another jar of mayonnaise. They both knew that the end of their relationship wouldn't kill them, but it was sad. A tear crept into her pillow, as she lay awake. She could hear him snoring, and he had already left for the gym when she woke up the next day. She tried to remember what had happened and what they'd said. Was it over? Is that what they had agreed to? He was leaving for London in a week, and she had to be out by the time he got back. She had no idea where to go. She wanted to tell Peter, but she needed time to digest it first. She needed to mourn it, just for a minute.

She had a missed call from Peter at noon when he was on his lunch break at work. He didn't call her again until he was on his way to Arthur's at five o'clock. Ava had gone for a long walk, and she sounded serious when she answered. Peter blurted out his news as soon as he heard her voice.

"Arthur says you can stay here whenever you want to." He sounded jubilant, and she laughed at the irony of it. Whenever she wanted to? How many nights was that? She had to find a job and an apartment now, and had three weeks to do it.

"Joel and I broke up last night," she said in a flat voice, which masked the panic she was feeling. She had traded a known quantity for a total stranger. But she had also done it so she could be an honest woman. A month of lying to Joel was enough, she didn't want to lose herself.

"You *what*?"

"We broke up. It's over. I'm moving out."

"Did you tell him it was because of me? Is he going to shoot me?"

She laughed at the idea. "He was fine. This was only temporary for him. He always said that."

"Are you sorry?"

She thought about it before she answered, she didn't want to lie to him too. That was no way to start. "Actually, no. Scared shitless of what I'm going to do next. I have to find a place to live, and I haven't worked in two years, which is hard to explain, so people don't think you were in rehab or jail."

"I'm sorry. I know this is scary as hell, and it doesn't seem like enough. But I love you, Ava. We'll make it work somehow." He would get a better paying job than the one at the magazine. His hopes and dreams were focused on his writing, but he had to be practical now too, for her sake.

"At least we're starting clean. I didn't want to lie to him anymore. It's not right. You don't have to worry about me. I can take care of myself, and the crazy thing is, knowing you for a month, and without ever making love with you, I love you too." She was smiling when she said it. They were like two crazy kids in love. It felt like riding the roller coaster at the fair. They had ridden up, up, up the steep part, and now they were going to shoot down, screaming and terrified, clinging to each other . . . but if they survived, it was going to be fantastic. "We're both nuts, but I love you," she said, feeling breathless. "I'll come by to see you later, if that's okay," she said. She was going to start looking for an apartment the next day. The roller coaster ride had started, and as they hung up, she felt insanely happy and like an honest woman. It was the best she could do for now.

Chapter 8

*Two days after their dinner, Charles called Meredith and in*vited her to spend the day with him in the Napa Valley on Saturday. He had a small rented house there, set amid extensive vineyards on someone's property, with a river running through it.

"I go there when I can get away, to clear my head."

"It sounds nice."

"It looks like Italy, or France. And there are good restaurants up there." She agreed to go, and he told her he'd pick her up at nine in the morning, they'd make a day of it, and come home late that night, after dinner at Bouchon, one of the restaurants he thought she'd like.

When he picked her up, she was wearing a white cashmere turtleneck and a warm parka. He had warned her it might be chilly. They chatted easily on the hour-and-a-half drive. They picked up sandwiches when they got to Yountville, and then went to his house. There were vineyards all around them, as far as the eye could see. They walked down to the river and went on a bike ride through the vineyards, and then had a picnic on a table outside his house, looking out over the valley. There was an outdoor fireplace and he built a fire in it to keep them warm while they talked.

"I love this," she said, looking more relaxed than he'd seen her. "Every time I go out with you, you remind me of what I've been missing. This is heaven. Scott and I came up here a few times when we first moved to San Francisco, but one of us was always on location. Our lives were complicated then, and people followed us around wherever we went. That's why we bought the big house in the city. We figured we'd have privacy, and we did. Kendall hated it when people stopped us for autographs when we went out, or wanted pictures of us with them, or the paparazzi caught us in some private moments. I guess it was a hard way to grow up. She hated everything about our careers. It must kill her that her daughter is pursuing that life now. I was happy Kendall didn't want it. It's hard to lead a normal life with all that going on. And I guess the parents of her friends at school talked about us.

"She was older and already married herself in New York when Scott left me, but it was a nightmare. The press was after us constantly. He went to the Cannes Film Festival with Silvana, for the film they were in, and everything exploded after that. Kendall's take on it was that if I'd been home more, and not working all the time, it wouldn't have happened, but I think Scott would have done something like it anyway. He was bored and she was young, and I was gone a lot, and he had a hard time with my success. His affair with Silvana might have blown over, but he would have done it again with someone else. I filed for divorce right after Justin died, since I blamed him for that. Kendall thought I nearly destroyed her father with the divorce and never forgave me for it. But it must have worked out for them. He and Silvana are still together fifteen years later. Her career tanked after one movie, but I think being married to Scott Price was enough for her. I retired then, because of my son, but I was tired of the Hollywood hype anyway. The box office pressure. You never really know what the truth is. With or without Silvana, our marriage probably would have run out of gas at some point. It took me years to figure that out. Justin's death just made it all more dramatic and tragic, and finished us off. It nearly killed both of us. Scott stayed drunk and on drugs afterward for two years, and I vanished. You can't come back from something like that as a couple. Too much had happened. He got his career back on track though, after he went to rehab. He's done some very good films in the last few years. He's a talented director. He's a Hollywood legend now," she said to Charles, and there was no bitterness in her voice. It was the story of her life, and she accepted where it had led her. She had learned to live with the losses. Scott was ancient history for her now.

"It can't be easy to have a decent marriage and bring up kids in Hollywood, with that kind of fame," Charles said sympathetically. He wanted to understand what had happened to her, why she had run away and hidden for so long. Their lives had been so different.

"That's why we moved to San Francisco. But all that crap follows you wherever you go. Fame is a hard game to play. You pay a high price for it, and even though we tried to protect them, so do your kids. Kendall married a very conservative young banker from a stuffy family with old money and she got as far away from it as she could. I don't blame her. And now her daughter wants everything we had. Hollywood families are like circus families. They love to dance on the high wire without a net. It's in their blood." Charles smiled at the comparison.

"People envy it, they have no idea what it's about, or the toll it takes," he said wisely.

"They envy it until you become too famous, and then they hate you for it. They only love you for a while."

They walked back into his little house then, and he lit a fire inside. She loved the smell of the wood burning as she snuggled up to him. The house itself was small and cozy, with a living room with a big fireplace, three bedrooms, and an inviting country kitchen. Charles said it was perfect for an occasional country weekend, or if his kids came to visit, which they didn't do often. He went to visit them instead.

At the end of the day, the October sun went down and the evening was cold. She had brought a skirt to wear to dinner at Bouchon, but Charles told her she didn't have to change. She lay on the couch next to him, totally relaxed, as he leaned over and kissed her, and then sat up, admiring her.

"How can you still be so beautiful?" Charles said, as he cupped one breast with his hand and she didn't pull away.

"Daphne says I'm a good witch." She smiled at him.

"Then you've bewitched me. That I'm willing to believe." It was dark in the living room as he slowly unbuttoned her blouse, unhooked her bra and bent to kiss her breast. Making love was barely a memory for her now, but she wanted him, and reached out for him, and then he took her hand, and they walked into his bedroom, and he peeled her clothes away, as she held her arms out to him, and they lay on the bed together, and made love as though everything was new and the past faded away. She held him in her arms afterward, at peace.

He tried not to think of who she was, and only that she was a woman he cared about, but the moment he looked at her, she took his breath away again. He had just made love to Meredith White, it felt like a dream to both of them.

"I want to forget who you are," Charles said to her in a hoarse voice after they made love.

"What does that mean?" She looked happy and sated, and felt as though she was in the right place with the right man. She had no idea how they had found each other, but she was glad they had.

"It means I want to forget that I'm making love to the most famous movie star of all time. It intimidates me."

"You know better. You know who I am now. That's all that matters and all there is." She felt as though they were on equal footing, and she liked that too. Neither of them was bigger or better or more powerful or important than the other. They were just a man and a woman who were falling in love with each other.

"I keep thinking that I would never have met you if the earthquake hadn't happened. You'd still be a recluse, and I'd be puttering around at loose ends."

"I wouldn't exactly call your life 'puttering.'" She smiled. His security business was a solid success with important clients, and he kept busy doing other things, like the OES. "I'm happy I'm not a recluse anymore," she whispered to him, and they made love again before they got up and showered together and dressed. She was still surprised by how comfortable they were with each other, as though they had been together for a long time.

"Did you do nude scenes in your movies?" he asked her while they were getting out of the shower. She seemed so at ease with her body and with him. She laughed at his question. It seemed so long ago.

"I had a body double for that. I never did my own nude scenes. Scott did, which is probably how he wound up with Silvana. She did her own nudity too. I didn't want to embarrass my kids if they saw the films later when they were older, so I always had a body double in my contracts. Maybe I should have one now for you," she teased, but her body was still beautiful, and a lifetime of exercise and careful eating had paid off. Charles had stayed trim and athletic after his military career too.

"You don't need a body double, you're gorgeous, Meredith."

She put up a gentle hand and kissed him. "If you start again, we won't make it to dinner," she warned him. He laughed and made a quick decision, they went back to bed and canceled dinner. It was a beautiful, romantic night, and they drove back to the city under a harvest moon, which hung in the sky like a movie set. He was beginning to forget who she was, and she was slowly becoming his, a woman he loved, not a movie star, or a legend.

They got back to the city at one-thirty in the morning. There had been no traffic, and he followed her into the house. She let him in with her key, and she knew that the night security man was watching them on one of the screens.

"Do you want to sleep here tonight?" she asked him, and he nodded. She took him up to her bedroom, and they piled into her enormous canopied bed, and they snuggled like two children and fell asleep within minutes.

They woke up early, and she took him down to the kitchen to make him breakfast. Jack and Debbie were off on Sundays, so she knew they'd be alone. She handed him *The New York Times* that the night man had left on the kitchen table. He read it while she made him fried eggs and bacon, and poured him a mug of steaming coffee, and then she sat across from him with a mug of her own.

"This is perfect, isn't it?" she said as he glanced over at her and thanked her for breakfast.

"Yes, it is." He looked as peaceful as she did.

They went for a walk on the beach after breakfast, bundled up in the wind, and came back at noon for something to eat, and wound up in bed again.

He hated to leave her that night, but he had an early meeting the next morning, and he didn't want to deal with Jack and Debbie snarling at him the next day.

"Are you keeping an eye on them?" he asked her when the subject came up, and she smiled.

"I don't need to. They're as honest as I am."

"I hope you're right," he said, but it was obvious he didn't believe her, and she didn't argue the point with him. The two days she had spent with him had been perfect, and she didn't want anything to spoil it. Nothing could have. They felt made for each other, and he was right, the eight years between them didn't matter at all.

* * *

"Son of a bitch!" Debbie exploded when she walked into their living room, where Jack was watching *Sunday Night Football* on TV. He looked up in surprise at the vehemence of her comment. "I talked to Harvey the night guy, and the colonel spent the night here last night. They came in at one-thirty in the morning, and he just left. Shit, we'll never get rid of him now."

"I can't believe it." Jack looked shocked. "She hasn't gotten laid since Scott left her."

"Yeah, now she's friends with half the neighborhood, and gives block parties, and she has a boyfriend. What are we supposed to do with that?"

He thought about it for a minute and shrugged. "What we've always done I guess. A little here, a little there, some kickbacks. We're there for her whenever she needs us, and one day she gratefully leaves us a nice fat pot of gold in her will."

"It's not as simple as that," Debbie said, pouring the last of a bottle of Chateau Margaux into a glass in front of her. They'd been drinking all day. "If he sticks around, he'll be watching us. He has some kind of a security business and she won't be lonely the way she was before. And she's not that old. It could be a long wait."

"He may not stick around for long. She's older than he is, and her life is pretty dull."

"She's Meredith White," Debbie reminded her husband. "What guy wouldn't want to show off with that? And what if she marries him?"

"At her age, she won't. What does she need to get married for?

Sooner or later he'll find someone his own age to play with. The star factor doesn't last forever." He dismissed it out of hand.

"I don't like the guy. I've got a bad feeling about him," Debbie said somberly.

"I don't like him either, but he's too busy to pay attention to us. We just stay below the radar for a while," Jack said. But Debbie didn't like the way things were going. It had all been so much easier when Meredith had no friends, no man, no kids, no family. But Debbie knew she was loyal, and wouldn't forget the time she had spent with them. They had enormous influence on her, and she frequently asked Debbie's advice. But it still made Debbie uneasy that Meredith was broadening her life. She could slip right through their fingers now and everything they'd built by careful, deliberate, constant, steady theft could come to an end. What a terrible thought, Debbie said to herself.

Ava was having dinner with Peter and Arthur that night. They had ordered food in from a nearby Vietnamese restaurant and were eating in the kitchen. Arthur was adept with chopsticks. He had just made a suggestion that stunned Peter and Ava.

Peter told him that Ava had broken up with Joel, and was looking for an apartment. Arthur approved of what she'd done. She couldn't ride two horses forever. She had done the right thing in a relatively short time and won his respect.

"Do you want her to live here with you?" he asked Peter when they were alone. "I'd be willing to try it, if she lives by the same rules you do. It makes more sense than her getting an apartment she can't afford, and then spending nights with you anyway." Arthur was willing to go to great lengths not to lose Peter, and he liked the girl from his few discussions with her while they were all at Meredith's. He knew Peter was crazy about her. They were the right age, Peter thought they were well suited, and she seemed like a bright girl. Now that she'd gotten rid of her narcissistic boyfriend, Arthur was willing to lend a hand.

Ava and Peter were both ecstatic with his offer that sounded like a dream to them. "You can move in here if you want," he'd said to Ava, as Peter grinned and hugged Arthur. She already knew that there were rules. They couldn't intrude on his space, practice or creative time, or make noise when he was playing the piano. Peter stayed upstairs most of the time, and his room was small. And he would have to be available for Arthur when he needed him. It sounded more than reasonable to them.

Arthur made the second part of his offer after dinner and surprised them both. In fact, they were stunned. They had just finished the meal when Arthur looked in Ava's direction and addressed her.

"I've been thinking, Ava. I need someone to arrange my travel, and I get a lot of correspondence that isn't in Braille. I need someone to handle it, answer the phones, so I have time to practice. I've been thinking of hiring an assistant. I was going to offer it to Peter, but he needs time to finish his novel, and he has a day job. You need a job now. Would you be interested in a job as my assistant?" He told her what he could pay her, and it was slightly more than she'd been making when Joel asked her to quit her job at the time.

She was speechless and nodded. He had solved all her problems. It was like a reward for doing the right thing with Joel.

"You're not answering," Arthur said after a minute of silence at the table. "Does that mean you're not interested?"

"She's nodding," Peter answered for her, "and she looks like she's going to faint."

"Fainting is not allowed, and she needs to speak so I can hear her," he said, and both young people laughed.

"I don't know what to say, Mr. Harriman. I would love it. And I can learn Braille, so I can answer all your correspondence."

"That might be a good idea." He looked pleased. He liked helping them. He was all in favor of young love. He was a romantic at heart, and had never had children, he had taken Peter under his wing, and he was willing to give Ava a chance and let her prove herself, to Peter, and to him. "When can you start?" he asked her as he got up from the table and reached for his cane, and she handed it to him.

"Tomorrow," she said without hesitating. It was perfect, just what they needed. She had a job and a place to stay, with Peter, and he didn't have to leave Arthur to be with her. If it turned out well, it could be a blessing for all three of them, and if it didn't, at least they would know they tried.

They cleaned up the kitchen after dinner, Peter and Ava went up to his room to talk, and make plans. She was going to move out when Joel left for Europe, but that was in a few days. She could spend the nights with Peter until then, and then pack her things once Joel was gone. It would be less awkward that way. She knew that Joel didn't like melodramatic farewells either. When it was over, he moved on, and she suspected that within a short time, she'd be replaced.

Peter and Ava were talking about how generous Arthur was to have offered her a job, and let her stay there with Peter. She was sitting on the small couch in his attic bedroom, when he came to sit next to her with a smile.

"You know, there's one thing we haven't worked out yet. We have all the practicalities arranged, your job, your salary, moving out of Joel's house, Braille lessons." She looked puzzled as he went down the list, it sounded like everything to her. In a sense, she was leaping from one man's bed to another, which made her somewhat uncomfortable, but they had spent a month living under one roof together, or three weeks. It had been long enough for them to fall in love.

"What have I missed?"

"Us," he said simply, with a boyish look.

"What do you mean us?" He kissed her in answer to her question, and slipped his hand gently under her sweater, and she smiled when she realized what he meant. "Oh . . . that . . ." They had something to celebrate, and nothing to stand between them or hold them back. Joel had ended it simply and cleanly, and she was stunned that she and Peter had rearranged their lives entirely without ever making love. He pulled her gently onto his bed, and undressed her in the simple attic room where she was going to live with him, and almost like a bride, he made love to her for the first time, first gently and then passionately, and she gave herself to him as though there had never been any man before him. It was simple and sweet and innocent and honest. It was everything she and Joel never had.

She spent the night with Peter, and texted Joel that she wasn't coming home, so he wouldn't worry. He didn't answer, and she didn't expect him to. A door had closed behind her. Joel was the past now, and Peter the future.

She stayed with Peter until Joel left town, and then she packed her things. Peter helped her move them to Arthur's house. She left Joel's home impeccable. She had spent two years there. She was alone when she closed the door for the last time, with a last look around. She didn't think she'd miss it. Her life with him had never been real. It had been a strange interlude in her life.

She walked to Arthur's house then, with her last suitcase, and walked the steps to the future. Peter was waiting for her. He took the bag from her, and they walked the rest of the way to his garret together. It felt like Heaven to her.

Chapter 9

*The morning after Charles and Meredith's first weekend to*gether, she told Debbie at breakfast that she was having the earthquake group to dinner on Saturday. It was a reunion of everyone who had stayed at the house. They all missed one another, and were eager to catch up on news, discuss the progress of their repairs, and just share a meal again.

Charles had to go out of town for three days to see an important client in Seattle before that, but he'd be back by Friday. Meredith and Tyla spoke almost every day, and she and Andrew were coming, with the children. Arthur and Peter accepted immediately, and Ava. She said that Joel would be in London. She was going to explain the situation to her later. It was too awkward to put in a text, and she said she'd come with Peter and Arthur. Meredith told Debbie there would be nine of them, and asked Debbie if she'd mind doing it. They could eat in the kitchen, which was easier for her.

Debbie reported it to Jack on her break at lunchtime.

"Christ, she's giving a dinner party for all of them. We're never going to get rid of these people, especially now if she's sleeping with the colonel. They're like the guests who stayed forever. We've lost her, Jack," she said miserably.

"Relax. Be patient. I told you. They'll get bored with each other. They're not that interesting. And the colonel will get tired of her."

"At least I don't have to babysit for those brats anymore. But they're coming to the dinner."

From Meredith's perspective, Jack and Debbie seemed in better humor since the houseguests had moved out. They didn't have more work to do, beds to make, meals to serve, and weren't worried about theft around the house. They seemed faintly chilly whenever she mentioned her former houseguests, but Debbie made an extra effort to be pleasant that week, made her all her favorite foods, and was secretly delighted there was no sign of the colonel. They had Meredith to themselves, just like old times. They didn't know Charles was in Seattle. Debbie was just grateful that he wasn't around, and hoped he was already bored, and none of the neighbors had dropped in to see her. Meredith and Debbie had several long chats in the morning at breakfast, and she said she was doing a research project, but didn't explain what it was. It had been gnawing at her since she spoke to Kendall. She hadn't heard from her since, although Kendall had promised to call again. But as usual, she didn't.

Debbie had the illusion that they were closer again. The Fabergé box hadn't turned up after the others left, but Meredith was sure it would, and that it had been put away for safekeeping. The aftershocks had been strong, and a few more paintings had fallen. Jack had taken them to the framers and they were getting a sizeable commission on all the repairs.

He had also found a structural engineer to check all the chandeliers. One had been slightly loose, and all the others were solid. Considering the force of the earthquake, they had suffered very little damage, unlike so many others. Bodies were still being found under collapsed houses, but no survivors now.

Unfortunately the repairs took time. Repair services were backed up for months, including the framers. Everyone was dealing with similar requests. The walls looked bare at the house in the meantime, with so many paintings missing. It couldn't be helped. Debbie and Jack had glued a vast number of small fragile objects back together, with meticulous, loving care. Meredith thanked them for doing it. They knew how much the small treasures meant to her.

For several days, and every night, Meredith combed the Internet, and even found the agent listed. She pretended to be a casting director for an independent film. She wanted to see all the examples of her granddaughter's work that were available. She had them digitally transferred whenever possible, and FedExed. Finally on Thursday, she had several hours of viewing material. Auditions Julia's agent had sent, two commercials she'd done in New York, one in L.A. for a blue jeans company, and a shampoo ad plus a number of bit parts in series and TV movies.

She watched them all diligently, and ran some of them again. Her conclusion at the end of it was that Julia had talent. She used her grandfather's last name, and mother's maiden name, as a stage name, Julia Price, not her grandmother's. Her real name was Julia

Holbrook, Kendall's married name, which Meredith would have liked better than Scott's name.

Her audition tapes were excellent, and so were her small parts in the two series she'd appeared in. Meredith had a few of the tapes on her desk. She told Charles about it on Friday night, and showed him some of them. He said his trip to Seattle had gone well, and he was fascinated by the video material Meredith showed him. Her granddaughter was tall, like Scott, and beautiful like her grandmother, with long wavy red hair. She was only nineteen and had played both teenagers and sophisticated women. One thing shone through every example. She was a born actress, like her grandmother.

"What are you going to do with all this?" Charles asked her, curious, after he'd watched it with her.

"Nothing. I just wanted to get an idea of whether she has talent, or is wasting her time in L.A. She's good. Could be great one day, if she works hard at it, and hones her skills. What I really want is to meet her. Maybe I can encourage her, or introduce her to some people. Kendall said that Scott is helping her, but I'd like to put my two cents in too, if she'll see me. She hardly knows me. I haven't seen her since she was ten, and she might not want to meet me again now."

"Are you going to invite her up here?" Charles asked her.

"Eventually. But I'd like to go to L.A. to see her. I have no idea if she'll even respond to a call or email from me. I think Kendall poisoned her against me for years."

"Try it. The worst she can do is refuse." He wasn't sure how hurtful that would be to her grandmother, but he thought it worth a shot and said so. He was excited that Meredith was reaching out instead of hiding. She had gotten braver and braver. "I'll go with you if you like," he offered. "I have several clients down there I can meet with while you see her. And we can have a little fun ourselves." He wanted to do things with her, and get her back out in the world she had abandoned. He was encouraging her gently, but didn't want to push her.

"I'm thinking about it," she admitted. "I'm not ready to write to her yet, but I will soon." He wasn't sure what she was waiting for, but suspected she was just trying to muster the courage to meet her granddaughter. It wasn't easy after so long, or even to explain.

She and Charles were happy to see each other again after his trip to Seattle. It had gone well. He had devised a massive personal protection plan for a very important CEO who had been receiving death threats for several months, because of the environmental stance of the company he worked for, and he was afraid for his wife and kids. The people who were threatening him had bombed someone else's home, and he didn't want it happening to them. It was exactly the sort of thing that Charles was good at. His agency did some industrial counter-espionage work too, which Meredith found fascinating. He was modest about his work, but he had had the highest security clearance given by the government, and was highly respected in his field. He had made a few suggestions to her, and she was planning to implement them with her own security people. He thought that she needed even more protection than she currently had, and underestimated the danger to herself. Charles had tried talking to Jack about it, and he dismissed it, and said they had all the systems they needed in place.

On Saturday, she was excited about the dinner. She arranged the flowers from her garden herself, and had picked the menu with Debbie. They were having lobster bisque to start, Cornish game hens, and chocolate soufflé for dessert, with whipped cream and crème anglaise. It was one of the things Debbie did well.

She told Jack that she hated to waste her talents on Meredith's intrusive neighbors, but Meredith had thanked her profusely several times, and was grateful, so maybe it was worth it to solidify their bond with her again. Things had deteriorated considerably between them while the neighbors were staying there, and Debbie made it clear how much she disliked them.

"You need to lighten up on that," Jack advised her, and she thought he might be right. As soon as Debbie put some effort into the menu, Meredith was happy with her again. She obviously wanted to impress her new friends. Or that was Debbie's take on it. In fact, she just wanted to spend time with them, and good food and great wine were part of it. Debbie was making pizza margherita for Will and Daphne, with French fries and ice cream sundaes. Meredith was delighted with the menu and Charles was impressed by how beautiful the table looked, with Meredith's magic touch. There were candles on the table, and she had used some pretty plates with a floral design in bright colors. It all looked very festive.

As soon as the guests arrived, it was even more so. They were offered martinis, margaritas, or champagne, with hors d'oeuvres Debbie had made. They congregated in the living room and the library, and Tyla noticed very quickly how close Ava and Peter seemed. They followed each other from room to room, and spoke in hushed tones.

"Is something going on with Peter and Ava?" Tyla asked her, and Meredith smiled mysteriously, and then whispered to her.

"Arthur offered her a job as an assistant. She's living there now, and she and Joel broke up."

"Holy shit! There's a major change," Tyla commented. "When did that happen?"

"Last week, I think."

"Is that why Joel's not here?"

"She says he's in England, but maybe he wouldn't have come anyway. She says the breakup was bloodless and very civilized." Tyla knew Andrew would be disappointed not to see Joel. He arrived late, and asked for him immediately. Ava gave him the party line about his being in London on business, and didn't explain the rest. They weren't ready to announce anything, but preferred to acknowledge it when people guessed. It seemed tasteless to Ava to make any big statements so soon after the breakup with Joel.

"What a whore," Andrew commented to Tyla under his breath. "Joel goes out of town for five minutes, and she's crawling all over Peter again."

Tyla didn't like to hear him talk about her friend that way, so she straightened him out. "They broke up. I think she may be seeing Peter now." She didn't tell him they were living in the same house, but he figured it out when Arthur said she was his new assistant. Andrew's eyes glittered with hatred and envy as soon as he heard.

During dinner, which everyone praised to the skies, they all got the very clear impression that Meredith and Charles were dating. He beamed every time he looked at her, and she seemed peaceful and happy. They all loved the food, and Daphne said it was the best pizza she'd ever eaten. Will ate a whole plate of fries. They devoured the ice cream sundaes, just as the adults did the soufflés.

Meredith made Debbie take a bow for the delicious dinner, and she positively glowed at their compliments, which were well deserved.

They had after-dinner drinks in the library, which were left on a silver tray. Charles helped Meredith bring in coffee, while Debbie and Jack cleaned up the kitchen. Debbie was mellower than she had been for a long time, with everyone so appreciative of her cooking, and they gave her a round of applause. She was preening like a peacock when she told Jack, and Meredith had hugged her for the first time in weeks. They were slowly sliding back in.

Everyone left after midnight, since they didn't have to work the next day, and she and Charles sat in the library alone afterward, discussing the evening. It was one of the things Meredith had always liked when she was married, being able to talk about a party afterward, and they both thought it was sweet that Peter and Ava were together and looked so much in love. When they'd exhausted the subject, they went upstairs to her bedroom, climbed into her bed and turned on the TV to watch a movie, but they were both asleep halfway through it, after agreeing it had been a lovely evening.

* * *

Andrew's take on it was different. After Tyla put the children to bed, after the big meal they'd eaten and the late hour for them. Daphne was already asleep when Tyla tucked her in, and she joined Andrew in their bedroom on their bed, where he was watching TV. He turned to Tyla with a sneer. He'd had a lot of wine to drink with dinner, a martini first, and the cognac afterward in the library had probably been one too many, Tyla realized.

"What a little whore Ava is," he commented, "moving in with Peter. She's probably fucking both him and Joel, and giving Arthur blow jobs." Tyla hated it when he talked that way. She considered Ava a friend now, and felt honor-bound to defend her, which with Andrew was always a mistake.

"She broke up with Joel before Arthur asked her to move in with them," she said primly. "She hasn't seen Joel since they broke up."

"Not likely. She looks like a whore and acts like one. Shit, she was standing naked on the sidewalk the night of the earthquake."

"She was wearing a bathrobe," Tyla corrected him.

"Yeah, and what do you think they were doing right before that, which is more than I can say for us." Tyla knew better than to answer him, particularly when he'd been drinking. He was capable of flying into a rage stone cold sober, and worse when he was drunk. "She's such a little slut," he went on, "and so are you." He rolled over at lightning speed, grabbed Tyla by the throat, and pressed her down on their bed, choking her. It crossed her mind instantly that she'd have marks from his handprints on her throat the next day, if she survived it. "Are you fucking Joel now? Is that why he didn't come tonight, because he was afraid to face me? Is that it?" He tightened his grip on her neck, dragged her up to the headboard, and started banging her head against it. It made a terrible sound, as she struggled against him, but she was afraid to wake the children if she screamed.

She did the only thing she could think of and kneed him in the groin. He doubled up with pain, and hit her so hard in the face that it threw her against the headboard even harder, and then he dragged her out of bed and she fell to the floor. And then he kicked her as hard as he could. "Don't you ever do that again, you bitch!" he shouted at her. She was dazed from the pain and could taste blood in her mouth. Her nose was bleeding, and then he slammed her head into the floor for good measure. She felt as though she was underwater, and then realized there was so much blood in her eyes she couldn't see. He continued to kick and pound on her as she came in and out of consciousness. She was sure he was going to kill her and she didn't care. She had no way to stop him or defend herself. There was no one to help her. She just didn't want her children to see it happening, but she forgot about that too as she lost consciousness. Everything went black as she went down, down, down to the ocean floor and swam away in a river of blood. It was the only way to get away from him.

The bell on the front gate rang about an hour after the guests had left. Charles and Meredith were asleep with the TV on, and she stirred when the intercom rang in her room. When she answered it, it was their night security man on duty that night. He was new. A service provided them on a rotating basis.

"I'm sorry to disturb you, ma'am," he said politely. "There's a child here. She rang at the gate, she says she lives down the street, and she needs your help. Her mother is sick or something."

"What's her name?" Meredith asked as she jumped out of bed.

"Daphne. She's very upset. Should I call 911 for her?"

"No . . . yes . . . I'll tell you in a minute. Tell her I'm coming right down." She shook Charles awake, and he was fully conscious quickly. "Charles . . . wake up . . . I need your help . . . Daphne's downstairs, something about Tyla. Andrew must have beaten her again. Should I call the police?"

"Yes." He grabbed his phone on the bedside table, called 911 and told them they had an injured person down, attacked by an intruder, gave them the Johnsons' address, and jumped into the clothes he'd worn to dinner. Meredith had already put on jeans, slipped into shoes, and put a sweater on, on her way down the stairs. He was right behind her. Daphne was sobbing in the front hall, barely able to speak, in her nightgown and bare feet, as Meredith grabbed her hand and they flew out the front door. The security guard opened the gate for them, as all three of them ran to the sidewalk.

"Tell me what happened," Meredith said to Daphne as they ran.

"I think he killed her . . . he hit her and hit her and I think Mommy's dead." They could hear sirens by then, and two police cars converged on the Johnson house at the same time from opposite directions. The policemen jumped out with guns drawn. Because Charles had told them it was an intruder, they drew their weapons, but for domestic violence they would have taken twice as long to come, which he knew.

"There's an eleven-year-old boy in the house," Meredith told them quickly. They had no way to get in. The door had locked behind Daphne when she left. They were sturdy young officers. They broke the door easily, as Charles followed them, and told Meredith to stay on the sidewalk with Daphne. She put an arm around her and held her close, and thanked God that Daphne had come to get her.

"Are they going to shoot my daddy?" Daphne sobbed. Meredith didn't know what to answer while they waited. Two more officers arrived and entered the house at a dead run, talking into their radios, and they came out two minutes later with Andrew, his hands cuffed behind him, his shirt and hands bloody, and for a moment Meredith was afraid that Daphne was right, and her mother was dead. They pushed Andrew into a squad car, and took off. He never looked at Daphne once. Meredith thought he hadn't even seen her. He was screaming at the officers and fighting them, and they were rough with him, as Daphne hid her face against Meredith. Two minutes later an ambulance arrived and three paramedics rushed into the house. They still didn't know what had happened, or if Tyla was alive, as Daphne buried her face in Meredith's sweater and sobbed. A minute later, Charles came out with Will. The boy was ghostly pale, he had been hiding in his room under the covers, but he could hear his mother's screams while Andrew beat her.

"Your mom is alive," he told both children, and then looked at Meredith with a grim expression. "I'll take the kids back to your house. You go with her in the ambulance." She nodded, and wanted to ask him how bad it was, but couldn't with the children present. A moment later, they brought Tyla out on a gurney, her face and head drenched in blood, her identity unrecognizable. She was just a bloody blob. She had an oxygen mask on, an IV in each arm, and was unconscious. Meredith gently handed Daphne off to Charles, and she went with him, as Meredith followed Tyla into the ambulance. They pulled away with lights flashing and siren screaming, and she saw Charles close the front door, and then head up the hill to her house with both children. After that her whole focus was on Tyla.

"How bad?" she asked one of the paramedics working on her. He shook his head in answer. She barely had a pulse, and was hardly breathing. Meredith heard one of the paramedics say that she had a severe concussion. They took her to the trauma unit of the nearest hospital, and Meredith never left her side for a minute. Meredith gave them all the information they needed that she knew, and when they asked her relationship to her, Meredith said "mother" so they wouldn't send her away.

It took them half an hour to assess her, superficially, and by then her blood pressure was a little more stable. They sent her for CT scans then, an MRI and X-rays, and by four A.M. they knew that her skull was intact, and not crushed or fractured, but she had a severe concussion. Her nose, cheekbone, and jaw were broken, and one arm. She had internal bleeding from where Andrew had kicked her in the stomach, but she was alive and was going to survive. She had surgery for the nose, cheekbone, and jaw performed by a plastic surgeon. They set her arm, and she looked like a mummy when she came back to the room swathed in bandages. They told Meredith that they had photographed all her injuries, since there would be criminal proceedings. Tyla was heavily sedated, and they told Meredith that her "daughter" would sleep now for several hours.

They suggested that she come back around noon, but to expect her to be groggy for the first day or two. They were giving her morphine for the pain.

Meredith realized as she was about to leave that she didn't have her purse with her or her phone so she couldn't call a cab or an Uber. They let her call Charles from the nursing desk. He called a cab for her, and told her he would pay for it when she got home.

He was waiting in the courtyard when she got there, paid the cab, and she told him the extent of Tyla's injuries. They both looked sick about it, as he followed her into the house. The children were asleep in her bed, in front of the TV. She left them in her bed, and she and Charles went to her study and spoke in whispers, and then he went home and Meredith slept on the couch in her study to be near them.

She told them a modified version of their mother's injuries when they woke up in the morning, and promised them she'd be okay.

"Can we see her?" Will asked. Meredith could see he had one of his stomachaches. He was doubled over in pain.

"Will my daddy go to jail?" Daphne wanted to know. Meredith didn't tell her that he was already there and she hoped he'd stay there forever.

"I'm not sure we can see her today. They said she's going to be very sleepy. Maybe tomorrow."

She took them both downstairs and fed them cereal and toast, and Charles arrived. Before they reached the kitchen, he told Meredith that as soon as the police cleared the crime scene, he would arrange for a special service that would clean the blood off every surface where it was smeared. That afternoon, he called and got the rundown on Andrew's situation. He was to be arraigned the next day, and they were going to charge him to the maximum extent of the law in view of Tyla's condition. He was being charged with battery under two sections of the California penal code, for "inflicting serious bodily injury" and for "willful conduct leading to corporal injury resulting in a traumatic condition" and making criminal threats. If convicted, he could serve up to four years in prison. A judge would set bail at the arraignment, and later there would be a trial, unless he pled guilty. Charles added that he would probably lose his medical license. He would be forbidden to come anywhere near Tyla, and possibly his children too. There would be a restraining order to prevent him. "I want Tyla and the kids to stay here," Meredith told him.

They took the kids to the park for an hour after they dressed, and they spent a quiet day. Meredith cooked them dinner. Charles stayed with them when she left to see Tyla briefly at the end of the day, but she was sleeping. She was still unrecognizable under her bandages. Her condition was serious but stable, and her vital signs were normal.

The following day, Charles got the cleaning service in, as he had promised, and afterward Meredith and the children were able to go to the house and gather up some things. She settled them into a room together, with two double beds and a big TV. She took them both to school and picked them up. And at the end of the day, Charles had the results of Andrew's arraignment. He had pleaded not guilty, was represented by a reputable criminal attorney, and the judge had released him on his own recognizance, since he was a respected physician and it was his first arrest. His lawyer had pleaded well. Pending further hearings there was a restraining order to keep him away from Tyla, the children, and their home. The next hearing was set in a month. Meredith felt sick as she listened, but she thanked God that Daphne had come to get her. If she hadn't, Meredith was certain her mother would be dead.

The children settled rapidly into a routine, and it was Wednesday before Tyla was coherent enough to recognize Meredith and talk to her, which was difficult, since her jaw was wired shut.

"You're staying with me," Meredith told her, and Tyla tried to smile and didn't argue with her.

"Kids okay?" she asked.

"Yes," Meredith said. The rest of what she wanted to say would have to wait until Tyla was feeling better.

Meredith told Ava, Arthur, and Peter what had happened and they were horrified, and deeply sympathetic to Tyla. "I hope he goes to prison," Ava said with feeling. And that weekend, they all went to visit her. She came home to Meredith's house the following week. She had to take it easy until the concussion was better. And she had to drink her meals through a straw, until her jaw healed. Meredith tended to her as though she was her mother, and little by little Tyla got better, and Will and Daphne calmed down.

Meredith had encouraged Tyla to seek legal counsel herself, although the state was pressing charges. The lawyer she consulted presented a request in family court, attaching one of Andrew's bank accounts for temporary support for Tyla and the children until the disposal of the case. The judge in family court granted it immediately. And the lawyer Meredith had found for her suggested starting a civil suit for permanent support if Andrew was convicted and he suggested suing him for the house. He assumed that Tyla would divorce him, whatever happened next.

"Christ," Debbie said to Jack on the day Tyla came home from the hospital, "now we're running a nursing home. First an earthquake shelter for the neighborhood, now this. She can only drink liquids and they have to be nourishing. And the two brats from hell are back."

"Don't let Meredith hear you," he warned her. "This is a chance to show her how much you care for her and her friends."

"Do I have to?" Debbie looked at him pleadingly. She had never liked children.

"Yes, you do, unless we want to go to jail with Andrew." They'd been skimming money off the top of all her house accounts and stealing objects of value and as much cash as they could get away with for fifteen years. Debbie might choose to forget it, but Jack never did. And he had no intention of going back to prison, ever again. Debbie was playing with fire with her attitude, and he knew it. They were going to have to win her confidence again, remind her how much they cared about her, and hope she got bored with her new friends soon, so he and Debbie could get back to business as usual.

Chapter 10

Tyla's convalescence from Andrew's last attack on her took longer than she had expected. The concussion gave her a headache if she read or watched TV, tried to read emails or looked at a computer screen. She wanted to play with her children, but they exhausted her. The broken arm was an inconvenience, and she hated having her jaw wired shut. The only plus in the whole experience was that she whispered to Meredith when they took off the bandages and she looked in the mirror, "Wow, I love my new nose!"

"I'm happy to hear it," Meredith said, rolling her eyes. "Next time you want a nose job, let's just call a plastic surgeon and schedule it, shall we?" There was no question in anyone's mind that she had escaped within an inch of her life, and if there was a next time, Tyla might not be as lucky, if you could call it that.

She told Meredith several times that it had happened because he drank too much that night. He wasn't normally as violent.

"'As violent'? What does that mean? A little less violent is acceptable? Tyla, you have to be done with him. He's too dangerous. You need to file for divorce. You can't play games with him anymore. What if he hurts one of the children?"

"He won't. He's a wonderful father." But a terrible man.

"He's dangerous!" Meredith didn't know how else to say it. Andrew was calling Tyla several times a day, and begging her to give him another chance. He wanted her to drop the charges. If convicted, he would lose his medical license. But charges had been filed by the state, not by Tyla. He wanted her to convince the police to drop theirs.

Will never mentioned his father, but Daphne wanted to know how he was, and if he was okay. Meredith said she was sure he was.

At least they were all safe now at Meredith's house. She told them they could stay for as long as they wanted, and hoped they would. Child Protective Services had come to talk to Tyla, Meredith, and the children, and they were satisfied that as long as Tyla and her children stayed with Meredith, the children would be in good hands. Andrew had been forbidden to see them until further hearings and a psychiatric evaluation.

Meredith tried to leave the room when Andrew called Tyla, but when she didn't, she could tell he was always wheedling and pleading and begging, and apologizing. He kept reminding Tyla that he was a doctor, and swore he would take anger management classes. Meredith hated that he was manipulating Tyla, and hoped it wasn't working.

Things began to unravel then. Will punched a boy at school who called him a name. It was the first time he had exhibited violent tendencies, and they didn't have far to look for the example for that. He was suspended from school for three days, which had never happened before. Jack complained that someone had taken his Swiss Army knife, and Debbie found it under Will's pillow in his room. Will swore he hadn't taken it, and Meredith wanted to believe him, but the evidence was damning. And worst of all for Meredith, there was a beautifully carved ivory horse that had belonged to her parents. She kept it in the library, and Debbie found it smashed to bits on the floor, as though someone had destroyed it intentionally. Everyone in the house knew how much she loved it. Debbie wasn't even allowed to dust it. It was broken into a million pieces, beyond repair. That time Meredith wondered. And worse still, Debbie said she had seen him do it. She swore it was true. Will sobbed piteously, promising he hadn't done it.

Meredith brought the subject up gingerly with Tyla, one morning when they were alone, and pointed out that there had been a number of violent incidents involving Will recently, and she was concerned about him.

"Do you want us to leave?" Tyla looked crushed. She believed her son. She swore to Meredith that he had never been destructive.

"He also never saw, or heard, his mother beaten nearly to death by his father. I don't want you to leave, of course not. But maybe he needs therapy of some kind, someone neutral he can talk to."

"He's not disturbed," she insisted.

"He's suffering," Meredith said. "That's different." They all were and had suffered an unspeakable trauma, physically in Tyla's case, and emotionally for all of them.

Meredith talked to Charles about it, and he agreed with her that Will should have counseling, and Daphne too. They'd been through a lot, and it wasn't over yet. If Andrew was convicted, he would go to prison for many years, which would be heartbreaking for them too. "Although I will tell you that I don't trust Debbie as an objective reporter of these incidents."

"You still don't trust her?" Meredith looked shocked.

"No, I don't. She would love it if Tyla and her kids went home, and if she can help that to happen, I think she'd say damn near anything to achieve it." Meredith looked sad when he said it.

"You don't know her." He didn't argue with her about it. He knew that she had a soft spot for them and was loyal to them.

"There's one thing I do want to remind you of, though. Most women who have been abused by their husbands or partners go back to them, even if they're separated. It's tragic. And they don't always survive a second round." The thought of it made her shudder, and she hoped he was wrong. She thought that Tyla talked to Andrew far too often, and was too sympathetic to him, after what he'd done. And she lied to Meredith sometimes and claimed she wasn't talking to him, and Meredith could tell she was. She didn't think that Tyla was always truthful with her, but she did believe Will when he said he hadn't destroyed anything. But Debbie wasn't a liar either. Emotions in the house were running high.

There was another incident a week later. A valuable piece of delicately carved jade vanished out of the drawing room. Debbie reported it to Meredith immediately when she noticed it was missing. It didn't turn up in Will's bedroom. It was nowhere to be found. This time, Charles was skeptical, and flatly didn't believe Debbie.

"That's not the kind of thing a kid would want. You can't do anything with it." It aroused his suspicions, and that afternoon, Charles wandered into the kitchen, took some Ziploc bags, and dropped some common objects into them. The salt cellar Debbie used often from above the stove, a coffee mug she'd used and he emptied and dropped into the plastic bag, a pair of kitchen scissors, a glass he'd seen Jack drink out of an hour before and no one had washed yet. He took half a dozen ordinary items, put all the Ziplocs in a paper bag, and went out to his car with it. He came back an hour later. Debbie was already complaining that someone had taken her scissors and the salt by then. Charles made no comment and no one had observed his little treasure hunt around the kitchen. He'd have one of his employees take it all to the police lab for fingerprinting.

He got a call from one of his police contacts the next morning and nothing he heard surprised him. It was what he had expected, and it was painful sharing it with Meredith, who had been betrayed by people she loved before.

He told her what he'd done, and she looked shocked at first, when he said he had sent the objects he knew had their fingerprints on them to the police, to run them through the interstate computers, and the California Criminal Justice System to check for criminal records and prior convictions.

"I hate to say this to you, but Debbie and Jack both have prison records, for stolen credit cards, credit card fraud, shoplifting, possession of drugs with intent to sell. They have a list of convictions an arm long. They've both served time. They were suspected of stealing money from two previous employers, but both couples died before it could be proven, and their families chose not to pursue it. The couple you love, who became your best friends, are crooks. They're convicts, convicted felons. And I'll bet that if you go through your house accounts carefully, you'll find that they've been stealing money from you too. They're not who you think they are. I'm really sorry, Meredith." She looked heartbroken, and he hated to give her the bad news.

"They can't be what you say," she said with tears in her eyes. "They came to me with glowing references."

"They probably wrote them themselves. Did you call the people who wrote them?" She shook her head.

"They were so good, I thought I didn't need to."

"From what I've seen and what you've said to me, I think they've manipulated you and isolated you, and controlled you, or tried to, until I came along, and you made new friends, and weren't as vulnerable as before. I think that's why they hate any of your neighbors staying here, and me probably. They want you alone, and they don't want anyone watching them. I've had a bad feeling about them since the day I met them. I want to do something with you now. Where are they right now?"

"I don't know. I think Jack went to the hardware store, and Debbie wanted to buy milk. The kids drank it all."

"I want to go to their room with you and have a look around."

"I can't let you do that," she said, horrified. "I respect their privacy. They're decent people," she pleaded for them, with the affection of fifteen years of loyalty on both sides.

"They have prison records," he reminded her. "They're criminals, with arrest records a mile long." The facts were impossible to deny, although she was sure they had never stolen from her. She would have sworn to it. She wanted to prove it to Charles.

Reluctantly, she stood up and followed Charles out of her study. They went downstairs, and Meredith took a key from a locked key rack that was only to be used in emergencies, like in case of fire. She unlocked their door, and almost shuddered as she did it. She trusted them, and she was sure that they wouldn't find anything that had been missing. She was violating them and fifteen years of their kindness to her.

They walked into the living room of their apartment, where Jack and Debbie knew they were safe and their employer hadn't set foot in fifteen years, and never would. She was too respectful and proper to do so. The piece of carved jade was sitting on a coffee table, amid a bunch of newspapers, with some nail clippers, and a pack of cigarettes. The Fabergé box that had been missing since the earthquake was sitting on the chest of drawers in the bedroom. Meredith's breath caught as her eyes swept the room. There were two extremely valuable small French paintings that she and Scott had bought in Paris. They were hanging above their bed. Apparently, they liked them enough to steal them, and they knew she would never come into their room. She couldn't remember when the paintings had disappeared, she'd never even noticed they were missing.

Charles pulled open the closet door, and there were four alligator handbags that Meredith had forgotten she ever owned, and hadn't seen in ten or twelve years. She couldn't help wondering if they had shattered the ivory horse on purpose and blamed Will, and planted Jack's Swiss Army knife underneath his pillow. They were cruel, evil people who had played her for a fool. She wondered if Charles was right, and they had intentionally isolated her and tried to influence and control her, or simply took advantage of the fact that she had isolated herself, and she had no other friends left except the two of them, two petty criminals who had used her in every way they could.

"I'm sorry, Meredith," Charles said when he saw the look on her face. "If you let me, I can do some research with the stores and services you do business with. Creaming money off the top of your accounts is how a lot of these people operate. The stores won't like to admit it, but faced with the police, they will. You've been profitable for Jack and Debbie, more than you intended." She nodded. "They've probably stolen money from you in other ways too." She thought of the car Jack had bought recently, a new Mercedes. She'd been impressed that they'd saved enough money to do so.

"I'd like to know," she said to him in a choked voice, and sat down in their living room, to wait for them. Charles sat in a chair across from her. They sat there like stone statues until they heard Debbie and Jack come in. They were talking and laughing, and Debbie screamed when she walked into the room and saw them. She looked as though she didn't know which direction to run. Her eyes darted to the piece of jade on the table, to Meredith's face, and then she ran into the bedroom and came back again.

"Game over," Charles said quietly. "You've had a profitable little business running here, haven't you?"

"What the hell are you doing in our apartment?" Jack shouted at him, advancing on him menacingly, and Charles looked unimpressed and didn't move.

"I wouldn't do that if I were you. I've gone through the police files, they have your fingerprints, and we've seen the arrest records for both of you. We'll be giving them a list of what you've stolen from here. What we can find records for. We'll cross-check Ms. White's insurance records to see what's disappeared over the years. I imagine you sold a lot of it. You had a nice little cash flow going for yourselves, didn't you? I've got two of my operatives on the way over. They'll watch you pack, and you'll be escorted out of the building as soon as you're packed. You're finished here. Ms. White will press charges, and there will be a full audit of all her household accounts." Meredith had just told him that Debbie could write checks on one household account. He was going to have all the locks changed too.

"You're a bitch to let him do this," Debbie shouted at Meredith, as she sat motionless watching the woman who had pretended to comfort her for so many years. "We were the best friends you ever had." Meredith didn't speak to her. She didn't know what to say. She was crushed and speechless for a minute.

"Friends don't steal from each other, and cheat and lie and manipulate," Charles said to her. "You've got half an hour to pack. We'll watch you do it. We'll report this to the police today. It's up to Ms. White if she's going to prosecute you. I'm going to advise her to. And I suggest you don't leave town," he said in an ice-cold voice.

"Screw you!" Debbie spat at him as though talking to a prison guard. They had nothing to lose now. They had turned into people Meredith didn't even recognize. They always had been, she knew now.

Jack ambled into their bedroom and took out a suitcase while Charles watched what he put in it. He brought the Fabergé box back to sit in front of Meredith, where she could keep an eye on it, and he was watching the two paintings to make sure they didn't disappear. There wasn't a sound in either room while they packed. Two of Charles's operatives came to the back door ten minutes later and Meredith let them in. They crowded into the small apartment with them. One stood a foot away from Debbie, and the other next to Jack. They knew there was no room left to maneuver. Charles was right. The game was over. Meredith looked as though someone had died as they zipped up their bags, looked around the room, and stared at her. There was no apology, no thank-you, no regret on either of their faces. Just two nasty, sick people, sociopaths, who had had a heyday with her, and exploited the tragedies in her life for fifteen years.

Charles's operatives walked them out into the street, where their car was parked. Meredith made no attempt to say goodbye to them. She couldn't say a word. Charles directed one of his men to call a locksmith, while Meredith collected the stolen items they'd retrieved and laid them on the bed.

"I'll bring them up to you later," Charles promised, and then they left the small airless apartment and went back upstairs. It had been one of the most unpleasant, saddest hours she'd ever spent. All of her illusions about humanity had come crashing down around her. She didn't say a word to Charles on their way upstairs. The only words she could finally get out were "Thank you." She walked straight into Tyla's bedroom then and spoke to her, standing at the foot of the bed, as Charles waited in the hall for her.

"I owe you an apology, and Will. And I want to tell him myself. We found the jade, and the Fabergé box, and a number of other things. I'm sure he didn't break the horse or take the Swiss Army knife. Charles discovered that Jack and Debbie have criminal records, and we found a stash of stolen items in their room. Some of them have been gone for a very long time. They just left." She felt dead inside as Tyla looked at her and nodded, and then Meredith went to her study, and sat thinking about them. Charles sat next to her as tears of grief and disappointment rolled down her cheeks, and he took her in his arms and held her, as her heart ached and she sobbed.

She went to find Will after that and solemnly apologized to him for questioning his honesty at all. He hugged her after she told him and swore he would never take anything of hers. Charles checked with her suppliers that afternoon, and he was right about that too. She nodded when he told her that they had gotten sizeable kickbacks for years. They knew how to work the system, and were total con artists.

"I'm sorry I was right, Meredith," he said when he told her and handed her a list of suppliers who had paid them handsomely at her expense.

"So am I." She smiled sadly at him. "But I'm glad you told me. They don't belong here. I guess they never did." It was a rude awakening for her of who they really were.

He took her in his arms again and held her. She didn't cry. She never wanted to think about them again. She had no tears left for the bad people in her life.

In the end, after she thought about it, she knew what she wanted to do. Charles disagreed with her. She decided not to prosecute them. It would be too complicated to try to figure out everything they'd stolen, and the cash they'd taken. There was a statute of limitations of three years, the police told her, so they couldn't even be prosecuted for twelve of the fifteen years, and the kickbacks had been paid in cash, which was impossible to prove. They'd gotten away with it and she didn't want to spend years of pain and grief trying to get money back and put them in jail. It was enough that they were gone, and she'd been able to save a few items, and stop them, thanks to Charles. They weren't worth the money or the time to pursue them for years for only a fraction of what they stole, and made from their kickbacks. There was no stopping people like them. They would probably find another victim somewhere. She felt sorry for the next person they fooled. Meredith and Charles were sure they would do it again. And Meredith would get little or nothing back. They had been so convincing, and seemed so kind, she had believed every word they said, and all it had ever been, she knew now, was a lie. Nothing about them had been true, and their so-called friendship had been a ploy to manipulate her. It broke her heart, and all she wanted now was to turn the page and move on. There was no way to stop them, or replay the past. She put it down to a terrible experience and a betrayal she would never forget. And it was clear now that the agency she'd hired them from hadn't done a criminal check. People like Jack and Debbie knew how to work the system, and were adept at finding innocent victims, just as they had victimized her, and her circumstances had played right into their hands. It was a terrible blow to realize how gullible she had been, and just how bad they were.

Chapter 11

Charles waited a few days after Jack and Debbie left before talking to Meredith about it again. He was spending most of his nights with her now. He had dealt with similar problems professionally, for his clients, but never in his personal life. So in some ways, this was new to him too. It was an old story for Meredith, who over the years had been cheated on and lied to and stolen from by people she had trusted. She saw clearly now that Jack and Debbie had never been her friends. They were frauds and petty criminals to the end. She had no idea where they were now and didn't care.

Charles and Meredith were alone in her study one night, after Tyla and her children had gone to bed. The house was quiet. She had interviewed a couple that afternoon, who had real references that she and Charles had both checked out. She had hired them, and they were going to start on the weekend. The wife was a warm woman from Guatemala, and her husband was Peruvian. They had worked in several fine homes, most recently in L.A. They were very polite, and looked immaculate. Their previous employers were moving to London, so they had let them go.

"I wanted to talk to you, Meredith, about some of your security systems," Charles said quietly. "Everything you have in place is state-of-the-art, but technology changes every day. I'd like to update what you have a little for you, not at great expense, just to fine-tune it all a bit. But I'm worried about something else. Because of who you are, you're a much bigger target than you realize for scams and dishonest people. You don't need to be paranoid, but I want you to be really careful. I love you, and I don't want you to get hurt." He didn't mention Jack and Debbie by name, but she understood.

"Thank you." She smiled at him for the "I love you." It was good news to her. She was in love with him too, and had said so to him when they were in bed. "I must look like a fool to you. Six months after Jack and Debbie got here, my whole life fell apart. I was out of my head for a couple of years. I couldn't think. I didn't care. I was an easy target. I'm not anymore. God knows how much money they stole from me, or cheated me out of. I'm awake now. They hit me at my lowest point. It was lucky for them."

"I've seen heads of large corporations unwittingly become victims and prisoners of their employees. The right circumstances, a death in the family, the loss of a spouse, an illness, a change of fortune, a weak moment, a hard time, and suddenly the tables turn. I want you to know that I'm here for you. I won't let that happen to you again as long as I'm around."

"I know that about you now, and you were right about them," she conceded. "I thought you were crazy. It turns out that I was."

"No, they were just very evil people, and clever about how they did it. It's usually a very simple system that works best. The rest of us just don't think that way. It's sad to have to be so careful, but in your position, you have no other choice." She nodded agreement, and they went to bed shortly after that. She nestled into his arms. He was a tall, powerful man, and in every possible way, she knew she was safe with him. He wasn't going to let anything bad happen to her. It was a wonderful feeling, and she was glad now that Jack and Debbie were gone, and pleased too that Tyla and her children were living with her for now.

Meredith dropped Will and Daphne off at school the next morning.

Two hours later, the school called Meredith to pick Will up. He had a stomachache again. Meredith was worried about him, and he went straight to his room when he got home. It was the first stomachache he'd had since the night his father had almost killed his mother. He asked her an odd question on the way home.

"Do you think Mom would ever go back to Dad? Or meet him somewhere?" he asked her.

"I hope not. At least until your father gets some very serious help. Meeting him now would be a very foolish thing to do." He nodded, and when he got back to the house, he disappeared to his room. Meredith tried to be careful not to malign their father to them, for their sakes.

"I think I'll sleep for a while," he told her. And when she stopped in to see Tyla, she was in particularly good spirits, the best she'd been in a long time. Meredith told her about Will's stomachache, and she looked surprised.

"Maybe this time it's something he ate."

"I didn't think of that." Meredith smiled, and then remembered. "Justin used to get stomachaches when he was upset too. He also wasn't above faking it, to get out of school, like the day of a test."

"Will has done that too," Tyla admitted, "though he's a pretty good student, except for math. Andrew is always hard on him about his grades. Maybe he was afraid of a bad grade today."

"Maybe so," Meredith said, and went back to her study. She had a mountain of papers on her desk. She liked taking Tyla's children to school. It reminded her of happy times, and they were such sweet children. She hoped things would settle down for them soon.

Meredith was still at her desk when Tyla slipped out of the house. She was going for walks now, to get some air. She felt stronger, and her wounds were healing. She was still talking to Andrew on the phone more than Meredith thought she should. She didn't think she should talk to him at all. He had told her about an anger management class he had signed up for, and told her he wanted to see her and the kids. He said he missed them terribly, and was so deeply sorry about what he'd done to her. He had begged her to take him back, or at least see him, and talk to him in person. Tyla said she felt sorry for him when they talked. He said he didn't even have a picture of the kids with him, he was staying in a dismal furnished room at a hotel, and missed their home. He had been temporarily suspended by the medical board, pending resolution of the charges against him, and he was deeply depressed about it. Tyla and the children were still receiving support by court order and Andrew was terrified about what he would do if he could never practice medicine again. How would he support himself? And what if he went to prison?

Will was watching at the window when his mother left the house. She walked down the street in the direction of their home. He had noticed that she headed in that direction most of the time on her walks. He wondered if maybe she missed their house too. He missed his toys. They'd only brought a few with them and he wanted to go back for more. But his mother didn't want to bring too much to Meredith's and clutter up their room.

Meredith came to find Tyla a few minutes later, to ask her something, and was surprised to find that she'd gone out. She had said she was tired that morning, although she was in a cheerful mood. Meredith peeked into Will's room to see how he was feeling, and if he was asleep. Instead he was standing at the window, looking out.

"Hi, Will, how are you feeling?" she asked with a smile.

"I'm okay," he said as he turned to look at her, and his eyes were sad.

"Do you know where your mom is?"

"She went for a walk, that way." He pointed toward their house.

Meredith thought about it for a minute after she'd left the room, and she got a queasy feeling in the pit of her stomach. Why had Tyla been almost euphoric? Was it a coincidence, or did she have a plan? Was she going to see Andrew?

Meredith went downstairs and grabbed a coat out of the closet.

She didn't know why, but she wanted to make sure Tyla was okay. It was a gray, foggy day. Meredith was in front of the Johnsons' house a few minutes later, and she saw that the lights were on in the living room on the ground floor, and suddenly panic set in. She was sure that Tyla had gone to meet Andrew. Maybe he had wanted to see her there. She hoped that she was wrong. But why was the light on? Or had Tyla just gone to spend a little time in her home, to try and exorcise the ghosts there?

She rang the doorbell, and a second later, the door was whipped open and Andrew was standing there. He looked ragged, with dark circles under his eyes. He needed a haircut, he hadn't shaved, and he was wearing running clothes. He looked angry and disheveled with wild eyes.

"Is Tyla here?" Meredith asked him in a cool voice, trying not to look surprised to see him there.

"Why don't you see for yourself," he said, and as he did, a powerful arm yanked her inside, and she could see Tyla cowering in a chair, with a trickle of blood running down her chin from her lip. His eyes looked crazy, and Meredith could see that he was going to do the same thing again. He had already hit Tyla, at least once.

"Andrew, why don't we just let it go for today," Meredith said calmly. "You don't need more trouble, and neither does Tyla, or your kids. You've all got enough to worry about."

"Oh listen to Little Miss Goody Two-Shoes. I wouldn't be in trouble if you hadn't filled her head with a lot of crap. She knew how to behave before. If she doesn't drop the charges, my medical license will be revoked. How am I going to make a living if that happens?" His eyes probed Meredith's. The terror of being poor again was devouring him.

"Then let's not make it any worse than it already is," she said quietly. She wanted to get Tyla out of the house and escape herself before he exploded and lost control.

"I didn't come here to cause trouble," Andrew said. "I came here to get pictures of my kids. She said she'd give them to me. I don't even have a picture of them with me, and I'm living in a hotel that's a dump, thanks to her." He pointed angrily at his wife. He was a madman, and Tyla had fallen for whatever promises he had made, or her own misplaced guilt for his situation, which he accused her of every day on the phone. That this was all her fault. And like most abused women, she believed him. Meredith wondered if what Charles had said was true, that women who had been abused almost always go back to their abusers.

"I'm sure you've got things to do," she said clearly, "so do we." She beckoned to Tyla, but she was too afraid to move. Tyla was terrified of what he'd do if she tried to get past him to the door. She knew what he was capable of. They all did now.

Will had already called Charles by then, as soon as Meredith left the house. He kept Charles's cellphone number in his wallet. He spoke as fast as he could when Charles answered.

"I think my mom went to meet my dad at our house, and Meredith went after her." He was talking fast, and sounded breathless.

"Did they tell you that?" Charles questioned him, and sensed the urgency in Will's voice.

"No, I'm guessing. I saw them go." Charles didn't hesitate for an instant. He promised Will he'd call him back and called the police. Charles called an inside number he had for law enforcement officers, for emergencies, and he didn't hesitate to use it when he needed to. He told them the possible situation, that Andrew was dangerous, under a restraining order, and awaiting trial for a brutal attack on his wife, and he might be holding two women captive in his old home.

"Come on, Tyla," Meredith said to her again, easing toward the door herself so she could open it, before Andrew got violent with either of them. Meredith had barely moved when Andrew grabbed her by the throat, jammed her up against the wall, and banged her head hard.

"You started all this, didn't you, you bitch," he said to her. "You filled her head with ideas about freedom and independence and not listening to me, and now she won't let me come home. She's not even living here. She's living with you, and your fascist boyfriend who thinks he runs the world."

Meredith didn't say anything and was wondering how they were going to get out of the house, as she saw two police officers approach the front door with caution, and suddenly the window exploded, with broken glass flying everywhere, and the two officers broke in. One of them jumped through the ground floor window, the other one reached inside, opened the door, grabbed Andrew, and they had him on the ground within seconds, and handcuffed his hands behind his back, as Tyla came running toward Meredith, and threw her arms around her. Andrew was screaming obscenities at Tyla from the floor as they dragged him out of the house, and saying what he was going to do to her if he got his hands on her again. Meredith looked at her and rubbed her head. Andrew was out by then.

"How did you know I was here?" Tyla looked mystified, as she wiped the blood off her face. She had told no one she was coming to the house to meet him.

"Will told me you'd gone for a walk and had come this way. He was watching you. I think he knew. And when he said it, I knew too, so I came to check on you."

"Did you call the police before you left the house?" Meredith shook her head.

"Maybe Will did. Tyla, you can't see Andrew again. He's going to kill you." Everyone knew and believed it, except her.

She hung her head in shame. "I know that now. I felt sorry for him, so I agreed to meet him."

"You can't afford to do that. You have two children who need you, and he *will* kill you the next time, or one of these times."

"I won't see him again." The police were outside, when Tyla turned off the lights in the house and closed the door. The lock was broken and the window. Someone would have to come and fix them. She had seen this movie too many times. They all had by now. The police said they'd come to Meredith's later to get a statement from them both.

Tyla and Meredith walked back to her house, and Charles pulled up when they arrived. He had been at his home nearby when Will called him. "Are you both okay?" They nodded, but Tyla had a cut lip where he had slapped her, and Meredith had an egg on her head from hitting the wall.

"Did you call the police?" Meredith asked him, confused about how he knew.

"Will called me. He thought you were going there, so I called the hotline. Was Andrew there?"

Tyla looked embarrassed and remorseful as she nodded. "I agreed to meet him to give him some photographs. He looks terrible." The police had taken Andrew to jail.

"They won't let him out on bail now," Charles told her. "They'll send him for a psych evaluation, at some mental hospital with a locked ward, where he belongs. They may not let him out until trial." Which would be a relief for all of them.

They walked into Meredith's house together, and Tyla went upstairs to Will's room to tell him they were okay. She came out a minute later, holding a scrap of paper, with Will's writing on it in pencil.

"Oh my God," she said. She held it out for them to read as tears filled her eyes. It said, "Don't let him kill my mom." And there was no sign of Will in the room. "I think he ran away," Tyla said, panicked.

"He's afraid you're going to go back to his father and he'll kill you. He told me the other day," Meredith said. "I think he's overheard some of your conversations with Andrew."

Tyla sank into a chair, feeling faint. "What do we do now?" She was frightened for Will.

"We drive around looking for him," Charles said, which was sensible. Charles never panicked in a crisis. They went back to the courtyard to his SUV. He got in quickly and started the car. "He can't have gone far. We'll find him," he reassured her. She had started another tidal wave by meeting up with Andrew.

"I'll come with you," Tyla said, and got into the passenger seat next to Charles.

"I'll look around too," Meredith said, and got out the key to her car sitting in the courtyard. They followed each other out, drove around the neighborhood separately and came back to the house. They returned within minutes of each other, two hours later. There was no sign of Will. And a few minutes later, Meredith went to pick up Daphne, after school, and brought her home.

"Should we call the police?" Tyla asked Charles.

"I think we'd better. I don't want him hitchhiking or out alone at night." He was eleven years old and had led a sheltered life, other than his father's violence. He knew nothing of life on the streets and would stick out as someone who didn't belong there. He'd be easy prey for predators of all kinds.

"What's he wearing?" Charles said, surprised that they hadn't found him, as he reached for his phone to call the police.

"He was wearing his school uniform. Gray pants, navy blazer, white shirt, navy tie," Meredith said. Her heart was beating faster. What if they didn't find him? Or something happened to him? She had been stupid to meet Andrew, and Will was so upset by it, he'd run away. Or maybe he'd been planning to anyway. So much had happened in a short time and he had no control over any of it.

The police arrived at the house half an hour later, took down the information, and put out an all-points bulletin in the Bay Area. Many areas of the city were still closed with no power. But most of the city was functioning again, and all bridges were open, so if someone abducted him, it would be easy to leave the city. The police put out an Amber Alert for him, just in case, warning motorists of a possible abducted child. It would be up in lights on every freeway in the state.

"Now what?" Meredith looked at Charles after the police left.

"We wait." And pray, he didn't say out loud.

Chapter 12

The wait for news from the police about Will seemed interminable. Tyla racked her brain, but couldn't imagine where he'd gone. She got out the school roster, and called the mothers of all the boys he was close to, but no one had seen him. He hadn't shown up at their homes after school. The other parents had heard rumors that there were problems at the Johnsons, and that Tyla and the children were staying at a friend's. Will had said it was because there was damage to their home from the earthquake, but there had been whispers that Will's parents were separated. No one knew the full details of the story, and miraculously it hadn't hit the press.

By seven o'clock, Tyla had called everyone she could think of, no one had heard a word from him. He had a cellphone Tyla let him use occasionally, but he had left it in his room. Meredith and Charles had helped her comb the room for clues and they found none.

He had been through so much, the constant tension in their home for years, in fear of Andrew's explosions, the physical abuse their mother had endured and he and Daphne were aware of. The secrets they had to keep. The terrible beating Tyla had had recently, and he couldn't protect her. Will's fear that she'd go back to him and the nightmare would start all over again. And worst of all, the fear that his father would kill his mother, which was a real possibility.

Charles and Meredith talked about it quietly in her study, while Tyla waited for news in her bedroom, with Daphne, and tried to reassure her.

"There's a terrible contradiction in these situations," Charles said seriously. "The women who are being abused stay for the sake of the children, to not break up the family, and what the children go through as a result is worse than any divorce, and damages them far more than if they'd gotten out of the marriage. The statistics on it are terrible, sometimes even including child suicide. The children feel helpless to protect their mothers and don't know how to handle it. It's hard enough for the adults involved, but kids are overwhelmed by circumstances they have no control over."

"You don't think Will would hurt himself, do you?" Meredith looked devastated.

"I don't know him well enough to judge it," Charles said honestly. "I hope not. I think he's more likely to get hurt on the streets, dealing with situations he's not familiar with, tough older kids, street gangs, drug addicts, dealers. He's a little innocent out there, and if he's wearing his private school uniform, he's going to stick out like a sore thumb." He looked young for his age. And worse, he might have the misfortune to cross paths with a pedophile who would abduct him. It was a dangerous world out there, almost as bad as the one he grew up in, where the person he should have been able to count on, his father, was the most lethal and toxic of all. "If Will seriously thought that Tyla went to meet Andrew, or maybe even heard her say it, he might have figured that Andrew would kill her this time, and since he couldn't stop her, or protect her, he ran, feeling guilty or frightened. Tyla said he might have had ten dollars on him. That won't get him far. He'll be cold, tired, and hungry by now. If he turns up at a homeless shelter, or a free kitchen, like Glide, they'll call Child Protective Services to pick him up. They don't leave kids his age on the streets. At thirteen and fourteen they turn a blind eye to runaways, but not with a child of eleven." Meredith was grateful that Charles was there with them. He had done nothing but improve their lives, and hers especially, since she had met him. He was a solid, responsible, intuitive, resourceful person, the kind you needed in a crisis. And he made everything go more smoothly in normal times.

It seemed as though very little had gone smoothly since the earthquake. It had been almost two months now. Ava and Joel had broken up, Peter's life had turned upside down in a good way, and Arthur now had two young people in his home instead of one. Andrew had lost all control and was facing prison for attempted murder, Tyla had nearly lost her life, Meredith had had a steady stream of houseguests since the night of the earthquake, and had discovered that her most trusted employees whom she relied on and considered dear friends were thieves who had preyed on her for fifteen years. Even the children had been profoundly affected, and now Will had run away, and God knew what would happen to him on the streets. It was a lot for any of them to weather. For all of them, and the rest of the population who had lost loved ones and homes in the earthquake, it was a time of turmoil and change. In some ways, for Meredith, it was a good change, but a lot of baggage had come with it. Charles had been there to share in all of it, and had passed every test and met every challenge head-on. In many ways, Meredith felt very lucky, but she was also deeply worried for her friends. With Andrew's upcoming trial, Tyla and her children would have hard times ahead.

By eight o'clock, Meredith couldn't stand it any longer. Her head was throbbing from where she had banged it earlier in the day, when she went to rescue Tyla, but she didn't care. "Can't we do something?" she asked Charles. Anything would have been better than just sitting there, imagining all the terrible things that could happen to Will. Charles had called his police contacts several times, but so far there was nothing. The squad cars on the streets and patrolmen on foot were on the lookout for him, but no one had seen him. They had checked the homeless shelters and free kitchens, and had combed the homeless camps South of Market.

"We can drive around ourselves if you want," Charles offered, "but we're no smarter than the cops. Sooner or later, someone will see him. He can't just disappear into thin air." But they both knew that children did every day, never to be seen again, if they'd fallen into the wrong hands. If he had gotten into a car with someone, he could be anywhere by now, even in grave danger, or dead.

The news stations were going to mention him at eleven, and show his school picture, which Tyla had given the police, but at six o'clock, they thought it was too soon. There was still the possibility that he had gone to a friend's house, someone Tyla hadn't thought to call, and he would come home on his own eventually. It was Charles's fondest hope, that this was all a misunderstanding, but in his heart of hearts, he didn't believe that, and his thoughts were running along the same anxious lines as Meredith's and Tyla's. But he didn't want to make the situation worse by admitting it to them. "Why don't we look around South of Market," he suggested to Meredith. "Maybe we'll get lucky. He may be hanging around a fast-food place, hoping someone will give him something to eat." The thought of Will hungry and pawing through the garbage at McDonald's made Meredith feel sick. And one of the dangers in San Francisco was that ordinary neighborhoods drifted into bad ones with no boundaries and no warning. The high-end downtown shopping district at Union Square, with all the most expensive shops, was only a block away from the Tenderloin, where most of the drug deals went down, and it was full of addicts and flop-houses. The shopping complexes and malls of Market Street were two blocks from one of the most dangerous streets in the city, where people got shot almost every day. Benign neighborhoods and newly trendy areas were cheek by jowl with projects, where juvenile delinquents roamed, looking for trouble. And it was all in a small, compact area. If Will wandered into any of it, he was visibly an innocent, and could get very badly hurt or even killed.

Meredith went to put on jeans and a heavy sweater, and sneakers, and Charles went to change too. Meredith told Tyla what they were doing. Daphne was fast asleep on the bed next to her, and Tyla was staring at the TV, without seeing it. She realized even more acutely now how stupid she had been to go and meet Andrew alone at their house, and if Will suspected it, or overheard her agreeing to it, how terrifying that was for him. Thank God he had called Charles before he ran away, or she might be dead by now. And Will probably feared she was, and was afraid to know.

Meredith whispered to her that they were going to drive around for a while, and Tyla whispered back "Thank you," while she stroked Daphne's hair. She'd been thinking about Andrew's hearing the next day, and second arraignment, and what Charles had said about their not letting him out on bail this time, and she realized it was just as well. He was too dangerous to be loose on the streets, or hiding his violent nature under a thin veneer and seeing patients. She understood more than ever now that he was a very sick man.

Until his recent attack on her, Tyla had always felt guilty for making him angry and part of her believed him that it was her fault. She no longer did. She understood now that he would have beaten her whatever she did, or no matter how perfect she was. He had a pathological need to punish her for crimes she didn't commit, maybe for his own mother's sins against him when she abandoned him as a child. Whatever it was, Tyla knew the problem and the danger were bigger than all of them, and even bigger than Andrew himself. He had a demon in him that nothing could stop. Maybe Will had understood that sooner than she did, even though he was a child.

Meredith and Charles left the courtyard, with Charles at the wheel of her car. It was an unassuming, ordinary SUV that wouldn't draw attention in the area South of Market, where drug deals went down, homeless people roamed, people slept in doorways, and the worst element preyed on one another, and had lost all hope. It pained Meredith to think of Will there.

"Do you carry a gun?" Meredith suddenly wondered, as they drove south across town. It had never occurred to her before, but in his line of work, providing high-powered security, it wouldn't have surprised her. He smiled when she asked.

"This isn't Texas and I'm not a cowboy," he teased her. "Some of the men I employ do, if that's what a client wants, but I prefer not to. I've been armed at times, but I'd rather rely on my wits than a weapon. Why? Do you want me to?" He was surprised. She was such a peaceful person.

"No, I'm glad you don't. I just wondered." But they both knew that many of the people in the underworld and desperate element of the city did, even children Will's age. A twelve- or thirteen-year-old could buy a stolen handgun for twenty-five dollars, if he had the money, and many did. Will would have no idea how to deal with kids like that, and he looked ripe for the picking, with his neat haircut and clean clothes.

They crossed Market Street a few minutes later, with crowds of late night shoppers and bums on the streets. The Tenderloin ran parallel to it, with drug deals happening in every dingy doorway and on every corner. They crossed Mission Street, and Charles followed a zigzag pattern on a grid, going up one street and down another, up one avenue for a while and then down the next. There were heaps of garbage in the gutter that looked like lifeless forms, and humans crumpled in doorways who looked like refuse, until they moved, and drunks and drug addicts unconscious on the sidewalks. The police used to pick them up and send them to a hospital, or to jail for the night, but there were so many of them now, that for the most part they stayed on the streets. A few looked like they'd set up house with shopping carts and cardboard boxes, a mangy dog, or a couple of cats. It made Meredith's heart ache to see them. It was hard to even determine age or gender on the streets, with people filthy, bundled up, with matted hair and dressed in whatever they had found to wear.

"God, it's depressing down here," she said, and he nodded. "I hope he's somewhere else." She couldn't imagine Will surviving for a night there.

"We can drive out to the Panhandle in Golden Gate Park later, if you want. That's where all the teenage drug addicts and runaways are, but he won't fit in there either." It was at the edge of the Haight-Ashbury, the home of the flower children in the sixties, and it had degenerated severely over time. It was mostly just filth and drugs now, and ravaged people who had fallen on hard times, and runaways whose lives at home were even worse than risking their fate on the streets. Charles said that the young ones tended to band together, and could be violent if they felt threatened. The police tended to leave them alone, as long as they didn't bother passersby or hurt one another. Many of them were on hard drugs.

Charles made a point of stopping at every food place, and Meredith ran inside, and even checked the bathrooms, and asked if anyone had seen him. She had a photograph of Will with her to show them, but no one had seen him.

A police car pulled them over after their fifth stop, and asked what they were doing. Charles showed the officer his credentials, including his OES identification, and his Pentagon pass with his security clearance on it. The policeman handed it all back to him respectfully. "What brings you down here?"

He explained the situation, and made it sound more like a misguided adventure or a misunderstanding, and Meredith showed him Will's picture.

"We call CPS as soon as we see kids that age," the policeman reassured them. "They don't do well down here. Most of these guys in this area are all long-term homeless. They're all pros, a lot of them are high, and they don't want kids around either. Sometimes they tell us when they see a fresh runaway or a kid that doesn't belong. This is the jungle. The boy will go running home if he winds up down here," he said with a smile, handing Meredith back Will's picture. "I have a boy that age myself. I've given him a little tour, so he realizes that things aren't as bad at home as he thinks. You just want to be sure he doesn't fall into the wrong hands, sex trade, or drugs, or whatever." The idea of Will being drugged and kidnapped into the sex trade gave Meredith shivers. Charles handed the officer his card with his cellphone number on it, and asked him to call if any leads turned up. He promised to do so.

Two blocks later, he was checking a drunk for a pulse, lying face-down on the sidewalk when a young guy on a battered bicycle stopped to talk to him. On a hunch, he asked the boy on the bicycle if he'd seen any kids that age. The cyclist and the patrolman knew each other by sight, but had never talked before.

"There's a kid in a doorway on Mission somewhere, someone said he looks fresh out of Pac Heights. They were going to call CPS before he gets hurt, but they don't want the cops on their necks either. They've settled down for the night." They huddled in front of shops and banks and office buildings, and left in the morning before they opened for business.

"Thanks. I'll check it out." The young man on the bicycle sped away, while the patrolman waited for a van to pick up the unconscious drunk. He was still breathing. They came for him a few minutes later, and the officer got in his squad car and headed toward Mission Street, which was at least brightly lit and slightly less dangerous than the side streets, or the broad streets farther south, which were rougher. He was planning to cruise both sides of the street, and walk it if necessary. There were groups of homeless under blankets and in sleeping bags in every doorway. He called Charles on the off chance that he wanted to have a look too. They used to patrol the area in pairs, but with cutbacks, most of the squad cars went out now with only one man, which was more dangerous for them. If they needed backup, they had to call for it, and hope another car showed up in time.

"What was that?" Meredith looked at Charles after the call from the officer.

"The officer we just talked to. He got a tip that there's a boy on Mission Street in a doorway, and he doesn't fit. They don't want the police bothering them or chasing them off, because there's a boy who doesn't belong there. He's on his way to take a look. I'll head over there too." Charles drove toward the most populated part of Mission, and cruised slowly while Meredith strained her eyes to check every doorway, and suddenly called out to Charles and raised a hand.

"Wait! Stop! There's someone small in that group of people, it could be a child." She opened the door to get out and look, and Charles stopped her until he put his flashers on and could get out with her. They walked toward the doorway together, in front of a shop that sold tourist memorabilia, souvenirs, and cheap electronic gimmicks. There were five people crowded together in sleeping bags, four men and a woman, which was the standard ratio on the streets, and huddled next to the woman was a boy in a knit cap. His face was dirty, and he looked cold. He had no sleeping bag, and they had folded a cardboard box around him to keep him warm, and as he looked up at them, Meredith's eyes filled with tears. It was Will. He looked frightened when he saw them, and one of the men who wasn't sleeping turned to him. He had a bottle of cheap wine in his hand, but he didn't look menacing, and he sounded kind when he spoke to Will.

"Are they your mom and dad?" Will shook his head. He was still wearing his school uniform inside the broken cardboard box. "Do you know them?" He nodded, and the older wino smiled a toothless grin at Meredith and Charles. "He's a good boy. Don't be too tough on him. Go on home, son," he said to Will. "And don't come back here. You do what they tell you. You don't want to end up like me." He raised the bottle in salute to Charles and Meredith, and Will stood up and thanked him in a whisper so he didn't wake the others, and thanked the woman too. He left the box, and handed her the knitted cap, and when she smiled, she had no teeth either. It was impossible to tell their ages, they could have been anywhere from thirty-five to seventy. Will walked over to Charles, and he put his arm around Will's shoulders, thanked the people he'd been camping with, and walked him to the car, with Meredith following, overcome with gratitude that they had found him. The squad car with the patrolman they'd talked to slowed just as they were getting into their car, and Charles waved and mouthed "thank you" to him too. The policeman gave him a thumbs-up and a broad grin.

"I'll call it in," he shouted out the window, and Charles nodded. It was ten-thirty, and Will's photograph hadn't been broadcast on the news yet. He'd be registered as a runaway with CPS now, and Charles knew they'd be out to speak to all of them tomorrow, and to question Will about why he had run away in case he was being mistreated and needed to be removed from his home. They were going to be checking on the family regularly anyway, because of the nature of Andrew's violent arrest and attempt to murder Tyla. If they thought it necessary, they would remove Will and Daphne to foster care, but Charles considered it unlikely. Will would have some explaining to do to the social worker who would come to see him. It was for his own protection. Will looked at both of them as he got into the backseat. He was meek and shivering in the cold in his white shirt and thin uniform blazer. His shirt was dirty, and Meredith thought there was blood on his jacket and then realized it was ketchup.

"Is my mom okay?" were his first words.

"She's fine, but very worried about you. We all were," Charles said. He was enormously relieved, but didn't want to let him off the hook too quickly. Will had terrified them all, and Charles didn't want him making a habit of running away. Some kids did. And after the first time, it became easier each time they did. Meredith was already on the phone to Tyla, to tell her, and she said she'd call the police and tell them he'd been found. Charles knew the officer would report it too.

"I thought my dad would kill her, and I didn't know what to do," he said, looking deflated, as though the wind had gone out of him. He had seen a world that night that he didn't know existed and hoped never to see again.

"Running away is never a solution. But it was good that you called me before you did," Charles said seriously. "Your dad was at the house with her. You were right about that. But he didn't hurt her. He didn't have time. I called the police after you called me. They came within minutes. So you saved her this time." Will's eyes opened wide when Charles said it.

"I'm sorry I ran away," he said to both of them, and they could see he meant it. Then he turned to Meredith. "Were you there too?" She nodded, she didn't want to tell him more than his mother wanted him to know, that his father was in jail again, and facing additional charges. "They gave me dinner. They get it out of the garbage cans at McDonald's. I had a Big Mac," he said, and Charles tried not to smile. It explained the ketchup on his jacket. And the thought of him eating out of a garbage can on Market Street was profoundly depressing.

Will was quiet on the ride home. Tyla was waiting for them in the courtyard when the gate opened. She wrapped her arms around Will the moment she saw him, and they both cried, and so did Charles and Meredith watching them. Then they walked into the house together. They went down to the kitchen to get something to eat, but Will wasn't too hungry. He was mostly cold, and

Tyla took him upstairs so he could have a hot bath, as Charles and Meredith sat at the kitchen table, drained by the experience. It was a first for both of them. None of their children had ever run away. But they hadn't been through the traumatic experiences Will had either, with one parent trying to kill the other.

"I kept thinking about everything that could happen to him," Meredith said to Charles, looking like she'd been hit by a bus, now that the tension had eased.

"So did I," Charles admitted. "Some very nasty stuff could have happened out there. Thank God, it didn't."

"You were right. He knew Tyla was going to meet Andrew, and he couldn't handle what he thought would happen to her."

They turned off the lights in the kitchen and went upstairs. Meredith wanted to take a bath, but she was too tired. She changed into her nightgown, and collapsed onto her bed. Charles took a shower, and Meredith was already half asleep by the time he slid into bed beside her.

"God, what a day," he said. An incident with Andrew, and his arrest. Will running away, and looking for him all night, terrified of what could happen to him. "How's your head, by the way?" he asked. They had both forgotten about it in their worry over Will.

"It's fine," she said sleepily. "It hurts, but I'm just happy Will is okay and we found him." She put her arms around Charles and rested her head on his shoulder, and two minutes later, she was sound asleep. Will too was sound asleep next to his mother in the big, warm, comfortable bed. As he drifted off, he thought of the people he had met on the street and knew he would never forget them.

Chapter 13

When Daphne came bounding into the kitchen the next morning, she was beaming.

"I knew you were a good witch! You found him!" she said to Meredith, and she laughed.

"Charles helped too, and the police."

Neither of the children were going to school. A member of Child Protective Services was coming to see all of them, Daphne too.

Tyla confided to Meredith that she was nervous about it. What if they declared her an unfit mother and took them away?

"They're not going to do that," Meredith reassured her. "And Charles and I can tell them you're a wonderful mother."

"I let them live in an abusive household all their lives," she said remorsefully. Will had told her the night before when he came home that he never wanted to see his father again, and he hoped he would go to prison forever. "And Daphne is afraid of him. We all are."

"He's in custody now, so it's not an issue," Meredith said quietly, but it would be again someday. Meredith was doubtful that Andrew would ever change. He was too sick. Tyla had finally come to that conclusion too. And understood now it wasn't her fault.

"When things calm down, I want to go back to nursing school. I need a refresher course to bring me back up to speed, and then I want to become a nurse practitioner, not just an O.R. nurse like I was before." It was how she had met Andrew. "I should have left him years ago," she said mournfully. "I don't know how I could let it go on for so long. I kept thinking it would get better, and he kept promising. I believed him. I don't want to see him again either."

Charles had gone to his office before breakfast, to catch up, and he came back when he knew the CPS officer would be there, to speak to him.

They sent Jane Applegate, a young African American woman who was quick and intelligent and had a warm way with the children. She was more direct with the adults, and Tyla liked her. She told her honestly what they had lived through, and what she believed the children had seen. She had tried to shield them. She didn't seem shocked that Tyla had stayed in the marriage for so long, and had even gone to meet him the day before to give him one last chance to speak and be civil, and he couldn't handle it.

"Abuse is the hardest thing in the world to get away from. Worse than drugs. You keep staying to convince them that you're not a bad person." Tyla looked relieved when she said it. It was exactly what she had done. "You can't reason with an abuser. You just have to cut your losses and run, and not look back. In the end, it's better for the kids, for you and everyone." Jane had gone to UCLA, and had worked at CPS for fifteen years since she graduated as a social worker. She had seen it all. "I checked with the court this morning, and he's still in custody. The judge doesn't want to set bail for the moment, and he may keep him in custody until a trial. But I'm sure a smart lawyer can change that. But at least for now, we don't need to worry about visitation."

"He has never hurt the children," Tyla said in Andrew's defense.

"That doesn't mean he won't start," Jane said bluntly. "If he becomes eligible for visitation, it would have to be with a court-appointed observer present to satisfy us." Tyla looked relieved at that too.

"My son says he doesn't want to see him again, ever."

"I'll see what he says when I talk to him." She didn't commit either way. She was there to protect the children's interests, not the parents'. She asked why they were living at someone else's house, although she commented that it was certainly a magnificent house.

"Ours is being repaired after the earthquake. We were living there, but it's a mess, and now it has bad memories for all of us. The children miss it. I want to sell it when we file for divorce. I could never live there again. And Meredith was kind enough to let us stay here and take care of me after . . . when Andrew . . ."

"After the assault," the social worker said.

"Yes. She's been very good to us. She loves the children, and we like being here."

"I have no problem with it," Jane said matter-of-factly. "I wouldn't mind staying here myself," she said with a grin. "Who else lives here?" There was room for an army, many bedrooms.

"No one. She does. She lives alone. She has a boyfriend who stays here sometimes. They were the ones who found Will last night. He owns a high-end security service to protect important people and celebrities. And Meredith has a housekeeping couple."

"No children of her own?"

"A daughter in New York who's about my age," Tyla said, while Jane thought about how lonely it must be to live all alone in a huge mansion. But it was clearly a lucky situation for Tyla and her children.

Tyla told her about her plan to go back to school to become a nurse practitioner and Jane jotted it down.

She spoke to Will after that, and he told her what he had told his mother, that he never wanted to see his father again, and hated him for what he had done to their mother.

"He always hurt her. They thought we didn't know, but we could hear them."

"Did you ever see him hit her?"

"Yes, sometimes. She always tried not to make him mad around us."

"That must have been stressful," Jane said sympathetically, wondering if he'd say more, but he didn't. He didn't know her well enough yet. "Did he hit you?"

"A few times. Mostly he hit my mom. He's a doctor, he's not supposed to do that."

"No one is supposed to hit other people, doctor or not. How do you feel about living here, with Ms. White?"

"I like it." He smiled at her. "I like it better than our house. I don't want to go back. My dad would find us there and beat her up again."

"Why did you run away yesterday, Will?"

He hung his head when he answered, and wouldn't look at her. "Because I heard her say she was going to meet him, and I thought he'd beat her up. I should have gone to stop him, and I didn't. I was scared. I was too scared to stop him the night he really hurt her too. I hid in my room."

"You can't stop a man his size," Jane pointed out to him. "No one expects you to protect your mom physically. Adults have to do that."

He shook his head. "I should have tried. I was scared yesterday too, so I ran."

"He won't hurt you now, Will. He's in custody."

"But he'll come out again someday, and then he'll try to hurt her again. I hate him." She wanted him to see a therapist, but none of what he said surprised her. It was normal for the situation he'd been in for most of his life.

"I'm going to give you my card with my phone number on it. The next time you want to run away, I want you to call me. I'll come and get you, if you want. But if you run away you could get really badly hurt, or abducted. You were lucky yesterday. But let's not try that again. Okay?" He nodded, and she took out a card and handed it to him, and he slid it into his jeans.

They talked for a while longer, and then he left and Daphne came in, holding tightly to Martha.

"Who's that?" Jane asked her, looking relaxed as she watched her.

"Martha. She has a headache today," she said.

"How did she get a headache?" Jane asked.

"She fell down and she hit her head." It sounded like a scenario she'd seen or an excuse she'd been given for her mother's injuries.

"I'm sorry to hear that. Does she fall down a lot?"

"Sometimes. She broke her nose once."

"That must have hurt a lot." She had seen in the report that one of her mother's recent injuries from the assault was a broken nose.

"My mom got a broken nose too. She likes her new nose better," she said, and Jane had to make an effort not to laugh. She must have heard her mother say it.

"That's lucky for her, but it's not nice getting hurt and it's scary." Daphne nodded agreement.

"My brother ran away yesterday," she informed the social worker. "He ate a Big Mac out of the garbage can at McDonald's, and he got ketchup on his uniform jacket." She was a bottomless source of information, and a very funny kid. She was looking down at Jane's pink Converse. "I like your shoes. I have sneakers that light up when I run. I like to dance in them. And I go to ballet." She was very chatty, and seemed very much at ease despite what they'd been through. Will was more deeply affected by it, and felt more responsible for his mother.

"How do you like living here in this house right now?"

"I like it. Martha likes it too. Meredith is a good witch, but she doesn't have a magic wand. When my mommy got hurt, I came to get her, and she called the police, and a ambubus with lights and a siren came to take her away." She got that Daphne meant an ambulance.

"You came to get Meredith all by yourself?" Jane was impressed. That was a brave thing for a child her age to do.

"She's kind of like a grandmother, even though she's a witch. I rang the bell at the gate, and they went to get her." It was also possibly why her brother felt so guilty, because he had hidden in his room, and his little sister had run away to get help.

"Why do you think Meredith is a witch?" She was curious about that.

"My daddy said she's a witch, and when I told her, I said she's a good witch, but she doesn't have a wand. And I know she's a witch, because she fixes everything, and she always helps us, like she found Will last night."

"She sounds like a good friend to have. How does Martha feel about her?" Daphne smiled her big toothless smile in response. "She loves her. She's like Martha's grandmother too."

Jane walked Daphne back to her mother then, and met with Charles and Meredith briefly.

"You have a serious fan club here." She smiled at Meredith. "All three Johnsons, and Martha! And I understand you're a good witch."

Meredith laughed. "I'm not sure if Daphne's father called me a witch or a bitch, but either way I did my best to clean up my image!" All three of them laughed.

"It sounds like you've been wonderful to them."

"I love them dearly, and they've been through a very hard time."

Meredith answered Jane's questions about the children as best she could, and said they were weathering the situation well. She said Tyla was a wonderful mother, and Charles agreed. He expressed his concerns about the dangers Andrew presented for them, and the hope that he wouldn't have the opportunity to hurt Tyla again, or the children.

"It sounds like he might remain in custody now until the trial," Jane commented. She liked both of them, and she refrained from telling Meredith that her own mother was her most ardent fan. She didn't think it would be professional to say so, but she couldn't wait to tell her mother that she'd met her, and how beautiful she still was. And apparently, a very kind woman.

Jane told them she'd be dropping in from time to time, and she'd try to make it as convenient as possible.

"You're welcome anytime," Meredith said. They had nothing to hide.

The social worker left the house a few minutes later, more than satisfied with everything she'd seen. Tyla was a responsible mother, the children were well cared for and doing well, and they had devoted adopted grandparents on the scene, living in a house that was everyone's dream. She just hoped that Andrew Johnson didn't manage to slither out of the charges against him, and that he would go to prison for his crimes.

"How do you think it went?" Meredith asked Tyla after Jane left.

"I don't know, but she was very nice. She wasn't scary, and I thought she would be. I was terrified she'd want to take the children away and put them in foster care."

"I don't think you need to worry about that."

Charles kissed Meredith after Jane left, and rushed back to his office. He had a busy day ahead.

* * *

Peter called Meredith that afternoon. "We saw the police outside the Johnsons' house yesterday, and Ava said she saw that the living room windows were broken. Did they have a break-in?"

"No," Meredith said with a sigh. "It was Andrew again. Tyla agreed to meet him there, which was a mistake, and he lost control again. He was arraigned this morning, and is in custody without bail this time."

"Did she get hurt again?" He sounded horrified.

"Barely. The police came before he got too out of hand, but he was heading there. The police broke the windows to get in." They were being repaired that morning. "I think she learned a lesson. She can't get anywhere near him. He tricked her into agreeing to a meeting, and started going nuts when she showed up."

"I hope they keep him in custody this time," Peter said, and he knew that Arthur and Ava would be upset to hear about it too.

"How are all of you?"

"Wonderful," he said with a lilt in his voice. "Ava has turned my room into a closet. We got a storage unit for some of her stuff. Arthur loves having an assistant, Ava loves her job, and I'm the happiest man on earth. What about you?"

"We're fine." They hadn't seen each other in a few weeks, since Tyla was in the hospital. "Why don't the three of you come to dinner tomorrow night? We have a new cook, a couple actually, she's a very good cook and they're very nice. She makes fabulous Mexican food," which after living with him for nearly a month after the earthquake, she knew was a favorite of his.

"We'd love it," he spoke for all of them, and knew Arthur would be pleased to see them too. "Are Debbie and Jack gone?" He sounded surprised.

"They are. It's a long story, but we made some unpleasant discoveries."

"I thought they'd been there forever."

"They were. They'd been stealing from me for years. It was very upsetting."

"I'm sorry, that's awful. See you tomorrow," Peter said, and went to tell Arthur and Ava, and about a new incident with Andrew the day before.

Charles told Meredith that night when he got home that he had spoken to the police about Andrew's arraignment, and he was being sent to a psychiatric hospital with a locked facility for a thirty-day psychiatric evaluation, to see if he was competent to stand trial.

"Is that good news or bad?" she asked Charles, not sure how to interpret it.

"Both possibly. It means he's not going to be out wandering the streets for the next month, but it could mean that the charges would be dropped, and he would be sent to a mental hospital instead of prison. It depends what they decide, and if he has a good lawyer, they'll probably do everything to plead insanity to get him off, and then get him out of the psych hospital later and claim he's cured." She didn't like the sound of it and neither did he.

* * *

The next morning when she came down to breakfast, she saw what Tyla had feared since the beginning. The story of the charges against Andrew, and how severely he had injured her, was on the front page. There was an old photograph of him looking distinguished and intelligent and very handsome. It spoke of how prominent he was, and listed the charges, and said there had been a second incident yesterday. Several newspapers and a TV station had called Tyla on her cellphone for comment by nine A.M. It meant that all the parents of Daphne's and Will's school friends would be aware that Andrew was being charged with attempted murder. It added a sordid element to what was already a painful time in their lives.

"I'm sorry," she said to Tyla over coffee after the children had gone to school.

"I feel bad for the kids," Tyla said with a sigh. "It was bound to come out eventually. He's a prominent physician with a busy practice. It wasn't going to stay a secret forever, or even for very long."

Two news vans were parked in front of their house all day. They didn't know that Tyla and the children weren't living there at the moment, which was some relief. She was letting all her calls go to voicemail so she didn't have to talk to the press.

They talked about it with Peter, Ava, and Arthur after the children left the dinner table that night. Arthur was still shocked that an educated, intelligent man, who could be so pleasant and entertaining to talk to, could almost murder his wife.

"He should be hanged!" he said in a stern voice. Ava had just confided to Tyla and Meredith that she had seen Joel a few days ago, helping a pretty young blond girl who looked like a model carry a mountain of suitcases into his house.

"So I've been replaced," she said matter-of-factly.

"Do you care?" Tyla asked her gently.

"Not really," Ava said with a smile. "It feels a little weird. It never takes him long. The girl looks about eighteen. She's probably twenty-one or twenty-two. It's just a little awkward living next door to them. But we'll probably never run into them."

"Did he say hello?" Meredith asked her.

"He didn't see me. I was in the car . . . spying on him!" She laughed. "She's a pretty girl."

"So are you," Meredith said firmly. "Better than that. You're beautiful, and smart and interesting, and better than he deserved."

"I'm not complaining. If I hadn't been living with him, I would never have met Peter and all of you during the earthquake," she said, smiling. It was nice being together again, although two members of their earthquake group had disappeared from their ranks now, Joel and Andrew. In two short months, all of their lives had changed dramatically.

They talked about their plans for Thanksgiving. Peter, Ava, and Arthur were staying home, and so were Tyla and the children. Meredith hadn't seen Kendall for the holidays in years. She never invited her mother, and she had declined Meredith's invitations for ten years before her mother finally stopped inviting her. Meredith had spent all holidays, Christmas, Thanksgiving, and her birthday, with Jack and Debbie for years.

"Why don't we spend it together?" Meredith suggested. "You can all come here." It sounded like a good idea to all of them. None of them went home for the holidays usually, and they agreed that it would be fun to be together. Charles normally went to his daughter in Texas, but he was going to ask her for a pass this year so he could be with Meredith. He had told his daughter about Meredith, and she was happy for him.

As always, it was a wonderful evening, and Tyla felt strongly supported by her friends. She tried not to think about Andrew, who was going to be spending the holidays alone this year, either in a psychiatric hospital, or in jail. She remembered what the social worker said about abuse being the hardest thing to get away from, and forced her mind back to the present. She had her children, she had friends, she was living in a gorgeous home for the time being, and miraculously, in spite of Andrew, she was alive!

When Charles and Meredith woke up the next morning, after dinner with Arthur's group, they both admitted that they were tired. It had been a long stressful week, with Andrew nearly committing mayhem again and stopped in the nick of time, Will running away, their spending half the night looking for him, a visit from CPS, Charles's regular meetings to attend to, and Meredith breaking in new housekeepers, and Tyla and her children in residence.

"What do you say I spirit you away to my chateau in the Napa Valley?" Charles said good-humoredly. His small, cozy house there had special meaning to them, since they had made love there for the first time.

"That sounds heavenly." Meredith smiled at him. She still had a mild headache from the bump on the head Andrew had given her, but she was grateful it hadn't been worse. "I need some quiet time with you," she said gently.

"I thought recluses were supposed to have small, boring lives, with nothing to do. We haven't stopped for five minutes." And they had gone from one drama to the next. "Your recluse card is seriously out of date. How fast can you pack for the weekend?" he asked her.

"Give me twenty minutes and I'll meet you in the car," she said, looking delighted. It was a chilly, blustery weekend, but even sitting in the house set among the vineyards would be a nice break from city life, and the issues they had been dealing with all week.

True to her word, she was ready twenty minutes later. She had told Tyla they were going, and Charles drove out of the courtyard, and headed for the Golden Gate Bridge.

They both enjoyed the drive, and when they got to Napa, it was cold, but bright and sunny. They set their bags down in his house and went for a long walk through the vineyards, breathing the crisp air, and they could smell wood fires in the distance.

"I love it here," she said, taking a deep breath of the country air, which smelled of earth and recent rains. "I'm so happy you have this house." She'd been to his city home too, which was small and spare, and practical for a man living alone, but he hadn't put much effort into decorating it. He traveled a lot, and preferred to entertain in restaurants since he was no longer married. She liked having him spend nights with her. His city house was just a closet and a home office now. He rarely spent a night there since they'd been together. But his little Napa house had charm, and was a welcome change from the grandeur of her home and all the people in it on a daily basis, with security men, cleaning staff, workmen, repair people, and the new housekeeping couple.

"I'm thinking of going to L.A. the week after Thanksgiving," she said to him when they got back to the house. He lit a fire, and handed her a glass of wine. "I wanted to go before then, but things keep coming up."

"Would you like me to go with you?" he offered, and she smiled.

"I'd like that. But I want to spend some time with my granddaughter. Do you have something to do there?"

"I have two clients I need to see. I can see them when you're with your granddaughter."

"That sounds good," she said. Their plans and schedules had been dovetailing nicely. "I don't know if she'll see me. I want to call her once I'm there, and be casual about it. If I try to set it up in advance, she might turn me down. If she's anything like her mother, she's not warm and fuzzy. But I haven't seen her since she was a child of ten, when she last visited me in San Francisco, and I'd like to get to know her. She has an amazing talent, and she looks like an interesting girl."

It seemed sad to him that Meredith had to put so much thought into it, and done some careful juggling. His relationship with his own daughter was easy and effortless. Meredith's daughter sounded like a tough customer with an axe to grind about her mother, even a chip on her shoulder, which left Meredith almost daughterless, and she expected her granddaughter to be the same way. She was looking forward to meeting Charles's children, who seemed to have a friendly, relaxed relationship with their father. They called him once or twice a week, and often for advice, and it was obvious that he enjoyed them. But every family was different, and some family members were more difficult than others. Kendall had always been cool and distant, and aloof, even as a child, even before the divorce and her brother's accident. Meredith liked her husband, but never had the opportunity to talk to him. She was hoping to salvage some kind of relationship at least with her granddaughter. It was the only family she had.

The two days in Napa were just what they both needed. They went for a bicycle ride on Sunday, another long walk, bought cheese and pate at the Oakville Grocery, and by the time they went back to the city on Sunday night, Meredith felt as though she'd had a two-week vacation. They had slept late too, and made love when they woke up, without the intercom ringing every five minutes, and someone needing her attention.

She had discovered too how easy her house was to run without Jack and Debbie. They had always made a big deal about how complicated it was, in order to make themselves seem important and essential. Instead, as soon as they left, she realized how much easier it was, and less expensive, without them skimming the cream off the top, to put in their pockets, or inflating what they spent. The more she saw, the more she understood what crooks they had been, and was embarrassed she hadn't figured it out sooner. The new couple was simple and straightforward to deal with.

"How was the weekend?" Tyla asked them when they walked in. Their cheeks were pink, they looked healthy and relaxed in jeans and heavy sweaters.

"Perfect," Meredith answered with a smile.

"I knew I rented that house for a reason," Charles said, as they made sandwiches for dinner. "I thought I'd never use it."

"What about you?" Meredith asked Tyla. She could see that she was feeling better.

"Nice. I took the kids to the science museum and a movie." It was so wonderful not to have to worry about Andrew coming home, and having a fit about something. The children were more relaxed too. No one was going to get angry at them or beat their mother.

Another week flew by and then it was Thanksgiving. Arthur, Peter, and Ava came to dinner at Meredith's as planned. They all dressed nicely in suits and dresses, and the new couple served the meal in the dining room. Meredith had hired a chef to prepare it, and the turkey was delicious. The conversation at the table was lively and fun. Arthur was about to fly off to do another concert, and since he had someone who traveled with him, Peter and Ava would have a break while he was away. Peter had bought theater tickets to surprise her. They lived on a small budget, unlike her life with Joel. But they both enjoyed simple pleasures, and Ava didn't miss having a Ferrari. She thought about Joel at times, and wondered if he thought about her at all. He was part of her history now, but she felt as though she and Peter had been together forever, and it seemed like the perfect fit. Joel never had been. He liked to show her off like an object, but he had never valued her as a person. Peter did.

They left for Los Angeles the Monday after Thanksgiving. Charles had set up his client meetings. They were planning to stay at the Beverly Hills Hotel, and had taken a bungalow. The hotel had a charming 1950s Old Hollywood flavor to it. Important people and big movie stars still stayed there. She and Scott had stayed there often and loved it. She hadn't been back since they separated, because she was trying to avoid the paparazzi when they first split up and they would have had a feeding frenzy there. And since then, she had no reason to go to L.A.

They treated her like returning royalty when she and Charles checked in. He was as handsome as any actor, with his thick white hair, bright blue eyes, and trim, athletic figure.

"Wow! They never treat me like this when I stay here," he teased her. There was a magnum of champagne in the room, three enormous vases of long-stemmed red roses, all her favorite magazines, pastries, petit fours, chocolates, and caviar in the fridge, as a gift from the manager.

"This is mecca for old movie stars." She grinned at him. "They all come here to die, like ancient elephants." He laughed at her comment.

They had lunch at the Polo Lounge before he left for his first meeting. And there were two important stars and a flock of agents having lunch there.

When she went back to the bungalow after lunch, she opened the thick file she'd brought with her about Julia, with articles about her, some photographs, her agent's contact information, and a bio she'd gotten from the Internet. She'd even checked out her Instagram and liked it. As she sat looking at the pages in the file, she knew that she was stalling. What if Julia never returned her calls, wouldn't answer, or hung up on her? She might be a little diva, or the carbon copy of her mother.

She finally decided to call Julia's agent first. It was a woman, who was apparently young and had started her own agency after working for ICM, and handled mostly young talent.

A receptionist answered the phone, and Meredith put on her best Hollywood voice, which she hadn't used for years. It was fun for a minute.

She asked the girl for Julia Price's phone number, as though she had a right to it. The receptionist asked for her name, and that was the fun part.

"Meredith White," she said grandly, "I'm her grandmother."

"Meredith White? Meredith *White*?" The poor girl sounded as though she'd been struck by lightning. "Of course . . . oh . . . yes, right away, Miss White. Please hold while I get it for you. I won't be a minute." Meredith then got to listen to a rap concert while she waited, and three minutes later a young, crisp, efficient voice came on the line.

"Hello, I'm Sarah Gross, Julia Price's agent. Who is this?" She obviously didn't believe the receptionist, and Meredith didn't blame her. A lot of crackpots or opportunists called actors with crank calls. She was surprised that the agent was on the line herself, instead of an assistant.

"Thanks very much for taking my call," Meredith said breezily, feeling more like herself than a diva. "I'm Meredith White, Julia Price's grandmother. I'm in town for a few days, I'd like to get in touch with her, and I don't have her number." She was simple and direct and the agent was smart enough to recognize the real deal.

"Good Lord!" she said. "It really is you. I thought it might be a joke. It's an honor to speak to you. I'd forgotten that you're her grandmother, although it's in our press kit on her somewhere. I'll get you her number right away." She went off the line and was back in seconds. "If you have trouble reaching her, and need us to get in touch, let me know. You know how kids are these days, it's all text, they don't pick up their phones." Meredith hadn't thought of that. "I'll give you her email address too," which she did, and Meredith thanked her warmly. It had been a friendly welcome to the Hollywood scene, and the gatekeepers of Julia's career. She liked the sound of her agent. She seemed young, energetic, and engaged.

After what Sarah Gross said, when Meredith called Julia's number a few minutes later, she expected it to go straight to voicemail. Instead, a sexy young voice answered, which Meredith thought was a recording at first, and she was waiting for the ding so she could leave a message. But instead, Julia said hello again and Meredith was flustered when she answered.

"Julia? Is that you?" she asked. "It's your grandmother. I've wanted to get in touch with you for ages." She didn't know what else to say for openers, but it was true.

"Grandma?" She only had one since Meredith knew Kendall's mother-in-law had passed away.

"Yes, it's me," Meredith said, feeling silly. It was odd dropping into her granddaughter's life nine years later. "I've been following your career, and I've watched everything I could lay hands on. You're terrific, and I wanted to tell you that myself."

"Where are you? In San Francisco?" She sounded excited and thrilled to hear from her.

"No, I'm in L.A., so I wanted to call you while I'm here." She didn't tell her that she was her sole reason for the trip, so as not to pressure her. "I was hoping we could get together if you're not too busy."

"I'd love it! Of course I'm not too busy. Where are you?"

"The Beverly Hills Hotel." Meredith felt a little overwhelmed herself by the warm reaction.

"Can I come now? I've wanted to call you, but Mom says you never talk to anyone, so I didn't want to intrude on you."

"I'm here to see you," Meredith said honestly. "Come on over." She couldn't believe how easy it had been. It felt meant to be.

"I live in West Hollywood. I'll grab an Uber and be there in fifteen minutes. I'm so happy you called me."

"So am I. See you soon." When they hung up, Meredith looked in the mirror. Her still blondish hair made her look younger, but she felt suddenly ancient. She wondered if she should change her clothes or try to look elegant. She was wearing jeans, a black cashmere sweater, and Hermès loafers. She hadn't expected to see her so soon. There was no time to get dressed now, and play the grande dame, and she didn't want to anyway. She wanted to be real, down-to-earth, and accessible to Julia.

She kept walking around the bungalow nervously, and set out some nuts and snacks and petit fours that the hotel had sent her. She was still fussing and had brushed her hair twice and put on lipstick, when the doorbell rang. Meredith opened it, and there was her spectacularly beautiful, tall, sexy granddaughter with a mane of red hair and no makeup, wearing almost the same thing she was, except that she was wearing sneakers instead of loafers. And before Meredith could say anything, Julia was hugging her and they were both crying. It was more emotional than either of them had expected, and felt as though they had seen each other yesterday.

"I still have all the dolls you gave me. I kept them. And I wanted you to know that I'm an actress now too, or trying to be."

"And doing a damn fine job of it too. I loved you in the second series you did."

"We're shooting another season and they're going to make my part bigger." There was so much to say and nearly nine years to cover. Meredith took out her file and showed her all the articles she had collected, and Julia looked deeply touched. She was staring at her grandmother. "You look the same."

"No, I don't," Meredith denied it, "but thank you. I'm sorry we haven't talked in so long."

"I know, me too."

"It's my fault." Meredith took responsibility for it, but Julia knew better.

"No, it's not. Not entirely. It's Mom. She makes everything so difficult. Nothing is ever a straight line with her. It has to be complicated and convoluted and dark, and you have to jump through hoops of fire to get to her. That's why I'm here. I just couldn't do it at home anymore. She hates my wanting to be an actress. She hates everything to do with Hollywood. Grampa got me a few jobs, and she had a fit at him. He does what he wants anyway. My dad is an angel, I don't know how he deals with her. She overthinks everything, and she's so bitter. It's sad. She's poisoned our relationship," Julia confided in her. It was similar to what Meredith had experienced with Kendall.

"She hardly ever returns my calls," Meredith admitted. "She goes for months without calling me. She's still angry about things that happened fifteen years ago, or when she was a little girl. For some reason, after he was gone, she decided that I loved her brother more than I loved her. It's hard to cut through all that and have a connection with her. I just let her call me when she wants to, and call her occasionally and hope for the best. But I lost you in all that," Meredith said sadly.

"I told her I wanted to see you when I came out here, and she acted as though I was abandoning her. I think underneath that ice-cold exterior, she's a very jealous person. She's pissed that I'm out here and enjoying it. She keeps telling me that I'm just like you, as though that's a crime. It's a compliment." Julia smiled at her. "Grampa says you're the greatest actress that ever lived, and it's a tragedy that you stopped working. My dream is to be in a picture with you one day," she blurted out, and Meredith knew that was never going to happen, but she wanted to know all about Julia now, and it was comforting to know that she had the same kind of problems with Kendall.

"She blamed me for our divorce, and I wasn't the one who left, your grandfather did. And she blamed me for being too hard on Scott, when your uncle died." It was odd to think of Justin that way, since he had only been fourteen at the time, but he was Julia's uncle.

"I don't know," Julia said. "Mom's been angry all her life, and my dad is so patient with her. He's the one who let me come out here, and she was furious with him. She says she hated Hollywood growing up, and she wants nothing to do with it now."

"I was gone a lot then, but Scott and I took turns going on location, so one of us was always with her. She's forgotten that."

"She has selective memory about everything, and nothing is ever her fault, although I have to admit, we were talking about you a couple of years ago, and I asked why she didn't make an effort to reconnect with you, and she said it was too late, she had been terrible to you, and you can't repair that."

"Oh my God, she said that?" Julia nodded, and helped herself to a petit four. "I'm amazed."

"She'd rather be miserable and angry than fix anything. She's still furious with me for being out here. She considers it the ultimate betrayal, that I'm not in New York, still in college and dating who she wants me to, her friends' sons. I would die of boredom, and that's not me. So now she never calls me. And sounds like an iceberg when I call her."

"She forgets that she did the same thing." Meredith smiled nostalgically. "She dropped out of college after she and your father met in Florence. I did everything to keep her in school, and she quit anyway, and got married. But I have to admit, it worked out well. I don't see how she can be so hard on you about what you've done. You have real talent, Julia," Meredith said proudly.

"She's hard on everyone, Grandma. It's her way or the highway. I'm telling you, my dad is a saint. And she can hold a grudge for centuries." Meredith knew it firsthand, Kendall had never forgiven her anything. "I don't know why she's so tough, but she is. It ruined our relationship years ago. Grampa is the only one who doesn't pay any attention when she gets that way. Maybe he's like that too, because you certainly don't seem to be that way, or we wouldn't be sitting here today."

Meredith smiled. "How is your grandfather, by the way?"

"He's fine, working like crazy. He had some health issues last year, but he's fine now. I think he gets bored whenever he's not working, so he sits still for about five minutes and then goes back to work."

"He was always that way," Meredith said, remembering.

"And Silvana is pretty boring. She spends a lot of time in Italy, he bought her a house there. She eats pasta at every meal, and she's gotten fat," Julia said evilly, and Meredith laughed. Silvana was very close to Kendall's age, and too young to let herself go. "You look way better than she does," Julia said, and Meredith was more than twenty years older. She remembered distinctly.

"I haven't talked to your grandfather in a long time." It was odd too how Kendall had forgiven her father for breaking up their family and marrying a girl her own age, but had never forgiven her mother for any of her perceived crimes. Kendall had always been partial to Scott, and apparently still was. And it was interesting that she acknowledged to Julia that she had treated Meredith "terribly." Julia had given her a lot to think about.

Julia lay down on the floor while they talked. She had been there for three hours when Charles came back and let himself into the bungalow, and Julia looked up in surprise. His face lit up when he saw her and she stood up to her full height to meet him.

"Are you married, Grandma?" Her mother hadn't told her, if she was.

"No, this is my very special friend, Charles Chapman." They shook hands, and Julia giggled with her red mane stretching out.

"I love it. You have a boyfriend! You're so cool!" All three of them laughed, and Meredith blushed a little.

"We met during the earthquake."

"Good for you. I want to come up and visit you!"

"You are welcome anytime. You can have your own room, and come and go whenever you want," she said generously. "You can bring a friend too, if you like."

Julia cocked her head to one side, thinking about it. "Mom is going to think we're conspiring against her. That's the sad part. She can't just be happy for us that we found each other; she'll take it as a slight of some kind, but I don't care. I'm coming to see you."

"Whenever you want," Meredith reiterated.

Charles poured himself a glass of wine, and the three of them chatted for another hour, and then Julia said she was meeting friends for dinner and had to go.

"How long are you here for?" she asked her grandmother.

"Two more days." Meredith had allotted three days, in case it took a long time to connect with her, but it hadn't. It had been instantaneous. Meredith had loved her as a little girl, full of spice and bright ideas, and this was even better. They could get to know each other as adults. Julia brought a lot to the table.

"Can we do lunch tomorrow?" Julia asked her. "I have an audition in the morning, and I'm getting paid to go to some fashion event tomorrow night. But I'm free for lunch and all afternoon. They wanted to do my hair and I won't let them. This is me."

"Good for you," her grandmother said, hugged her when she left, and kissed her. They made a date to meet at the Polo Lounge for lunch the next day. She was smiling when Julia left.

"Well, that looked like a major success. No one would have guessed that you hadn't seen each other in nearly ten years."

"It was a success," Meredith confirmed, and then looked serious. "She has the same problems with her mother that I do, a lot of the same complaints. And apparently, Kendall has admitted to her that she treated me 'terribly,' but she never fixes it. She told Julia it's too late. It's never too late. And now she has alienated her daughter the way she did me. If she's not careful, she'll lose her too. Kendall is so hard and unforgiving, and she sets the bar so high for everyone, no one can live up to it."

"It's sad for her," he said. Meredith nodded and kissed him.

"She's beautiful, isn't she?" Meaning Julia.

"She's stunning. Actually, she looks a little like you. The red hair distracts you, but the fine features are very similar. You could be her mother."

"I hope she comes to San Francisco to see me, she said she would."

"She seems very excited to reconnect with you."

"I am too." Her eyes were sparkling and she was smiling. This was why she had come to L.A., and it had been a resounding success. Her only regret was that she hadn't done it sooner. She said it to Charles, and he pointed out that Julia wouldn't have been old enough. She was the right age to have her own relationship with Meredith now, and they had a career in common, which was a bond too.

She and Charles had dinner at Giorgio Baldi in Santa Monica that night, and people recognized her as she walked into the restaurant. Some just stared, but they knew who she was. No one had forgotten her. And one of the older headwaiters almost cried when he greeted her.

"Welcome back! Are you working again?"

"No." She smiled and shook her head. "But my granddaughter is," she said proudly.

"You must make another film. You are still beautiful!"

"I agree with him," Charles said when they sat down. "You are beautiful."

"You're blind, but I love you," she brushed off the compliment.

Julia and Meredith met for lunch the next day and spent another three hours talking, and made a date for breakfast the day after. Meredith was going back to San Francisco on a five o'clock flight, and had to leave the city at three. On her last day, they went for a walk, and she went to Julia's tiny apartment in West Hollywood. It reminded her of her own beginnings, although her career had shot into the stratosphere very quickly. Things were different then, when they "discovered" someone and put them in movie after movie with big stars, and spent a fortune on publicity. The studios were in control then. That had all changed, but she could see Julia becoming a big star herself in time. She was already on her way at a steady pace, and she had the talent that would keep her at the top once she got there, if she worked hard.

Meredith left her at her apartment with a pang of regret, and hugged her for a long time. "I love you, Julia. Come home to me whenever you want. Do you have a boyfriend, by the way?" She had forgotten to ask her, they had spoken of so many things, their careers, Kendall, Scott, Silvana, and mostly Julia's dreams for her career. She had big dreams.

"No. I had one last year but we broke up. He was a jerk. There's an actor I sort of like, but he's kind of a jerk too."

"There's a lot of that here." Meredith smiled. "Just have fun, and work hard. And, Julia, don't give up on your mom yet. I know how hard she is, but you only have one mother."

"I know. I love you, Grandma." It was music to her ears. It was the relationship she would have loved to have with her daughter, but never had, and probably never would. She had accepted it. And now here was Julia, like a big shining star in the sky, and a remarkable gift.

"I love you too," Meredith said again.

Meredith took a cab back to the hotel. Her trip to L.A. had been a resounding success. She and Charles talked about it all the way home on the flight, and Julia called her when they landed, to thank her. Meredith was smiling when she hung up. It had taken a long time, waiting for her to grow up, but her granddaughter had been worth the wait.

Chapter 14

Meredith told Tyla all about her trip to L.A. and the time she had spent with Julia.

"She sounds fantastic. I can't believe you haven't seen her in that long. And you're so good with kids. Your daughter was crazy not to let you be with her for all this time."

"Kendall is a hard woman. She remembers everything and forgives nothing. She sees it all through her own lens, whether true or not. I'm sorry for Julia that her mother hasn't softened over the years. Julia's given up on her for now. And Kendall never humbles herself, nor admits it when she's wrong." Meredith was amazed that her marriage had lasted. George really must be a saint, as his daughter said.

Meredith coasted on the joy of their L.A. visit for days, remembering things Julia had said and smiling. She called Meredith twice, to tell her what she was doing and maintain the connection and the bond they had forged. It was something Kendall had never learned. Maybe it had killed something in her when her brother died. But Kendall was already twenty-six then, and a mother herself, which should have made her warmer, more forgiving, and more compassionate. It was as though there was a piece missing in her, a link that didn't exist to connect her to others.

Meredith thought about it all week after she saw Julia, and made a decision that weekend. She didn't think it would make a difference, but that didn't matter. Kendall was never going to reach out to her. She had said so to her daughter. Meredith wanted to show her that it was never too late. Broken hearts mended. They had scars but they didn't have to be broken forever. Life was a patchwork of pieces and broken bits that became beautiful when you wove them together. The beauty is in the tears and the embroidery you put over them. It's the rents and the tears and breaks that make us who we are. Kendall had never understood that.

Meredith thought more about it over the weekend, and told Charles on Sunday night.

"I'm going to New York for a few days," she said quietly.

"I wish I could go with you, but I can't," he said regretfully. It was getting close to Christmas, and his work always heated up then, finding the right security agents to accompany his celebrity clients to their holiday destinations. "Are you going for fun? A little Christmas shopping?" He had a feeling it was something more serious and he was right.

"I might do that too." She smiled and kissed him. "I'll tell you about it when I get back."

"It sounds mysterious." His curiosity was piqued, but he could see that she didn't want to talk about it. She booked a ticket for

Tuesday, and told him she'd be back Thursday or Friday, depending on how it went. Or she might turn around and come back in twenty-four hours.

She thought about it on the flight east, and she had promised to bring Daphne a surprise. They were excited about Christmas, and this year they didn't need to worry about their father ruining it. Andrew was refusing to plead guilty, and was still at the locked psychiatric facility, being evaluated.

Meredith checked into the Four Seasons hotel in New York, and then she called her. She wondered how many days it would take to reach her, but it only took three tries. Kendall sounded surprised to hear her mother's voice when she called from the hotel phone. They hadn't spoken in three months. She hadn't called back after the first time, after the earthquake, which didn't surprise Meredith. She told Kendall she was in New York, and there was silence on the line. It was very different from Julia's jubilant reaction in L.A.

"Would you like to have lunch or dinner, if you have time?" Meredith asked her. Kendall was like an animal in the wild. You couldn't approach too quickly, or make her feel cornered. Like a panther or a leopard that would attack if you did. Or just walk into the brush and disappear.

"I think I can do lunch tomorrow," she said coolly. "I'll text you, I have to check. What are you doing in New York?" Kendall knew her mother hadn't been there in fifteen years, and didn't sound pleased to hear her.

"I had some things to do."

An hour later, Kendall texted her, and said she could make it for noon the next day at Harry Cipriani at the Sherry-Netherland. She had purposely picked a place where it would be loud and hard to talk. Intimacy was not Kendall's forte.

Meredith spent a quiet night at the hotel, thinking about what she wanted to say the next day. She called Charles to tell him she had arrived safely, and sent Julia a text to say hello. She got an instant response from Julia, saying hi and sending her love.

Meredith was waiting at the restaurant at noon the next day when Kendall arrived. She was wearing a serious black dress, pearls, and a mink coat, which aged her. She had grown up to be the society matron she wanted to be. And just as she had rejected who Meredith was, now Julia was rejecting her. It was the nature of life. Meredith hugged her and Kendall seemed awkward and stiff.

They were halfway through lunch before Meredith broached the reason she had come.

"I came to tell you that I love you. That however hard it's been for us to connect, however many mistakes you feel I made, whether I did or not, I love you. That's all. I know you're angry that I blamed your father for Justin's death. I don't hate him for it. I think it's sad that he let him go out in the boat alone. But destiny is what it is. And you were angry about the divorce, but that wasn't my doing."

"You could have let him come back," Kendall said, her eyes still full of black fire.

"He never wanted to, Kendall. He wanted to marry Silvana. He told me that when he left. And once Justin died, it was a moot point, but I wouldn't have taken him back anyway. The affair with Silvana had been too public. He wanted to burn all his bridges behind him, and he did. He's still married to her so he can't be too unhappy. You may have wanted him to, but he never wanted to come back to me."

"Maybe if you'd been around more he wouldn't have had the affair." It was still a heated topic for her fifteen years later. Meredith doubted it would have been as heated with Scott. They had gotten over it. Kendall never had. The sack on her back was so full and heavy with past grievances that she had no room in it for forgiveness or love. Meredith wanted to help her empty it now, if that was possible, for Kendall's sake, and Julia's, and her own.

"Maybe you're right. But his affair with Silvana, and how he conducted it, was his responsibility, not mine. In spite of it, I was fighting the divorce, but when Justin died, I knew I couldn't forgive him for that, so I filed. I couldn't stay with a man I couldn't forgive. It would have been wrong and unfair to him."

"Would you have stayed married to him otherwise?" she asked her pointedly.

"I don't know. I don't think he's ever regretted the divorce, and I'm comfortable now. It was never your battle. You were a married woman with a child of your own when we divorced. We didn't ruin your life. You had us at our best when you were a child."

"If you can call it that. You were gone all the time, being a big movie star."

"So was he. We alternated, equal time away. Why did that end up on my scoreboard and not both of ours? Why me?"

"I wanted you to be different than you were," she said honestly. She had never admitted it before. "I wanted you to be like all the other mothers, not different and special, with everyone asking you for an autograph wherever we went." Meredith nodded. She couldn't change that now, or even then. "And by the time you gave it all up and went into seclusion, I didn't care. It was too late for me."

"I retired because of your father and Justin, not for you. I can't sell you on how hard I tried to be there for you when I was working, and I won't try. If it wasn't enough for you, that's fair. You have the right to feel that."

"Why are you doing this now?" Kendall asked her, still angry. "Are you sick?" Her mother was shocked by the question.

"No, I'm not. I wanted to clear the air, to give us a chance to be friends, or whatever you want to be. We don't have to. We can stay just as we are now. I miss having a daughter, and a real relationship with you. And maybe you miss having a mother. I wanted to give us that chance." And Kendall would never have done it. Meredith knew it was up to her, and was willing to try.

"I have Julia and George," Kendall said harshly. "I don't need you. You weren't what I needed when I was young, and I don't need you now." It was a cruel thing to say, as Meredith looked her in the eye, but it was who Kendall was, and had always been, even as a child. She'd had a mean streak even as a little girl, and was harsh, except with her brother.

"I guess that makes it clear. Be careful you don't do the same thing to Julia you've done to me, shutting her out."

"If she's not up to my standards, I will," she said coldly.

"You're not building cars, you're talking about a mother and daughter. That's a special relationship." She was giving her every chance to reach out and she wouldn't, and Meredith suddenly understood what Kendall had said to Julia, that it was too late. It wasn't too late for Meredith. It was too late for her. She didn't want to repair it. She had closed the door on her mother years before. Meredith looked at her. She didn't feel defeat or despair, she felt pity for her. For whatever the reason, Kendall was someone who couldn't forgive, and couldn't love. You had to be able to forgive in order to love. She didn't have it in her. She had rocks in her soul. Her mother had given her every chance to connect, and she could see now that Kendall didn't intend to. Meredith meant nothing to her. She wondered if, when her brother had died, part of her had died too. Or all of her.

They both left their lunches unfinished, and Meredith paid the check. She understood now what Julia was up against, why she had fled to L.A., as her father had encouraged her to do. He was saving his daughter from his wife. She felt sorry for all three of them.

They walked out of the restaurant together, and Meredith looked at her gently. "I don't know if you can hear it, but I do love you." She had suffered so much when she lost Scott and Justin that it had increased the capacity of her heart. And with her lack of compassion and forgiveness, Kendall's had shrunk. Kendall just looked at her mother and shook her head.

"I can't, Mom. I'm sorry." Then she turned and walked away. She was a bitter woman. Meredith wondered if she'd ever hear from her again. Every contact between them for years now had been forced. Kendall really didn't want a relationship with her. It was a strange feeling as she walked back to the hotel. She wasn't sorry she'd come. In an odd way, it was like a viewing, where you look at the body one last time before they close the casket. But it's no longer the person you knew and loved. It's just an empty shell.

She went to her room, and changed her reservation from Friday to the last flight of the day to San Francisco. She sent a text to Charles to tell him she was coming home. She had only been gone a day, and wasn't in the mood to shop. And she sent a text to Julia that said only "I love you. Grandma." It was all she needed to know, and the only thing she needed to hear. They had bridged the generations when they met in L.A. Kendall couldn't do that, with either of them. She just didn't have it in her. The tragedy was Kendall's, not theirs. And they had each other now. She had lost Kendall, but she had found Julia.

Charles was waiting for her at the airport when she arrived. She hadn't expected him to be there, and he could see in her eyes that something had happened. He didn't want to ask unless she volunteered.

"Short trip," he said as he took her bag from her, and they walked through the airport to baggage claim. It was late in San Francisco, and later in New York.

"I went to see Kendall," she said on the ride home.

"I thought it might be that. How was it?" He hated to ask, but she looked peaceful and strong, so he hoped it had gone well.

"It was the way she needed it to be, and maybe I did too. We needed closure." He nodded, and Meredith didn't say more. She realized now that she had lost Kendall years before. She didn't feel loss now. She felt free from the pain her daughter had inflicted on her for years.

Chapter 15

When Daphne came down to breakfast the next morning, there was a little pink teddy bear next to her place at the breakfast table, and an even smaller one next to it.

"What's that?" she asked with a big smile.

"I promised you a surprise from New York," Meredith reminded her. "The bigger one is for you, and the tiny one is for Martha."

"She's going to love it!" Daphne picked them both up and held them. And next to Will's place there was a Yankees baseball cap. They both thanked her. It was the only shopping she had done in New York, at the airport. She didn't want to disappoint the children.

She had done the rest of her Christmas shopping before she left San Francisco.

She and Charles were celebrating Christmas early. He was going to spend the holiday with his daughter and her family in Texas. Meredith felt that it was the wrong time for her to go. She didn't want to intrude on their family Christmas. She and Charles were going to visit her for a weekend in the next few months. His son, Jeff, had just been transferred to Germany, and they were going to visit him later in the year. And Charles was coming back to spend New Year's Eve with her. They were going to Napa, to his little house.

Julia was meeting her father in Aspen, to go skiing. Her mother wasn't coming. Julia said she hated holidays and didn't ski, and she didn't like Aspen. Meredith hadn't told her about her trip to New York and didn't intend to. It was between her and Kendall.

She gave a dinner for the earthquake group before Charles left. Arthur was flying to Japan for a concert the day after Christmas. Peter and Ava were going to Tahoe while he was away, and Tyla and her children would be spending Christmas with Meredith.

They all toasted the earthquake that had brought them together, and exchanged small thoughtful gifts.

Meredith had a wonderful Christmas with Tyla and her kids. In the end, it was a peaceful, lovely Christmas. They went to mass on Christmas Eve, and ice-skating on Christmas Day in Union Square, and they made s'mores. Tyla and Meredith prepared the turkey together, and congratulated each other on how good it was. They watched Christmas movies with the children and ate popcorn.

Charles called her and told her how much he missed her and couldn't wait to see her. It was a very nice Christmas, nicer than any she had spent with Jack and Debbie.

When Charles came home on the morning of New Year's Eve, they drove straight to the Napa Valley, and toasted each other with champagne at midnight. He had told his daughter, Pattie, that he was seriously in love with Meredith, and she was happy for him. They were going to visit her soon in the New Year. Charles assured Meredith that she was going to love Texas, and she believed him. So far everything he had said to her had been true. And she was excited to meet his children.

Julia came up from Los Angeles in the second week of January, after she got back from Aspen. She was startled to realize that Tyla and her children were living there, and Meredith explained the situation to her. Julia liked her, and got along with her better than with her own mother. Tyla was starting her refresher course at USF nursing school in February, and her courses to become a nurse practitioner in September.

Julia sank into the comforts of her grandmother's home like it was a giant featherbed. She pitched baseballs at Will in the back garden, and helped Daphne dress her dolls, and she had loved Charles when she met him. She said again that he reminded her of her father. They were both very kind men.

Meredith was thrilled to have her there. Julia stayed for a long weekend, and promised to come back again soon, and she meant it. Even though the others weren't related to them, it felt like a family being with them. Ava, Peter, and Arthur came to meet her. She liked them a lot too. She loved the fact that her grandmother had created a world where people felt loved and at home. Her house felt like a warm embrace now that Debbie and Jack were gone.

And a week after Julia's visit, Meredith got a shock when she opened her morning paper. It was a small article several pages in, about a couple who had taken a job as property managers of a well-known estate in Woodside, near San Francisco. They had masterminded an art and jewelry heist, and hired thugs to do it, who had tied up the other employees. Over twenty million in art, jewelry, and personal property had been taken. An informer had told the police. Everything had been recovered, and the two ringleaders were now in custody without bail. Meredith stared at the names in disbelief. It was Debbie and Jack. They had obviously become desperate or overambitious, and it hadn't worked, and now they would both go back to prison, as they deserved. She showed it to Charles that night, and all she could think was how lucky she was that they hadn't stolen more, although she probably would never know everything that was gone.

The call from Sarah Gross, Julia's agent, came in the first week of February. She apologized for calling Meredith directly, but she had looked it up and discovered that Meredith didn't have an agent. She didn't even have a Screen Actors Guild card anymore. She didn't need one.

"Julia asked me to call you," Sarah explained to her. "She just got a part in a movie she's very excited about. I think this is going to be a big career step for her. She wants me to send you the script."

"I'd love to see it," Meredith said, excited for her. "Do you know who else is in it?" Sarah reeled off an impressive list of names. The stars were major box office draws. "Does she have an ingénue role?" It was what she'd expect at her age.

"She's the co-star," Sarah said proudly. "She earned it fair and square at the audition. She was fabulous. Her acting classes have paid off. She's grown a lot."

"By all means, send me the script, I'd love to read it." It amused Meredith too that the director was an actress she had worked with years before. She was a director now, and a good one.

"I want to be honest with you," Sarah said carefully. "We have an ulterior motive here. There's a part in the movie for a somewhat older woman. She ties the whole story together. It's a key character, and it will need a seasoned actress to pull it off." She told her who they were considering, which told Meredith it was an important role. "The actress who plays it won't be in the script for long. Possibly three weeks of shooting, but the scenes she's in are key. Julia wants you to do it. You're the right age, the right look, and God knows you have the talent. I know you haven't worked in a long time, but Julia tells me her life's dream is to work with you, at least on one film, and this one might be it. It's a part that's worthy of you, if you'll do it. It's a highly dramatic role. And if you don't have an agent, I'd be happy to negotiate it for you. Because of your stature, I think I can get you top billing, or lead billing, ahead of the rest of the cast. It would be an extraordinary comeback if that interests you, or a cameo appearance your fans will never forget." Meredith was stunned by what she said, and that Julia had suggested it. She was too startled to speak for a minute.

"I haven't worked in years, nor wanted to. I'm not even sure I could still remember lines anymore. My skills aren't exactly razor sharp after fifteen years in retirement."

"Will you think about it?"

"I don't know . . . I was finished with all that years ago."

"It would be incredible to have you and Julia in the same film." Meredith laughed at the thought.

"Julia making her entrance, and me making my exit."

"It doesn't have to be an exit. You can come back anytime you want. Your fans would go nuts."

"I don't want to make a comeback," Meredith said firmly. "Let me read the script for Julia's part, and the sheer pleasure of it. And I'll let you know what I think when I've read it, but don't get Julia's hopes up. I doubt I'll do it."

"Thank you," Sarah said, sounding grateful. She sent the script digitally a few minutes later, and Meredith read it that afternoon. The part for Julia was a fantastic opportunity, and the one for her was intriguing and challenging, a role she would have enjoyed doing, but she just couldn't see herself making a film, even for Julia. She tossed it on her desk, and Charles noticed it that night.

"What's that?"

Meredith gave him a rueful look. "A movie Julia is going to be in and I'm not. It's a great script for her. She'll be a big star after that, or well on her way."

"How do you figure into it?" He looked confused.

"They offered me a part too," she said in a choked voice. "It's a very interesting part. But I'm done with all that. I don't want to make a comeback, like some pathetic old thing trying to cling to fame."

"You don't need to 'cling,' you own it. Would you have to go on location to do it?"

"Just to L.A. They could shoot me in three or four weeks." Julia had sent her an email that afternoon, begging her to do it, once she knew Meredith had the script.

"I think you should do it," he said, excited by the idea. Meredith looked doubtful.

"I told them I'd think about it. I think it's a bad idea, for me. No matter how good the part is. The critics will stomp all over me for trying to make a comeback. I don't want to make a fool of myself, even for Julia."

"Can I read it?" She handed it to him, and he read it that night.

"Meredith, you *have* to do it. The movie is going to be fantastic. It's an all-star cast. Your granddaughter is in it. And I want to see you in it."

"You're crazy." She laughed at him, and he kissed her. "I'm *not* going to do it," she said stubbornly, and he ignored her and didn't comment. She wanted it clear. In her mind, she was no longer an actress.

It took her three days of long walks, hot baths, grumbling, and thinking of every reason why she shouldn't. In the end, Julia made the difference. If it was Julia's life's dream to be in a film with her grandmother, how could she resist? She sent Sarah Gross a text on the fourth day. "I'll do it. Top billing, or first name to appear alone on the screen, not billed as a cameo." She wasn't coming back to do a cameo after fifteen years. She wasn't dead yet. Charles laughed when she said it to him. And she agreed to let Sarah Gross represent her. She liked her, and it would be simpler than looking for a new agent, since hers had passed away years ago.

* * *

The producers treated her like returning royalty when Sarah told them she had agreed to do the film. The part was a natural for her. Charles said he was proud of her for having the courage to go back. Julia screamed when Meredith told her. Once she accepted, Meredith was excited about it too. It gave her something wonderful to look forward to. She was going to be making a movie in L.A. in June. It was due out at the end of the year, and the fanfare would be tremendous. And best of all, she was making Julia's dream come true, to work together. Daphne was right. She was a good witch after all.

Meredith hired a famous acting coach to work with her for three months before she had to be in L.A. to start shooting. She wanted to fine-tune her skills again, and try out some nuances for her interpretation of the part. In the end, she and the director were in such harmony about how they viewed it that Meredith felt she had delivered one of the best performances of her career. She finished her role in three weeks, and she had three days of shooting with Julia. It was a thrill for her to watch Julia grow and progress, as she sat on the sidelines on the set. It was one of the most fulfilling films Meredith had ever worked on and she was proud of the performance she'd given.

In July, she and Charles went to Europe for three weeks, after she finished, and after that, they visited his daughter, Pattie, and her family in Texas. They were nice people. And they visited his son, Jeff, in Germany when they were in Europe.

They spent as much time as they could in the Napa Valley in August. They had a lovely summer.

Andrew's trial was set for September, eleven months after his first arrest. They had combined the two cases, and he had hired a hot-shot lawyer to defend him. He was known for his ability to create doubt in the jurors' minds.

Andrew had been deemed competent to stand trial, and Tyla was dreading it. It was going to be a circus, and they all knew that Andrew was going to lie through his teeth.

Jury selection was scheduled to start right after Labor Day. The district attorney was still offering Andrew a deal if he pled guilty to a lesser charge. They were offering him two years in prison, but he would lose his medical license forever, and he wasn't willing to do that. His license was on hold for now, but he hadn't lost it yet, and wouldn't until he was convicted. He had been arrogant in all his court appearances. But if he went to trial, and was found guilty by the jury, he could get up to eight years in prison, if they ran all the charges consecutively. It was a tremendous risk for him, and Charles was surprised that his attorney would allow him to take the chance. He wasn't an appealing defendant. Beating his wife almost to death and terrorizing his children were not acts that would win the sympathy of a jury.

Tyla had met with the assistant district attorney assigned to the case many times in August. She was their star witness, and she'd have to hold up on the stand. She had lost ten pounds from worrying about it over the summer. Meredith was going to attend the trial with her. Peter, Arthur, and Ava had promised to be there to support her too.

Tyla was barely sleeping at night. Andrew's lawyer had finally gotten him released on bail in June. He had put up the deed of their house against five hundred thousand dollars' bail. Since he had paid for the house, the mortgage was in his name, and Tyla hadn't filed for divorce yet, so he could do that. She was going to file the divorce after the trial. Her lawyer had said she would get a better deal if he was convicted, so she had waited. And in the meantime, the court order was still in effect giving her monthly spousal support and child support from Andrew's considerable savings, although his legal fees were eating a massive hole in what he had.

His medical license had been suspended, so he didn't have anything to do, and couldn't see patients. Since his release from jail, he had been granted four visits with his children, with court supervision, but they had refused to go, and had begged their mother not to send them, so they hadn't gone. By the end of August, he hadn't seen his children in ten months and blamed it on Tyla.

Meredith and Charles were having breakfast with Tyla in the kitchen, two days before jury selection was to begin. Will and Daphne had started school the day before. Tyla was deathly pale as she sipped her coffee and read the paper, when Tyla's cell phone rang, and she saw that it was Angela Luna, the assistant DA. Tyla looked pained as she answered. The upcoming trial had been devouring her life for months. All she wanted now was for it to be over.

The assistant DA asked Tyla if she could see her.

"Now? We're just having breakfast."

"I'm already in an Uber, five blocks from where you're living." Tyla didn't particularly like her, and the assistant DA was furious at the deal the DA had offered Andrew, with only two years in prison, but he wanted to get rid of the case. She wanted to try him, see him convicted, and send him away for twenty years. She was a bulldog, but her heart was in the right place.

Tyla told Meredith and Charles that she was on her way.

"Do you want us to leave?" Meredith asked her immediately, and Tyla shook her head.

"There's nothing you don't know about the case." The doorbell rang as she said it. Charles went to answer it, and brought Angela into the kitchen. He offered her a cup of coffee and she declined. She looked serious and sat down across from Tyla for what she had to say.

"It's over, Mrs. Johnson. I wanted to come to tell you in person." Tyla was staring at her as though she'd seen a ghost.

"What do you mean 'over'? Did they dismiss it? Or did he take the deal?"

"Neither one," the assistant DA said solemnly. "The deal is off the table, as of two hours ago. Apparently Dr. Johnson has been seeing a woman since June, when he got out of jail. She's a schoolteacher at a Marin County school. He's been staying with her. Two weeks ago she asked him to move out, because he'd been threatening her and drinking to excess. He gave her a black eye last Monday. He put the threats in writing by email and text, and spray-painted the word 'whore' on the side of her house. He thought she was cheating on him. He broke into her home last night, and beat her unconscious. She was taken to Marin General Hospital. He was gone when a neighbor went to check on her and found her. They just picked him up. His prints are everywhere. She died two hours ago. He confessed. Because of the threats he made, it's first-degree murder, which could get him twenty-five years in a maximum security prison. The DA just offered him twelve years, ten for the murder of the schoolteacher, and two for your case, and the loss of his medical license. He'll never practice medicine again. He took the deal. It doesn't give you justice to the full extent of the law, but he can't hurt you again, he'll be in prison for the next twelve years and you don't need to go through a trial." Tyla looked shocked when she finished. She seemed dazed. Meredith and Charles were too stunned to speak.

"He killed her? What am I going to tell my children about their father?"

"It could have been you, Mrs. Johnson. What he did last night is a terrible thing, but he could have come here and killed you, or killed you last October. He belongs behind bars. He's in custody now. He'll be going to prison in a few days."

Meredith came to sit next to Tyla and put an arm around her shoulders. She looked as though she didn't understand. Andrew had killed a woman. Maybe he really was insane. She had no idea how to explain it to the children, but they were afraid of him too. And thank God he hadn't killed them.

The assistant DA stood up, and Tyla thanked her. She said she would be in touch about any further details. But her case had been resolved by his pleading guilty to both cases, and the assistant DA was satisfied with the twelve-year sentence, and hoped Tyla was too. It wasn't long enough but it avoided the agony of the trial. She still had to divorce him. Her lawyer had advised her to go after the remains of his savings and the house, and he believed she'd get it, which would give her financial security for herself, Daphne, and Will.

There was silence in the kitchen after Angela left, as the three of them looked at one another. Meredith was remembering when he had gotten her by the throat and banged her head against the wall, and the condition Tyla had been in when he'd almost killed her. She felt sorry for the schoolteacher in Marin, but she was grateful that her friend had been spared.

"Do you want to go upstairs and lie down?" Meredith asked her.

"No, I'm so relieved that I don't have to go through a trial, Andrew isn't walking around free, and he won't get out of jail for a long time." In twelve years, Daphne would be nineteen and Will twenty-three. They had a chance to grow up in peace now, and no one was going to beat her again. But all three of them were shocked about the woman who had died.

It was a terrible story, for Tyla, for her children, for the woman he had killed. But it was over now. They never had to see him again. She, Daphne, and Will would feel the effects of what they'd been through for years. But they could start over now and begin to heal. And miraculously, Tyla and her children had lived through it, unlike the schoolteacher. They were free of him forever. It was all she wanted, and felt like justice enough to her.

Chapter 16

The producers had sent a private jet to pick up Meredith and Charles in San Francisco. It was a G500, and they had a hairdresser and makeup artist on the plane with her. Meredith had brought a long black Dior evening gown with her, and high heels, and she was going to dress on the plane, and go straight from the airport to the premiere. Charles was already wearing his tuxedo. There would be both red carpet and a press conference at the premiere. Julia was planning to attend with an actor she knew. Her father had flown out from New York, and Kendall had sent her regrets, and said she had the flu. Julia said she was sure her mother had never intended to come, but maybe it was just as well. She would have been like the evil witch in a fairy tale, given how she felt about Hollywood. Julia was the fairy princess. Meredith was so proud of her.

She got her hair and makeup done on the short flight. It was in a sleek bun, and the dress was very flattering. The heels made her almost as tall as Charles. There was a black Rolls with a driver waiting for them on the runway, to whisk them to the theater. It reminded Meredith of the old days.

"You look beautiful," Charles whispered to her in the car. Their bags were being taken to a bungalow at the Beverly Hills Hotel, where they would spend the night, and go home on the same plane in the morning after a press breakfast Meredith had to attend with her granddaughter. The press had been playing up the multigenerational aspect, which had been the whole point of her doing it.

Meredith headed down the red carpet on Charles's arm as soon as they arrived, stopping to pose for photographers. There were easily two hundred of them, and the flashes were blinding, but Meredith never stopped smiling. It was like a long forgotten déjà vu for her. When her vision cleared, she saw her granddaughter coming toward her, with her red hair piled on top of her head with a diamond clip, her perfect body poured into a white satin Chanel haute couture evening gown, and a handsome young man at her side. The four of them posed for more pictures, and then several of Meredith and Julia together without the men, and then, waving and smiling, they made their way into the theater, where more photographers were waiting for them.

When they finally took their seats in the theater, Charles whispered to her, "Is it always like this?"

"If it's a major film, it is." He was enjoying it. Meredith looked radiant. She had been born to be a star. She really was movie royalty, and so was Julia now.

Charles had seen a screening of the movie with her, but he enjoyed seeing it again. They were inching out of the theater into the lobby with fans and gawkers waiting outside, photographers pushing and shoving them, while Meredith remained gracious and poised with Julia next to her, and her date at her side.

They were slowly making their way to the door, to get to the dinner and after-party when a man stepped in front of her. He had with him a blousy, heavyset woman, with a bad dye job. She was overflowing out of her dress, and the man was looking straight at Meredith as though he knew her. For an instant she didn't recognize him, and then she knew who he was. It was her ex-husband, Scott Price, and his wife, Silvana. She hadn't seen Scott since their son's funeral, and now she was face-to-face with him. Charles guessed instantly who he was from Meredith's expression, and he almost laughed when he saw Silvana. Talk about betting on the wrong horse for the long haul. Meredith was as slim and beautiful and elegant and graceful as ever. Silvana looked like a cheap waitress in a borrowed dress. It clung to her like a second skin that belonged to someone else. Scott paid no attention to her.

"You were wonderful in the movie," he complimented her. "You always were. I knew the part was for you the minute I read it. I'm glad you agreed to do it."

"Julia is our star," she deflected the praise as she always did, and then turned it on him. "I saw your last two movies. They were excellent. Oscar material." And she meant it. But what felt so odd was seeing him, meeting his eyes, the man who had broken her heart with another woman, risked their son, and had haunted her for fourteen years. He had caused her years of torment, and now he stood there, making small talk as though they were friends. Talking to him, she realized that he was nothing to her now, neither lover nor friend. They were barely acquaintances and didn't know each other anymore. He could no longer hurt her or cause her pain. He had no power over her. He gently touched her arm and she instinctively pulled away, and then the crowd separated them and he was gone.

"Are you okay?" Charles whispered to her as they were carried on the tide to the lobby.

"I'm fine. It was like we never knew each other." She had loved him so much for a long time. After that, in her heart, he was the man who had killed her son. Now he was nothing. "We're strangers now," she said about Scott, and Charles nodded, and held tight to her arm to remind her that he was there in all the ways that mattered and he would let no harm come to her.

It was a long night. The party went on forever, the meal was elaborate. The press stayed longer than usual, and it was entertainment headlines that Meredith White had come out of retirement to appear in a movie with her granddaughter, and they had both been fabulous. Meredith looked better than ever. She was almost more beautiful now.

Funnily enough, it was as though everyone had forgotten she'd ever been married to Scott. The years had taken a toll on him. He had aged badly. No one wanted pictures of him with Silvana. They photographed him alone. They left the party early, without saying goodbye to Julia. Meredith felt as though she had broken another spell that night. Scott no longer mattered to her. It was good to know.

Meredith and Charles had arrived at the premiere at six for the red carpet, and it was after one when they left the after-party, still crawling with press. This was a major Hollywood milestone. Meredith claimed it was a one-off she had done for her granddaughter, but everyone wanted to know if she was going to make another movie, if she was back.

Charles asked her the same question in the car on the way to the hotel.

"I don't know," she said in a soft voice, sitting regally next to him in the Rolls, and then she melted against him. "I'm not sure it matters. I have everything I want, Julia . . . you . . . friends . . ." She had Will and Daphne as her adopted grandchildren . . . Tyla had just moved to her own apartment a few blocks away, and had sold the house the court had given to her in full. She and the children were financially secure and safe at last. Andrew was in San Quentin prison, where he belonged. Peter and Ava were getting married. They were all going to a concert of Arthur's in New York soon, at Carnegie Hall. The two people who had hurt her the most, Scott and Kendall, had lost their power over her. She was happy with Charles. It was hard to imagine anything more. "I don't know if I need another movie. I had fun with this one," she said to Charles. But she wasn't afraid of that either. If she found another movie she wanted to do, she would. She could do whatever she wanted now, and it was amazing to think that an earthquake had started it all.

THE AFFAIR

Rose McCarthy is the legendary editor-in-chief of a New York fashion magazine. Following her husband's death several years ago, her four beloved daughters have grown even closer. Their eldest daughter Athena is a popular chef, while Venetia is a successful fashion designer, and Olivia is a court judge. Their youngest daughter Nadia is a highly sought-after interior designer married to bestselling novelist Nicolas Bateau. They seem to have the perfect life, living in a beautiful Paris apartment with two adorable daughters.

But when the tabloid press leak the story of Nicolas's affair with a beautiful young actress, Nadia's life falls apart. Heartbroken and humiliated, Nadia's mother and sisters come together to be the support she needs. Yet it seems that Nadia is not the only one suffering. As they spend time together, they discover that loyalty and being true to yourself are some of the most important lessons to learn.

Coming soon